Bagels FOR Tea

Also by Serita Stevens and Rayanne Moore:

Red Sea, Dead Sea

Bagels FOR Tea

Serita Stevens and
Rayanne Moore

St. Martin's Press   New York

Library of Congress Cataloging-in-Publication Data

Stevens, Serita.
    Bagels for tea / Serita Stevens and Rayanne Moore.
        p.   cm.
    "A Thomas Dunne book."
    ISBN 0-312-09348-9
    I. Moore, Rayanne.   II. Title.
    PS3569.T4527B3   1993
    813'.54—dc20   93-22115
                                                                         CIP

First edition: May 1993

10 9 8 7 6 5 4 3 2 1

Dedicated to
Our Significant Others:
Barrie Barr
William Rodgers

We acknowledge the assistance of
Robbie Patterson, of Manchester, England,
and
Denise Karlskind
for their advice
on English matters

One

*I*DARTED across the clay, frantic to get a racquet on that crosscourt smash from Amanda Klarner. Ms. Smarty-Pants Klarner couldn't possibly take the championship from me. Not after I'd held the *B'nai Brith* Northside Seniors Tennis Trophy for five seasons running.

Suddenly, pounding across the smooth surface, as unaware of the arthritis twinges in my joints now as I had been swinging from that balcony in Israel, I felt myself stumble.

No, I thought. Not like this. Not Fanny Zindel sprawled like an empty overcoat on the smooth clay while Ms. Smarty-Pants Klarner grinned and bowed to the crowd and accepted *my* trophy!

As I pitched forward, I batted at the ball with my last gasp. Too bad. I batted instead of trying to catch myself. I went down, skidding on both knees and the heels of my hands. I tried to remember my self-defense classes from the park. I tucked and rolled onto my side to protect myself from really being hurt. My new Donnay racquet had not been in those classes. It went flying across the court.

I had only one reaction. I looked for the ball.

It teetered on the top of the net. My side . . . her side . . . mine . . . I couldn't even breathe, not for a million— unless, maybe, breathing would push that ball over a bit. Moving as slowly as my Morris, he should rest in peace, on his way to get his bridge worked on, the ball dropped, at last, into *her* forecourt, not mine. Down the face of the net like a man in a barrel down Niagara Falls, and just as impossible for Amanda to reach.

I felt tears in my eyes and I can tell you, it wasn't from the pain in my skinned knees. The months of hard practice had paid off. "Game. Set. Match!" came over the loudspeaker. Yes!

The silence of several hundred people, each one holding his or her breath, broke into cheers, hoots, whistles. And all for me, Fanny Zindel, winner of the tennis trophy six times in a row.

The ball girls rushed to help me up. Was I all right? Sure—I was in no hurry to find out what I had scraped besides the frame of my Donnay Pro One and both my knees and palms, which already burned like an oven being koshered.

As my hands gripped the trophy bowl, its silver cool against my scrapes, the director of the country club that was our host for the tournament pushed through the crowd and tugged at my elbow.

"Fanny! There's an emergency call for you. It's long-distance."

"Long-distance?" I nearly lost my grip on my trophy. Nobody pays those charges in the middle of the afternoon unless it's bad news. I shoved my trophy into my friend Sadie's waiting hands and hurried into the main building.

"Hello?" I said, shakily.

"Fanny Zindel?" It was a man's voice. I didn't recognize it.

My first thought was that something had happened to Nathan. After all we had been through together in Israel, I had hoped his future assignments for Mossad would be less dangerous.

"Yes," I said.

"This is Joseph Bacha, Karin's husband."

2

Such a relief. Not Nathan. Then he told me about Karin's health. "Her gallbladder," I said. "So, when's the surgery?"

"That's the problem," Joe answered. "It's scheduled for Thursday, when Karin is *supposed* to be on a plane to England for the Clifford's Tower Memorial service, in York."

"Such a shame. I know she was looking forward to being the delegate."

"Yes," he said, suddenly sounding as awkward as if he were asking for my daughter's hand in marriage. "So, that's why I'm calling," he said. "We need you to be the replacement delegate." He rushed on before I could turn him down. "We really have no one else, Fanny. I know it's short notice, but you are the vice president, and you mentioned you would be going to England again."

"Joe, I just got back from there. A few months ago, only. My own house I hardly know anymore, the Hanukkah things barely in the cupboards, the Passover cleaning to be done, and the cats—"

"Fanny. We're desperate. You can have Karin's ticket, first-class, if only you'll set her mind at ease. I know it doesn't get you to New York, but you were going to come for the national board meeting next month. If you come now instead, I'll fill in for you at the meeting. I'll even see to it that *B'nai Brith* contributes something toward your hotel bill in England."

Well, I thought, a trip back to see my granddaughter Susan and the famous Clifford's Tower Memorial for practically free, I could hardly turn down. On my budget, another trip like that I couldn't have afforded for two years, at least.

"It wouldn't do for Karin to go into surgery with worry on her mind, Fanny."

That did it. Guilt. That lifelong Jewish curse. I should have her life on my conscience? Still, I could hardly believe my ears as I heard myself accept his offer. "I would love to go for her, Joe, but I have to see if Sadie could watch Susan's cats while I'm there. I can't just leave them to *nosh* on poor Mrs. Krepalski's canary."

I had been taking care of the little bird since my dear

3

neighbor had started with the Alzheimer's and started forgetting: her dear dead husband; that she was ever married; and breakfast, lunch, and dinner for herself as well as the canary. Last summer she'd still been at home, but now she was in a full-care place, the Jewish Home for the Aged. Her children couldn't help it they all worked and lived too far away to look in often enough.

That was just as well. I couldn't help her or look in enough, either. If she fell, who could have picked her up? A woman my size—a perfect ten, just like when I used to model at the department store in Chicago—get Mrs. Krepalski, who was no size ten, I can tell you, up off the floor? Never.

I realized Joe was shouting for joy in my ear.

"Oh, Fanny! Thank you, I was counting on your help." He sounded less like Mr. Gloom-and-Doom now, even with his Karin practically on the gurney already. "When will you know for sure?"

"Hang on a minute, can you?" I set the phone on the glossy mahogany desk and went to the window. Through the Irish lace I could see Sadie still clutching my trophy and taking my bows as if she had dropped that shot into Amanda's forecourt herself. "Sadie!" I yelled, and leaned over the bright window boxes, waved my headband at her. "Come!"

As she trotted over, my trophy dangling from her hand, I shouted: "I need you to look after the animals, Sadie."

She looked curious, but she nodded and kept coming. "What's going on?" she asked.

I gestured for her to wait a moment and hurried back to the phone. "How long will I be gone, Joe?"

I ran again to the window and called to Sadie: "I need to be in York, England, for about a week and a half."

She was so shocked she missed her step and almost tumbled into the hydrangeas. "Something's happened to Susan?" she shrieked, and began running and asking *HaShem*'s help before she even knew. I didn't have the strength or desire for shouting it all out the window. Sadie, always assuming the worst, I thought. I shook my head and turned back to the phone to tell Joe I'd see him in New York late the following

4

afternoon. While he went on thanking me some more, I looked around the director's office until he ran down. Such blessings as he was calling down on me I wouldn't want to interrupt, just in case God, *HaShem*, was listening for a change.

Like a palace that office. Paintings. Knickknacks of glass and china in fancy-shmancy cases with glass doors and locks! On one side was a wet bar with a solid brass sink and bottles, as many as the clubhouse restaurant I would have bet my *Susa-le's* favorite cat. And from cut crystal glasses? Enough to put a good chandelier to shame. Such a club we used for our tournament. Such a club some of our members belonged to! Me, I couldn't afford to have a glass of tea on their patio. Impressive. Looking at everything, I almost missed Joe saying he had made a reservation for me to New York.

"Yes. I'll call and confirm. Good planning, Joe." I wondered if he had been so sure of my help or if he had made a reservation because he knew he would find someone to take Karin's place no matter what.

I hardly had the phone away from my ear when Sadie burst into the room. "So, what kind of trouble is Susan in this time?" Worried as she was, she looked around at the office with her mouth hanging open like a door on a refrigerator when my son Marvin is around. A composer, sitting all the time at the piano and stuffing his face, he should be five hundred pounds. *Feh!* Like a rail that one. Maybe that was the trouble with his marriage. His wife, Sharon, would have had to be in the kitchen twenty-four hours a day just to fix him *noshes*.

I gave Sadie my offended look, like Alfred Hitchcock announcing a commercial. Last summer, *Susa-le* took a vacation from boarding school when she shouldn't have. So maybe she made Larry, her father, a little anxious. And her mother, Judith, was biting those precious talons of hers to the quick. But Susan was a good girl. Sadie had no call to think the worst. Of course, later, I wished I had known an omen when it sank its teeth into my ankle.

"My *Susa-le* is not in any trouble!" I said, taking my trophy from Sadie and buffing her fingerprints from the inscription with the hem of my tennis skirt. I should have recalled what a knack my granddaughter had; trouble was to Susan what dill is to a pickle.

As we walked back to the clubhouse, where the awards banquet was being held, I explained everything to Sadie. She was happy to watch the cats. Well, at least willing, she said, trying to look a little put-upon. An actress Sadie wasn't. Didn't Charlie Dickens, Susan's favorite Himalayan, jump into Sadie's lap every time she sat down in my house? Of course. And that one knew who liked him. The same with the rest.

The banquet hall was packed. We almost needed to oil ourselves to squeeze between the chairs to our seats. I moved toward the head table for the winners. Sadie was *my* guest.

I looked around the Viewridge Country Club. Fancy-shmancy like the office, and everything like an old English estate. Soon again I would be seeing the real thing. And Susan. I felt my *kishkes*, my insides, flop over with excitement. Travel my life hadn't exactly been filled with. Oh, my Morris would take me to the Catskills every year or occasionally to one resort or another around the country, but outside the U. S. of A.? Not until last summer, when I finally got my wish to see the Holy Land. Then I had taken Susan back to her school near York. Over a week Susan spent showing me the Lake District and around Yorkshire before she went back to classes and I flew home. Now I had the chance to go back. And for almost no expense!

I had such *shpilkes* I couldn't sit still through lunch. All I could think about was getting packed and calling *Susa-le* with the news. Winter clothes I would need; March in northern England was no place for shorts and a tank top. But I would take my tennis things. You never knew when you might get invited to a game, and wasn't England the home of Wimbledon?

Feh! How silly. It was the Memorial I should have been thinking of. Since 1190, the people of York had denied that a Jewish tragedy—the massacre—had happened there. Until

1960 there had not even been a posting to tell tourists about the deaths. All that had been said was that Clifford's Tower was Robert Clifford's contribution to defending the king from the Picts. Revisionist history, really. Now York and its people were finally willing to admit to the massacre, take responsibility for it and ask forgiveness at a worldwide memorial. And Fanny Zindel would see it happen.

At last the luncheon ended and I pushed past the crowd of well-wishers.

At home, I had hardly set my trophy in its place of honor on my mantel when the phone rang.

"Mother Zindel?"

Oh, good. It was my daughter-in-law, her Royal *Kvetch*ness. She thought maybe the cats answered the phone? Putting on my sweet mother-in-law voice, I answered, "Yes, Judy." She hates that name.

"You still keep a kosher kitchen, don't you, Mother Zindel?"

She should ask? A little less observant I might be now, because of my arthritis and since Morris was gone, but kosher I'd kept for sixty-five years, why would I change? "Yes, Judy, since before you were born," I said, trying to remain sweet, for Larry's sake. "Why?" As if I didn't know. Something there was she wanted I should make for her. God forbid she should break her own nails.

"Well, Mother Zindel, I was thinking." That alone was an experience I'm sure she would find different, but she soon went on talking instead. "You know those *kreplach* you make so well . . ."

"You mean the same ones I made so well for your sisterhood last year, and the year before and the year before that? The ones you told them you had slaved over for days?"

"I never exactly told them I made them, Mother Zindel. I merely said it was an old family recipe."

From *my* old family, I thought. Now I knew. Lazy. Didn't *kreplach* take forever to make? All those little squares of dough: roll out and cut and fold over the meat mixture; then boil until they float.

Now that her boy, Joey, was at school all day and her Susan away in England, Judith could take the time to do it herself. "So I'll give you my recipe," I offered.

"Mother Zindel, you know how much better you are at these things," she whined. "And I don't have a meat grinder."

"You can chop it by hand, Judy," I said. "It's the way my mother did the filling."

I heard the silence from her. I added, "Or I can drop off my grinder before I leave."

"Leave?" She sounded like she was strangling.

In spite of the training I had from two years in Yiddish theater, I still had to fight to put some sympathy in my voice. "I'm sorry, Judith. I'm going back to England tomorrow. I won't have time to cook you anything."

"England? You can't afford another trip."

"*B'nai Brith* is paying. I'm a delegate to the Clifford's Tower Memorial. I have to hurry and pack, Judith. Good-bye."

I hung up. The phone rang again. Almost immediately. Judith. I didn't answer.

Later, I would phone her husband, my Larry, at his law office and tell him I was going. Maybe he would want to send something along for Susan. My granddaughter I would call when the rates changed. I would have called her even without the trip. Twice a month I checked to see how she was doing. She'd been in therapy since that trouble in Israel.

I carried on with my packing. Tomorrow I would be in New York. The day after in old York. It seemed only yesterday that I was taking my granddaughter back to her school from our Israel tour. Tour? From tours like that one I never want to know. Guns, spies, fraud, blackmail, and kidnapping, never mind murder. The only good thing was Nathan. And him I wasn't so sure of right off, I can tell you.

While I packed, I made a few notes so I shouldn't forget anything in my rush. I wanted to be sure and call my cousin Doris when I got to England. A country estate, she had now, up near Easingwold. Only an hour north of Susan's school. Tourists came from everywhere to see her gardens and her Henry II Gothic chapel.

8

Doris was widowed now. Suddenly. She and her husband, Bernard, had been touring when I was last in England with Susan. My sympathies I should offer in person. Just a card doesn't do.

When my son Larry and his wife, Judith, had first decided to send Susan to a boarding school near York, it was Doris who sent them a list of good girls' schools. Of course, I had complained about the location at first. But my rabbi had assured me that the legendary rabbis' curse on York, the threat of *Harem*, hell, for Jews who went there, was only superstition. I folded another sweater into my suitcase. How things change.

Last summer I had felt so safe once I had gotten Susan back to school in York. Maybe that's why I was so excited to be going again. *Feh!* Safe? From now on, if I want safe I'll stay home and crochet, feed the cats, maybe play a little tennis.

Two

Such a deal. First-class from New York to England. I remembered trading my first-class ticket to Israel for a coach. I never regretted saving that money for shopping in the markets of Jerusalem's Old City. On this trip there had been no time for trading tickets. I was just lucky my New York flight was on schedule. Such a rush. Joe handed me Karin's ticket as I was boarding the plane for England.

From catching my breath, I can tell you, I didn't know. So first-class gave me a little luxury and eight hours of rest before I had to run through Heathrow airport to catch the plane to Manchester.

I needed that rest. In Manchester the airline clerk told me that I would have to wait over an hour for a train to York. I sighed and must have looked about like I felt. Disgusted and tired.

A pretty blonde tapped my shoulder. "Excuse me, did I hear you say you were going to York?"

"I am." I looked at her. In her forties but looking like thirties except for a few crow's-feet when she smiled.

"The conference?"

I nodded. "You, too?"

"Janet Percy," she said, sticking out a well-manicured hand. I was glad to see her nails were short but painted a pretty shell pink. I shook it and liked her firm grasp.

"Frances Zindel," I said. "But call me Fanny."

"All right, Fanny." She smiled. "There are commuter buses from here to the conference check-in."

"Oh, they didn't tell me. Where do we catch them?" I started to collect my luggage.

"Right over there." She pointed. "By the rental cars."

I thanked her and followed.

Janet held her ticket out to the driver of one of the buses.

"I don't have a ticket, yet," I said.

"This bus is full, ma'am. You can catch the next one. Fifteen minutes. Just pay the driver when you board."

I sighed. "See you there," I said, as Janet climbed onto the bus.

She smiled and waved. I sat down to wait. Fifteen minutes was better than an hour and the bus was cheaper than the train. And closer.

From the length of the conference check-in line, I was going to use all my strength just for waiting.

Digging a bagel out of my everything bag to keep up my energy, I took a bite and chewed slowly. Who knew how long my supplies would have to last? Of course, I still had the piece of fruitcake from the snack on the plane.

I glanced around the hotel lobby. Elegant. Marble columns—gold everything, from the carpet to the furnishings—and ceilings so high you could probably fly a plane up to the crown moldings for a closer look, which I'm sure they deserved.

So beautiful, but chilly. A gas fee for this place I wouldn't want to pay. Unfortunately, it would show up on my bill somewhere. How the palms survived the cold I couldn't imagine. A special breed, I thought, as I inched forward. I reached out. Yes. A special breed of silk! That explained it. A snowstorm these would last through.

The line barely moved. I sighed heavily. No one notices

11

anymore, offers you a seat. Nothing. When I was a girl, no one under the age of thirty would have sat while someone the age I am now stood. I looked down at my size-seven pumps. Were my ankles a little puffy? I eased my heel out of the right shoe and stuffed it down again. Good. Tired, a little sore, but no problems.

Occasionally, I have to pamper my ankles, what with my arthritis. Crippled I didn't want to be with so much walking ahead. York, I knew from my last visit, was a city of walking. Such narrow streets; who could drive? Yet always someone tried. People scattered up onto the shop-front stoops to avoid being run down. I know. I had been one of them.

Suddenly, from somewhere up ahead, such a commotion. Here at a religious conference? I raised up on my toes and cricked my neck trying to see. Looked like trouble, and for the only person who had been nice to me since I got to York.

Janet was leaning away from a man who was obviously angry at her. Her face was red and she stood as if facing a strong wind. The hotel clerk looked embarrassed for her.

I pressed to the front of the line and touched Janet's elbow. "You need some help, maybe? I could pay you back for telling me about the bus."

She turned her head, tears in her eyes. "Oh, Fanny," she said. "It's nothing. I'll handle it." She didn't look like she was doing too well in that department.

I patted her shoulder. "Fanny Zindel you helped. If this man—I won't say gentleman—is bothering you, I can go for a policeman." I fixed the fellow with my best Charles Bronson glare. He backed off a bit.

That surprised me. A gun you would need for this one, so mean he looked. Tall, with a suit that could have been a size bigger and still would have pulled at the buttons. Squinty eyes—I never liked squinty eyes in a man, or a woman, either—so that I could hardly tell their color, and dishwater blond hair that waved and kinked thinly across his balding scalp. The conference tag stuck to his lapel said: PROFESSOR STEIN.

"Police won't be necessary, Fanny. He'll leave now, won't you, Kenneth?"

12

"Janet, we have to talk. You can't do this to us. To me. We had plans for that money and—"

Janet cut him off. "Not here, Kenneth, please. I'll speak with you later. You're making a scene."

"Oh, right. Now you don't want a scene. In front of *your* friends. How typical. It's always you and what you want. So damn selfish!"

"Kenneth!" Janet's voice had a real edge to it now. Like a schoolteacher talking to a problem student. I could have told her it was no way to calm him down.

To my surprise, it worked. Kenneth backed off.

"I'll make sure you meet me later, Janet." It sounded a little like a threat to me.

I watched Kenneth. He was getting more upset. I could tell from the way his fingers gripped the bowl of his pipe. The knuckles were white and the tips left sweaty smears against the dark wood.

Janet turned her back on him and spoke with the hotel clerk. The clerk started filling out papers.

Janet explained. "We've been divorced nearly two years. I never expected him to come to the conference and make a scene." She glanced over at him. A pretty good imitation of Tipi Hedren backing down Sean Connery in Hitchcock's *Marnie*, if I did say so.

Kenneth shoved his pipe into a jacket pocket. Then he turned away. "This isn't the end of it, Janet." He marched off into the crowd.

I patted Janet's shoulder as the clerk at the check-in asked something about assigning her a roommate for the conference.

"Look," I said, quickly. "You're going to need someone to help keep that lunatic away from you. Why not let me share with you? We'll get on fine, and I can help if that *meshuge* comes back." I whipped a knitting needle from my everything bag and poked it into the air, narrowly missing the desk clerk, who jumped back. "Sorry," I said, and held the needle out to Janet. "A good thing to have a defense with someone like that running around loose. I can teach you how to use one. I've got a spare."

13

Janet burst into laughter and gave me a hug. "You are wonderful, Fanny. I'd be happy to share a room with you." She took my papers from me and handed them to the clerk, but refused my offer of a knitting needle. No matter, I knew I would get her to change her mind. I hadn't been taking that self-defense class at the park with Sadie for nothing. I had signed up as soon as I'd gotten back from Israel. Who would know travel could be so dangerous these days?

"I don't think I'll need that kind of help with him, though. He's just emotionally unstable. I think I can handle him."

I shook my head. "So many women who think that end up dead. You see their pictures in the newspaper later," I said.

"Fanny, I'm an M.F.C.C. I've handled a lot of agitated people."

I looked at her. "A marriage and family counselor? As a delegate to the conference?"

She smiled. "I do a lot of work for a church. Most of my clients are church related and I occasionally act as a lay minister."

Such an important lady my new roommate was. I was impressed. We collected our luggage and headed for our room.

So many stairs but the lift was slower and older than I ever wanted to be. Janet insisted on carrying my heaviest bag. I took one of her small ones, and after huffing and puffing up two flights, I was reminded of climbing up stairs like these in Tiberias to deliver the letter that got me in so much trouble.

"Oh, what a pleasant room!" Janet exclaimed, dropping the bag and throwing open the drapes.

"And so big," I added. It looked out on to a court and wonderful gardens. Across I could just see the spire of the famous York Minster. "Such a lovely view." I set my everything bag on the bed nearest the door. First thing I would do is clean it out and pack it with things for walking around York. A few *noshes,* a water bottle, my Sony tape recorder, and a few tapes. Naturally, my knitting needles, for self-defense, and my crocheting.

"You take the one by the window, Fanny. You'll love waking up to that in the morning light."

"Thank you very much, but me, I've been here before. I have a granddaughter in school not far from here. You take the view."

Janet picked up my suitcase and plunked it firmly on the bed by the window. "I, too, have been in York, Fanny. And if you take the window, you and your knitting needles can defend me if Kenneth tries to come in unannounced." She looked down at the trellises, now winter-bare.

I looked, too. "You really think he might try something?" I whipped out my needle and took a few practice lunges in front of the full-length mirror. My form was improving. Must have been my fencing lessons at the park. So good for balance.

When I turned back, Janet was sitting on the window seat and crying softly. I hurried to comfort her. "It's all so ugly, Fanny. Why does divorce always have to be so ugly?" She pounded her fist against her thigh.

"Janet, you should only calm down a little. I heard him mention something about money. It's the number one thing people fight over in a marriage. I'm sure I don't have to tell you."

"I know. Money and sex. You'd think after all my experience as a family therapist . . ."

"It's hard to keep your distance when it's your own husband."

"*Ex*-husband." Janet looked quite fierce as she said that. "And it's not as if the sex didn't come into it. Kenneth's a college professor. Everything they say about profs being appealing to students is true. Kenneth had so many young girls following him everywhere," she paused and looked down at her lap.

I didn't know what to say. So humiliating it was to be cheated on, betrayed. I thought of my Susan and her shattered faith in the boy from Israel. The bad experience now required her to see a therapist once a week. I thought of how lucky I had been with my Morris and his long love affair with me. I waited to see if Janet would tell me about the other problems between them, but she seemed stuck on his affairs.

"You should have seen that last girl, Fanny. Twenty, blond,

15

and built like a movie queen. How in hell can a wife compete with an endless supply of that?"

"A lovely figure you have, Janet," I said, and it was true. More revealing clothes she could have used, but maybe she was still at that stage where she wanted to put men off. It happens.

I stared at her a moment, then I filled the electric teakettle the hotel had provided and plugged it in. These teakettles were one of the things I liked best about hotels in England. All through Israel I'd had to carry my hot pot with me in my luggage. Such an inconvenience. Enough weight I had with clothes, let alone kitchen goods.

I set out the cups and dug in my everything bag for my bagels and some of the jam containers I'd taken from the plane. "What you need is something in your stomach," I said. "Then we can talk."

I found out, to my surprise, that Janet was now from New Jersey. No accent at all. I mentioned it.

"Actually, I was born over here but went to school in New Jersey, Fanny. I think one accent erased the other." She laughed. "Then I took some of my internship for my counseling degree in the South. The drawl is really infectious and I sounded like Scarlett O'Hara for almost two years." She sipped the tea and nodded her thanks. "I worked with prisoners in the southern justice system."

"So, such a strong lady and still you have this business with your husband?" I refilled her cup and nudged the bagels closer.

Janet took one with the raspberry jam. A good choice.

"I think it all started because of the interfaith marriage."

"Interfaith?"

"Kenneth is Jewish. He was so angry at his parents' disapproval, he decided to convert. That really caused a commotion. I was always the ruination of their baby boy. After the divorce, Kenneth returned to his faith, but the rift was unbridgeable. His parents couldn't forgive or forget. He still blames me for the distance between them."

"You have children?"

Janet shook her head. "We wanted some, but when he started with his students . . ."

"Very wise." I patted her hand. "So here, at the conference, maybe you'll find someone with your own beliefs."

Janet laughed. "I'm not looking, Fanny. There's no one out there for me anymore."

"*Feh!* You're a beautiful woman, smart, and most important, nice. Don't tell Fanny Zindel there's no one out there for you. I'll find him myself if I have to!"

I began unpacking some of my things. "I'm meeting my granddaughter, Susan, tomorrow for lunch. You'll come with me. And maybe one afternoon we can go to see my cousin Doris at her country estate. You like gardens? She's got gardens!"

"That's a nice idea, Fanny. Thank you. Is Susan coming into York?"

"No. When I called to tell her I was coming, she told me she was grounded. I don't know what kind of a mess she got herself into, but knowing my pretty *Susa-le*, it's probably a boy. We'll take a cab out to Taddington." In my heart, I hoped Susan had recovered from her bad experience enough to be dating again.

"Taddington Agricultural Boarding School?"

"You know it?"

Janet hesitated a moment. "Yes. My parents sent my sister there for several semesters while I was in college in the States. It's built incorporating the ruins of an old abbey."

"Yes," I said. "That's the one. There's still some old stone arches out behind the school buildings. Susan seems to like it there.

"A shame I can't take Susan into town. There are some nice little coffee shops. They have pastry. It's delicious. Of school food I'm sure she's had enough." I picked up my purse and my tidied everything bag. "I'm going down to get a newspaper, would you like to come along?"

Janet shook her head. "I'll just rest a bit, if you don't mind, Fanny, thanks."

"Right. Better you shouldn't take a chance of running into

17

your crazy ex so soon again. You want I should get you anything?''

Janet shook her head and sat on the edge of her bed. As I closed the door behind me, I could hear her using the telephone. So, if she wanted a little privacy for a personal call, I could give it. She had only to ask me.

Downstairs, the lobby wasn't quite as crowded as it had been before, but there were still a lot of people walking in and out, clutching their conference packets and talking in small groups. Such a crush when the conference was still a few days off. How many were attending? I wondered.

Like summer camp it seemed, only for grown-ups. So clear the memory came all of a sudden: Camp Herzl, eight of us squealing girls, and Harvey. Harvey, a senior counselor, had been to die for. Three of us, Rachel Green, Sharon Feferman, and myself, all had such a crush. We all followed him everywhere, our knees melting, our tongues hanging out, *chalishing,* drooling we were, and Harvey ignoring. Until Rachel came back on a parents' day and brought him a cake she *said* she made.

Feh! A cake that nice Rachel still can't make, but it got her a real date with Harvey. Sharon and I weren't ever going to speak to her again. A week we lasted, until he threw poor Rachel over for a long-legged, blond water-skier who was really more his age.

I sighed and wondered what ever happened to Harvey and his skier. Did they ever marry? Were they the smiling grandparents of lots of little water-skiing grandchildren? Reunions they should have had for my camp like they have for some others, so you can find out.

I stepped around a clump of people in front of the phones and dug Susan's number out of my everything bag. As I dialed my *Susa-le* to let her know I was here safely, I wondered why Janet had used the phone in the room. Didn't she know they charged you an arm and a leg for the convenience? Made of money, she could have been for all I knew, but it wasn't from being a counselor, that I was sure. Of course, a lot of people didn't know that it costs so much more from the room. I made up my mind to tell her. Maybe with all her work for the church, she had to watch her pennies. Didn't most counselors do that sort of work for a reduced rate?

After arranging to meet *Susa-le* at her school the next day, I wandered over to the small gift shop, where I got a paper and a box of Cadbury's chocolates, just in case my sweet tooth put in an appearance during the evening. As I left, I dropped a few pence into a ceramic Labrador retriever. FOUR PAUSE ANIMAL RESCUE, it said. Cute, I thought, to use the *pause* instead of *paws*. I supposed, like in the States, the rescue people thought of themselves as a pause along the way to a good home.

Peeking out into the cool night air, I decided I would take a walk before returning to the room. After all, the last time I visited York with my granddaughter, we mostly went places *she* would enjoy.

Going outside, I looked at my map and then hurried across the bridge and entered the cobblestone streets by the Micklegate. As I walked, I took the little tape recorder out of my everything bag and clapped on the headset. What would it be this evening, Israeli folk songs or the music of the big bands? Tommy Dorsey, I decided, and snapped the tape into the player.

The sound of horns backed by an old-fashioned orchestra swelled through the earpieces. I hummed as I stepped along toward Bridge Street and the crossing for the Ouse River. St. Michael Spurriergate loomed to my left. I jumped when its bells started tolling the eight-o'clock curfew. I thumbed my guidebook again.

A benefactor, it said, *decreed the curfew to toll in honor of that bell guiding him into York from the forests of old when he was lost.* Loud. Right next to it like that, I can tell you it was enough to guide me all the way from the States.

The darker Nessgate Street caused me to remove my headset and turn off my music. I needed all my senses alert. No one was going to sneak up on Fanny Zindel in the gloom. I felt for my knitting needle. I was almost at the junction to Castlegate, the final leg of my pilgrimage to see Clifford's Tower with its dramatic evening lighting, when I heard shouting.

I hurried toward the noise, my knitting needle out of my bag and at the ready, in case someone needed help. As I rounded a corner, the sharp point glinting in my hand, I caught words from the argument. A woman's voice was saying she didn't love the man. This was private. I was being a buttinsky. I turned to go back the way I had come, sticking my needle back in my bag.

Suddenly there was a *thump*, as if someone had fallen against something. I stopped cold and heard a sound like my mallet makes when I pound chicken breasts for schnitzel. A real slap it was. Then a shadow broke from the dark of the doorway and ran down the side street.

Calling out, "Are you all right?" I hurried toward the sound of sobbing.

Before I could see more than a mop of blond hair and an expensive coat with one sleeve ripped open at the armhole seam, the woman was up and running from me.

"Wait!" I cried. "Let me help you. Get you to a doctor."

I chased for a moment, but the woman didn't stop. If she could run like that, how badly could she be hurt? Since my heart was pounding worse than in the final set of my tennis match, only the day before yesterday, I decided she could do without my help.

At sixty-five, I should run like a gazelle, over cobblestones, maybe twist my ankle in the dark? *Feh!* For what? But still, I was uneasy as I walked the rest of the way to the tower. Less scary the dark street would have looked had there been more people around. I hurried back to the hotel. Too upset to think of dinner, I went straight upstairs.

Janet was sound asleep when I got to the room. I spent some time soaking in the big, claw-footed bathtub before getting into bed. While I soaked, I thought about that fight I had seen. So much trouble relationships caused. First Janet. Now this girl in the black streets. Well, if Kenneth got violent like that fellow in the alley, I would be ready to help Janet and call the police.

I tossed and turned until late. With any luck, I would be able to sleep in to recover from jet lag and my restlessness.

Sleep in I did, but not too late. Janet was up and asking me to have breakfast with her in the hotel restaurant. A leisurely meal. A good way to relax after all the rushing, and get to know my roommate a bit better.

A nice surprise at breakfast, Janet told me she'd rented a car for our trip to the school. "After we visit with Susan," she said, "I thought we might tour a little. I'd love to see the town of Acaster Malbis, the home of the evil Baron Malabestia."

"Hard to think of such a monster as having a home like anyone else and still plotting such a massacre," I said.

Janet smiled. "I imagine that Benedict Arnold, too, had a nice living room and hearth fire at one time. Would you mind if we tried to find the baron's home?"

"That suits me just fine, Janet. Better than a taxi, but can you drive on these roads? Everything right to left and back to front?"

Janet laughed and led the way to the parking lot. "I took my first driving license in England, Fanny. I'm rusty, but driving on the left isn't such a big deal." She grinned at me. "Of course, if your afraid to trust me . . ." She started the engine and looked out at me.

My roommate was beginning to know me already. Nothing like a challenge. "Fanny Zindel isn't someone who mistrusts her friends," I said, smiling at her and winking to let her know I knew what she was up to. I got into the passenger's seat and we were off.

On the way, Janet asked me if I had spent much time at the school when I was here last.

"Oh, yes. It's a nice boarding school. For me, I would have kept her in the States. My daughter-in-law Judith insisted England would give Susan polish.

"*Feh!* A veterinarian that one will be, like her aunt, my daughter, Deborah. I know all the signs. Like Deborah, Susan brings home anything with four legs. Such a zoo Deborah made of my home. Horses, dogs, cats, even wild things. That kind most people hire someone to keep away. Raccoons, squirrels, even mice. I had to learn to take care of everything that breathed. Deborah was good about them, but still I had to help sometimes."

"Maybe she should have you as a partner in her animal

21

hospital now," Janet said, smiling and taking a sharp turn in the road.

I laughed. "Don't think I haven't done it. When Deborah had her first practice, who do you think helped when she got sick?"

"So you're wondering: if Susan's going to follow in her aunt's footsteps, what does she need with so much polish?" Janet said, taking my words right out of my mouth.

I shrugged. "Sterling from plated she'll only know because of the decorations on her bridles in the tack room. Judith would have her telling her horse which leg he needs to use to eat his hay."

Janet laughed.

"Stop!" I said, as she turned down a pretty side road.

She slammed on the brakes. "What's the matter, Fanny?"

I jumped out of the car and sloshed through the dirty snow under the trees. "Here, baby," I called, holding out my hand to the skinny black Labrador. It froze, then bolted away on three legs, leaving even more bloody tracks in the snow.

"It's okay, baby." Slowly, I reached into my everything bag and pulled out a bagel. "You need a little something," I said. "Every rib I can count on you."

The dog raised his ears and cocked his head to one side. One hind leg was still in the air. "So, if you'll come to Fanny, I'll take you to a doctor." I tore off a piece of the bagel and tossed it gently toward him.

He jumped away, then came slowly back to sniff the food. He wolfed it down.

"More?"

He whined and limped closer. I held out the rest of the bread, flat on my palm. He wouldn't come. He cried and I could see the injured leg had an ugly gash across the thigh. Either a fight with a much bigger dog or barbed wire, I guessed. It needed to be stitched.

"Please come to Fanny. I only want to help." I crouched down in the snow and waved the tuna-filled bagel at him. "Look, fresh. I made it this morning."

He dropped his head and I thought for a moment he might

slink closer. Then Janet honked and he scrambled away into a bush.

"Okay," I said, "at least you'll have a meal." I set the bagel sandwich on the ground and moved away.

Sadly, I walked to the car.

"My God, Fanny, what's going on?"

"Nothing anymore," I said, a bit too sharply. "That dog is injured. I almost had him. Then you honked."

"Fanny, he probably lives on one of the local farms."

"With a gash in his leg you could practically see the bone?" I snapped, feeling angry that my friend didn't have more compassion.

"Fanny, we have to go. I'm sorry I honked, but he'll never come to you now." She started the engine.

I climbed in and watched in the mirror as we pulled away. The dog came out from behind the bush and hopped up to the food. He didn't even sniff this time. He dived in, grabbed the roll, and fled. I had done what I could.

Janet sighed. "You're a bleeding heart, Fanny. It can get you in trouble. My mother was the same."

I shrugged and we drove on. Since when was feeding the hungry and helping the injured a crime? I tried not to think less of Janet. Perhaps it was all her own worries that were hardening her heart. Besides, I knew I was one of the more extreme rescue people, even in my group back home. Who had more animal placements on her card than Fanny Zindel? No one. Who sometimes practically had a zoo in the yard of her own home? Me.

Soon we were turning into the wrought-iron gates at Taddington. Here and there, the grounds were dotted with remains of the crumbling old abbey walls.

My Susan was sitting out in front of the English Tudor home that served as the administration building. Across the grassy area to the left and right, newer buildings in that same style were classrooms and dormitory buildings. The barn, farther away in a field, had obviously been part of the original estate. Not that it was shabby, but the modern paddock with

23

bright white fences made the barn look ancient. Nothing at Taddington was shabby. Old, yes, but kept up nice.

Glad I was that Janet was driving. I would have had a hard time keeping my eyes on the winding cobblestone drive and Susan at the same time. So tall. Had she grown so in just a few months, or was my grandmother mind refusing to remember how tall she was now that she was turning seventeen? A joy to celebrate her birthday with her on Friday. Especially if I could do something about her being grounded.

Susan ran to me before I was completely out of the car, nearly knocking me back into the seat with her hugs and kisses. *"Faygele!"* I cried, and embraced her. "You're not such a 'little bird' now, are you? More like a beautiful swan!" I held her away from me to look at her while she blushed.

"Just as well, Gram. I prefer you call me something else, anyway."

"Why? What's wrong?" I held her away from me a little and studied her.

She glanced over at Janet. "I'll tell you later, *Bubbe*."

I sighed. "At least I'm still your *Bubbe*."

Janet got out of the car.

"Janet Percy, this is my granddaughter, Susan Zindel. Susan, Janet and I are roommates at the Royal York."

After making all the right noises, Susan insisted that we come to the barn and see her favorite horse. Alexander, she said, was almost her very own horse here at school, and one of the main reasons she wanted to be at Taddington.

A beautiful Thoroughbred. Tall and sleek, his gray coat shining even in the dim light of the barn. Such a good smell, horses, hay, and leather. I breathed it in and smiled. Then I sneezed as the dust got to me.

Susan grinned. "I love it too, *Bubbe*." She twitched her nose and inhaled deeply. "I could live in here."

"If I know my granddaughter," I said to Janet, who was being a good sport about it all, "she probably does." Susan leaped up onto the sleek back and trotted Alexander out the barn door into the paddock. Without any tack but a halter, Susan put the big horse through his paces for us while we looked on, amazed.

24

At last, she jumped down and put Alexander back in his stall, shoving a carrot into his mouth, and led us off to see her room at the dorm. Then she took us to the refectory for lunch.

A big hall it was, with tapestries on the walls and a dozen different family crests displayed with crossed swords or spears. So warlike. It nearly took my appetite to think of what those symbols really meant.

I was hardly in my seat when Susan nearly gave me a heart attack.

"Oh, guess what *Bubbe*, Nathan will be here sometime later today."

"My Nathan?" I clutched my chest. "What would my Nathan be doing here?"

"Well, when I spoke to him on the phone, I happened to mention that you would be coming over for the memorial service and he—"

"*Faygele!* On the phone?"

Susan glared at me. "Please, Gram, don't call me that."

"All right, *Susan*. Just who called who?" I gave her my Columbo stare.

Susan laughed, "Oh, *Bubbe*, Nathan called me." She paused. There was a Zindel twinkle in her eyes. "After I left a message for him."

"A *shadchen*, a regular little matchmaker," I said to Janet, and shook my head. Janet was smiling into her napkin.

I had only started explaining to her about Nathan, the adventure in Israel, when Susan put a finger to her lips. So quiet it got all of a sudden that the whole room would have heard me if I'd whispered. I looked up to see a stern-faced man in a black suit march to the front and stand behind the heavy, dark oak podium. Susan's headmistress, Miss Gwendolyn Kentworth, introduced him as the Reverend Malbys, who would lead grace.

We bowed our heads, but I was to get a crick in my neck before that man said amen. He managed to work in everything from the birth of Christ to the present-day Middle East crisis, not to mention comments about the memorial and the 1190 massacre before he wound down. Like a river, he ran on and on until all the hot food got cold and the cold food warmed up.

I was watching my iced-tea glass lose the last of its frosty coat when he finally called a halt. The room echoed with grateful amens and forks went to work.

"Isn't he something, *Bubbe?*" Susan whispered, and made a face. "We have to tolerate him every weekend and all special occasions." She passed me a covered basket of rolls.

As I suspected, cold. I took two anyway. I'd put them in my everything bag, just in case I should need a little something to settle my stomach from the winding roads later on. Maybe I'd leave one for the injured black dog on the way home. "Yes, *Fay—*" I caught myself. "Susan, he is something, but I don't quite know what."

She giggled, then fell silent when the headmistress came up with a handsome young man.

"Mrs. Zindel, may I introduce Mr. Hamilton Craig, our Latin master. He also teaches a course in the classics and tutors the girls in English when they fall behind. We can't have our girls getting so horsey that they muddle their more academic studies, can we?" She gave me a grin much like those horses she spoke of might have given. Unfortunate teeth, but I guessed maybe the National Health didn't do orthodontia.

Mr. Hamilton Craig took my hand and bowed a little as he shook it. "My pleasure, Mrs. Zindel."

Too smooth, with his slicked-back blond hair and his neatly trimmed moustache and goatee. I never trusted a goatee.

"I see Susan gets her budding beauty from the parent rose," he added.

Now I really didn't trust him. Such a line. He thought I was a fish, maybe? "Thank you, Mr. Craig. I'm sure the girls are learning a lot from you." I hoped he didn't try to charm all these young girls with his flashy manners. My Susan, I could tell, liked him. A schoolgirl crush on this one? I hoped not. To tell the truth I was glad to see them move on. Miss Kentworth continued around the dining hall.

Susan jumped up and hurried over to another nice-looking

hunk of a man. She began leading him toward our table. A large woman in a severe tweed suit followed closely behind him.

"*Bubbe*, I'd like you to meet my history master, Mr. Barry Barr, and Ms. Westenbury, who is our gamesmistress."

We all shook hands and said our hellos, Ms. Westenbury having, by far, the firmest grip.

"Master Barr has arranged our field trip to the opening ceremonies of the memorial."

"How nice," I said, beaming at the man, wondering if he was married and who I could fix him up with. Too old he certainly was for any of these girls, but maybe Sadie's daughter, the one whose husband just took a hike, the *momzer*. Such a bastard to betray a loving wife and mother like Rochelle.

I saw Susan looking at me as if she knew what I was thinking. "His fiancée is going to help chaperone us at the ceremonies."

I sighed. I had been wondering how to get Rochelle to England. You win some, you lose some. Susan giggled. She knew me too well.

"I understand you're here as the *B'nai B'rith* representative from the States, Mrs. Zindel. I'm impressed, and Susan must be very proud."

"I am," Susan said, hugging me. "And you should see her tennis trophies. Six times now she's won the North Side Seniors Tournament."

Ms. Westenbury grinned like the famous Cheshire Cat and stuck out her hand with the formidable grip again. "A woman after my own heart. Well done."

My arm I could hardly get her to stop pumping. "Is tennis your game also, Ms. Westenbury?" I asked, smiling and pulling my hand away to save it, my lunch I would be needing it to eat yet.

"Yes," she said, drawing back her arm and executing a powerful forehand stroke that threatened to take my water glass off the table. "Maybe we can play a set or two while you're visiting." She also showed a horsey set of choppers.

I smiled politely, glad that the rest of the food was coming

27

around. I gave Ms. Westenbury the number at my hotel, and, excusing ourselves, Susan and I turned our attention to the meal.

Before we had finished our salads, another gentleman tapped Susan on the shoulder. I looked up. He was tall and nicely built. Long-waisted and longer-legged, with a neatly trimmed full red beard and a Scottish brogue. He introduced himself as Susan's mathematics instructor.

"So nice to meet you, Mr. MacMurray. I hope you're not going to tell me all about how much my Susan dislikes your courses."

"No, actually, she does quite well. It's no love I've been able to foster for the subject in her highly resistant heart, but I have m' hopes up. We Scots are a stubborn lot." He grinned and patted Susan's shoulder. "I hurried over here because I couldn't believe that such an attractive and youthful woman could be Susan's grandmother."

I nodded my acceptance of his compliment, but I shook my finger at him. "And I thought the Irish were supposed to have all the blarney, Mr. MacMurray."

He laughed, a hearty, happy sound. He held a match to the bowl of a handsome meerschaum. How my Morris would have envied him that pipe. A Sherlock Holmes style was the only lack in my late husband's collection. Unfortunately, he had died before the Hanukkah I had planned to give one to him. Now Morris's entire collection belonged to my nephew Raymond.

"Actually, I believe a smooth tongue to be a Gaelic trait in general, Mrs. Zindel." He excused himself to talk with some of the other visitors.

I took a deep breath of the aromatic tobacco Mr. MacMurray was smoking. What memories. Maybe it was just the connection with Morris, but I felt as if Mr. MacMurray and I could be friends. "Such a nice-looking man," I said.

"Aren't they all just hunks, *Bubbe?*" Susan had a dreamy smile on her face.

"Yes," I said, "they are. *Older* hunks."

Susan made a face at me and started to eat her meat loaf. "I just had fish yesterday, *Bubbe.* Don't be upset."

"Upset? Me? Maybe when you're older you'll change your mind about kosher. For now, you live your life."

Nice it looked, the meat loaf, but obviously not kosher. I was glad the school, like this country, made allowances for vegetarians and others with diet needs.

I had the salmon, so fresh, I wondered if Mr. MacMurray caught it on a recent trip home to Scotland.

I was about to ask Susan why she couldn't get time off to tour with me when I saw her giving such a look as I wouldn't have turned on my worst enemy.

Curious, I glanced behind me. All I could see was Miss Kentworth leaning forward over a gorgeous young lady at the end of the next table. The girl stood up. A figure she had, it should never be owned by one so young. I looked back at my Susan.

Before I could ask her what was wrong, the pretty blonde hurried from the room. She met a young man by the refectory door and bent her head to talk with him. Thick hair fell over one eye, like a young Veronica Lake. Maybe that's why the girl looked familiar, so many old movies the cats and I had watched since I got that American Movie Channel on cable at home.

There was a scraping clatter and a piece of Susan's meat loaf shot across her plate and onto the tablecloth. Some gravy spattered into my lap. *"Susa-le!* Temper is making you careless," I said, mopping at the stain with my napkin. "You're so angry you let that one take your manners when she left the room?"

Susan blushed and hung her head. "I'm sorry, *Bubbe.*" She dipped a corner of her own napkin into her water glass and helped me with the gravy spot. Suddenly tears were rolling down her cheeks. I hugged her and the dam burst.

"You want to take a little walk with me, maybe?"

Susan sniffled and pulled herself together. "Later, *Bubbe.* Mary Louise just makes me so mad."

Hurt I knew she was, but I also knew better than to keep after her. A *nudzh* I wouldn't be to my own granddaughter. I chatted pleasantly with Janet until the lunch was over. One eye I kept on my *Susa-le.*

29

We were almost out the door of the refectory when Mr. Craig offered to show Janet and me around the grounds. "You go, Janet," I said. "I want to visit with Susan until her class starts." Besides, I thought, Mr. Craig gave Janet a look. Janet was too smart to be taken in by such a smoothie, but maybe he could help her forget that nastiness with her ex.

Alone with Susan in her room, I insisted she explain her actions at lunch. "It's not like you to have such a temper, Susan. With such short notice, I didn't pack enough skirts for you to spill on out of anger."

Susan didn't look at me but stared across the narrow space between her bed and the armoire. Her right leg banged back and forth against the edge of the mattress. "I'm really sorry, *Bubbe*, but that spoiled little prig just makes my blood boil. She's practically failing all her subjects and *she* got called out of lunch to work with Joshua."

"The boy who met her at the door?"

"No! That's the groom. Joshua is a horse. A hunter-jumper I've been taking care of since he hurt his leg. Now they call in Mary Louise, who couldn't put a Band-Aid on a cut without screwing up!" Susan jumped to her feet and paced. So cramped it was in here, I had to pull my pumps out of her way so she could pass.

"Maybe they think she needs the practice?"

"She sure needs something. She had to cheat to pass her last two math tests."

"So, it's skin off your nose if she's not getting the education her parents are paying for?" I patted her shoulder. "What are you really so mad about?" I lifted my feet again, she shouldn't step on my corns.

Susan whirled around with such a look I wouldn't have recognized my own granddaughter. "That bitch got me gated!"

"Gated?"

"You know, *Bubbe*, restricted. Grounded. That's why I can't tour with you. She reported me to Miss Kentworth. My grades are all As. I could have had time off with you but for that little whore."

I flinched at the word. "And what were you doing that she should report you?"

"Geoffrey and I were just kissing good-bye near the entranceway—"

"Must have been some kiss," I interrupted.

"Well . . ." Susan blushed. "You'd like him a lot, *Bubbe*. Really."

"What I'd like is for you not to be caught necking by your headmistress."

"I wasn't necking! It was just one kiss. But the boys aren't allowed on the grounds during the week."

"He snuck in? This I should like him for?"

"No. You should like him because he's the first boy I've gotten close to since Israel!" Her eyes were dark with hurt and I felt ashamed for pushing her about this.

She was right. I was happy to have her beginning to trust again where boys were concerned. "Your therapist approves?"

She nodded. "Geoff was nice enough to come to meet Doctor Schneider without making me feel like a complete fool. You don't know what that means over here." She looked a bit frantic.

I shrugged. "It's such a big deal for your boyfriend to meet your doctor and learn a little bit about a girl he's supposed to care for?" This didn't sound like such a hot prospect to me.

"*Bubbe!* People over here frown on psychiatry. It isn't like California."

I gave her a look. "For heaven's sake, Susan. Home everyone and his dog has a shrink. Even I know the English don't rush their pets to a doggy psychiatrist once-a-week regular."

"*Bubbe*, over here, *people* don't go with once-a-week regularity. It was a big thing for Geoff. I think he's sweet."

She looked angry, but I had to ask. "So, what was he doing sneaking into a girls' school?"

"It was just for a minute, *Bubbe*. He wanted to give me something." She went to her drawer and took out a pretty filigree Star of David on a thin gold chain. "His parents brought it back from Israel for my birthday."

I nodded. "But your birthday isn't until Friday."

"He won't be here then." She looked stricken. "His parents are picking him up at noon Friday after half-day session and they'll be in London for the whole weekend, then skiing in Switzerland for spring break."

My granddaughter's emotions were loosening her grip on the facts. I gave her a little nudge back toward the real world. "So, you two did something wrong and you got caught, and now you're paying for it. This is something to get so mad at someone else for and call her ugly names?" I held up my hand so she shouldn't interrupt me. "True, she shouldn't go telling tales, but you did break the school rules. That's no one's fault but your own."

"It isn't just that, Gram. Mary Louise Malbys gets away with murder and it's just because her father's the vicar. Maybe I was kissing Geoffrey, but she does a lot worse. I didn't just call her a whore. She is one. She sleeps around, *Bubbe.*"

"*Susa-le!* What a thing to say. Do I have to remind you about *Lashon Hara?* You know the spreading of gossip about another is against our religion." I was shocked at her behavior.

"It's not gossip when it's the truth!"

"You have proof of what someone does in private? You bug her room, maybe?"

Susan sighed and sank down on the edge of her bed. "Oh. *Bubbe!* It's not just boys she plays around with. It's anything in pants! And the vicar doesn't have the kind of money she spends."

"You're sure that isn't maybe your grudge talking, *Susa-le?* A little jealousy?"

"You don't understand."

Susan turned her back on me. Me, her grandmother. After all we had been through just a short time ago in Israel? This wasn't like my Susan. "I do. But we'll talk about something else so I can have a nice memory of this trip, all right?"

"All right, *Bubbe,*" she said with a sigh.

"Maybe you'd like to tell me why I shouldn't call you what I've called you almost since you were born?"

32

"Oh. *Bubbe*. Even my brother knows. *Faygele* means some guy who's a little light in his loafers."

"What?"

"You know. Gay. A homo."

My mouth dropped open. "What a way to talk. Polish your mother thought you would get over here."

"Over here has nothing to do with it, *Bubbe*. All my girl-friends are writing me from home. *They* warned me I should have you start calling me something else."

I shrugged. "Whatever you want. Maybe I'll ask someone at my *Hadassah* group what the Yiddish is for 'swan.' "

Susan laughed. "Whatever *you* want, *Bubbe*. I do have good news. We get to go to the opening service at Clifford's Tower on Thursday morning. It's for history class. Maybe we can meet before that."

I thought maybe I would change the topic to something I knew Susan would like. "Why don't we walk back to the paddock and you can show me Alexander some more."

It worked like a charm. Susan looked at her watch, grinned, and started for the door. "We have just enough time."

I leaned my elbows on the railing and watched Susan and Alexander move as one. So beautiful they both were, it made my heart ache. Susan would be an excellent vet. Maybe she would go into practice with her Aunt Deborah. Of course, that would mean moving to the Bay Area and I wouldn't see her as much. But if she was happy . . .

"Beautiful sight, isn't it?"

I turned to see her math teacher, Mr. MacMurray. His pipe was out now, but still in his hand. "I know, such a love she should only have for calculus."

Mr. MacMurray laughed. "I wouldn't go that far, Mrs. Zindel. Susan is adept enough and it's obvious that her heart is already taken."

"Yes, but she comes by it honestly. Her Aunt Deborah, my daughter, is a veterinarian in the San Francisco area."

"That explains it," he said. He smiled with his eyes as he watched her.

I was beginning to like this Scot. Compassion he had for his students. He must be a good teacher. "Susan will do well enough with her math to get into vet school, won't she?"

"No doubt about it. If she only had some affection for the subject, she could be a mathematician."

In the ring, Susan headed Alexander toward one of the higher jumps. I held my breath. Surely she would fall if she took such a jump bareback. My hands gripped the rail and even Mr. MacMurray stood rigid as Alexander, Susan sitting lightly on his back, soared into the air.

"Beautiful!" Mr. MacMurray shouted and clapped his hands as Susan completed the jump and rode over to us.

"Thanks, Mr. MacMurray," she said, beaming.

"You ride like a Cossack, lass."

She grinned, pleased with such a compliment. Even I knew that Cossacks were considered the best horsemen, although I shuddered, inwardly reminded of pogroms.

"I have to get ready for class, *Bubbe*. Excuse me, Mr. Mac-Murray." Susan hurried off to the barn.

I turned to the teacher. "If I wanted to take Susan to Scotland for spring break, where would you suggest?"

"Ach! Would you think me foolish if I told you my heart was in the Highlands?"

"Certainly not. You don't impress me as a foolish type, Mr. MacMurray."

"I am about Scotland. The Highlands offer the most breathtaking landscapes in the world. And you must see Nessie. She's a national treasure y'know." He winked at me.

"Loch Ness was on my must-see list."

"Fort Augustus," he said. "There's a most comfortable bed-and-breakfast farmhouse right there on the old pier, not a hundred feet from the *loch*. Mrs. Mackinzie's. Her daughter's a world-class harpist. They have horses there, too. And Highland cattle. The ones with hair in their eyes and great shaggy coats. Susan will be wild about it."

"Thank you, Mr. MacMurray. Fort Augustus it will be."

He turned to leave and I saw Janet coming across the pas-

34

ture. "I'm not interrupting anything, am I?" she said, looking from Mr. MacMurray to me and back again.

"No," I said. "Mr. MacMurray was telling me the best place to visit in Scotland. I hope to take Susan there for spring break, after the conference."

"Well, ladies, I have a class," Mr. MacMurray said, giving us a nod and striding off across the campus.

Susan came hurrying out of the barn. "Hi, Miss Percy. Did you enjoy your tour?"

Janet nodded.

"Susan told me that she wants to meet us for the opening services, maybe a little breakfast beforehand," I said, putting my arm around my granddaughter's shoulders.

"Wonderful," Janet said, and smiled.

"And tomorrow I have a half-day off, *Bubbe*. Would you and Miss Percy like to go riding with me? I'm sure I can get permission to use extra horses."

"What a lovely offer," Janet said. "But I don't ride, Susan."

"A horsewoman I'm not," I said, hoping to encourage her. "So we'll all have an adventure. It'll be fun, and we have Miss Expert Horsewoman here to help us." I waved at my *Susa-le*.

Janet shook her head. "Sorry, it's not my idea of adventure anymore. Not since I took a fall. I should have gotten right back on then, but I didn't. You go with your granddaughter, though."

I shrugged. "I'll do it. Years since I rode in the park with your grandfather, he should only rest in peace, but maybe it will come back to me. Enough horses I've handled with your Aunt Deborah. Promise you'll get a tame one, yes?"

Susan laughed and hugged me. "Yes, *Bubbe*, a tame one."

I nodded. "What time should I be here?"

"About six?" She looked at me.

"The horses are awake so early?"

It was good to hear my Susan laugh. "You always told me you were a morning person, *Bubbe*."

"I am. I just want to make sure the horse is a morning person as well. One of us should have his eyes open when we ride. Mine I'll have closed from fright."

"I'm sure you'll do splendidly, Fanny," Janet said

35

That wasn't what I would have called it. Splendid I knew my first time back on a horse wouldn't be. It wasn't until after our outing that I knew what a disaster a simple picnic could become.

Three

S o pretty the town of old York looked in the early morning. Mist rose off the river in clouds and dew sparkled on everything, even in the half-light. But cold. I pulled my scarf across my mouth and nose and zipped my jacket. If England's March had teeth, I can tell you, she kept them next to her bed in a glass of ice water!

Except for the milk delivery truck and a few vendors who hurried along empty streets with large boxes or pushcarts, I didn't see a soul. I played my tape of Israeli folk songs on my Sony as the cab rolled through the walled city. With all these buildings, walls, and cobblestone streets right out of the thirteenth century—and some even earlier—it was easy to imagine that instead of being here for a memorial, I had been sent back in time to witness the real Clifford's Tower Massacre.

That thought made me shiver so I began singing along with "*Boker, Boker*" and stared at the glittering river while I tried to think of something pleasant. With that view, it was more difficult to imagine anything ugly happening here.

Outside the town, the streets gradually filled with the city-bound cars of workers while my driver wound his way out to Taddington. My feeling of being a time traveler faded.

When the cabbie let me off at Susan's school, I could see that my granddaughter already had two horses groomed, saddled, and waiting. I tucked my Sony into my everything bag and headed toward her, smiling. So beautiful they looked. Fit and healthy. All three of them, my Susan included.

Alexander was there, of course. Bigger he looked up so close, me standing right next to him. His coat, that lovely gray, I now noticed was blotched all over with darker gray, and so shiny in the morning sun that I almost expected to see my face in the satin of his side.

"What a handsome boy he is."

Susan beamed like a new mother. "He's the most beautiful dapple gray anywhere in England! And very smart."

I agreed with her, naturally, and then eyed the horse she'd selected for me. Also a beauty, but shorter and heavier, and coal black.

"His name's Samson," Susan told me as I edged closer. "Go on, *Bubbe*, pet him. Here. On the neck." She rubbed the horse's sleek black coat and motioned for me to do the same. I reached out my hand.

Samson glanced around and snorted. In the chill morning air it looked like smoke coming from his nose. I jerked my hand back. More like a dragon he looked than a horse. "You're sure he's a tame one, Susan?"

"Quite. He's a baby-sitter horse. We even put little children on him and he's good as gold."

The only gold he brought to my mind was what my doctor bills would cost me if I fell off. I shivered a little and this time not from the cold.

She led him over to a big wooden box with stairs at one side. "Come on, *Bubbe*, you can mount from here."

Hesitantly, I raised my leg and put my left foot into the stirrup iron she held for me.

"Okay, *Bubbe*, balance your weight in this and swing your other leg up and over the horse's back."

I tested the iron loop. It wobbled. "Standing on one leg on something that moves isn't for a mature woman with arthritis."

"*Bubbe*, don't be a chicken. Think of that motorcycle ride in Israel."

"Mounting that, I had at least one foot on the ground, which, God willing, never"—I thought of California's last earthquake—"hardly ever moves."

"I'll help you swing your leg over."

Susan came up on the mounting block with me. It wasn't easy, but between us we managed to pile my old bones onto the animal's back. So wide he was, like a barrel. Susan walked around and adjusted my foot in the other stirrup. "Good," she said, pulling a pack onto her shoulders. She sprang up onto Alexander's back just like in the movies. So easy she made it look: *National Velvet*, and my Susan was Elizabeth Taylor, dark and pretty and fit.

From the school grounds, we pressed between some bordering hedges and set out across a field. Samson rolled beneath me like the deck of a ship. And a calm day on the ocean it wasn't. I gripped his mane and hoped I wasn't pulling his hair too hard. "You sure it's okay to hold on here?" I asked Susan for the third time. My fingers cramped inside my gloves.

"Just sit back and relax a little, *Bubbe*. Samson will do all the work." The muscles in my legs said different. *Oy*, would I ache tomorrow. But the scenery was lovely. Such fields and trees like I never saw in California. By March there, or even earlier, all the hills were brown already and dry and the fire department was sending brush-clearance notices to all the homeowners. Such a mistake to try to make a desert green with borrowed water. Rationing we had now at home and still, wealthy complexes kept *their* lawns green. My own was a beige that crunched when I stepped on it.

By the time we reached the first gate, I was getting used to the motion of the horse. "I think it's coming back to me," I said, as Susan jumped down, opened the gate, and waved me through.

"Great, *Bubbe*. How was your tour of Acaster Malbis yesterday?" She led Alexander through and latched the gate. Back up she leaped, like nothing.

39

"A disappointment. I thought for sure we'd see at least ruins of the Baron Malabestia's castle. Nothing was left. A modern pub they built next to the river where the castle used to be."

"The castle of the Evil Beast may be gone, *Bubbe*, but the chapel he probably used is spooky enough for me. Did you see it?" Almost before I could nod she dived into a new topic. "So, how's Nathan?"

"*Feh!* More disaster. He telegraphed he was delayed. Not till late tonight will he be here. We have a date for breakfast tomorrow." Susan grinned a bigger grin than I thought she had reason for.

The horses paused at the edge of a small stream. "They can cross this?" I asked, clutching Samson's mane in my fists.

"Sure. They like water."

"Even when some of it is still frozen?" I looked at the bits around the rocks. Like broken glass reflecting the morning sun off its sharp edges.

"Just give him a kick and ease up on the reins, *Bubbe*," Susan instructed.

With a sudden lurch, Samson plunged into the water, splashing and pawing with his front hooves until I thought there'd be no water left to run through the meadow. Most of it was soaking into my pant legs. "What's he doing?" I asked, kicking at his sides as much to warm my chilled calves as to get him to go on across. I admit my voice was a little shrill with fright, but my granddaughter just laughed.

"He's playing, *Bubbe*. Just like a big kid under a sprinkler in summer." She rode Alexander back into the water.

"Summer I can tell you it isn't!" I said, as he pawed more water onto my pant leg.

She tapped her palm with the flat-bladed crop, making a popping sound. Samson's ears twitched and he lunged the rest of the way out of the water and up the far bank with a speed I hadn't suspected. He nearly dumped me. I'm afraid I screamed and yanked at his neck hairs without mercy.

"Oh, how cute!" Susan said, laughing again. "He's getting playful in his old age, aren't you, you old teddy bear?" She leaned to pet his neck.

"Cute? The headlines at home will read GRANDMOTHER OF FOUR DIES OF PNEUMONIA, DUMPED INTO ICE WATER BY CUTE HORSE," I scolded, near laughter myself at the way Samson seemed to listen to my granddaughter's every word.

Susan talked some baby talk to the horse and then patted Alexander, just so he shouldn't be jealous. Such a way she had with animals. Susan should have been Deborah's daughter, not Judith's.

I looked up to see a huge, black-and-white-spotted cow staring at us. "Is that cow going to charge?"

"No. The cows don't mind us a bit. They're used to us riding through their pasture."

"It wasn't the cows' feelings I was worried about."

Susan laughed and led the way past one mooing face and then another.

I worried that the mother cows might be afraid of us, since a few of them had calves with them. But they just put their weight on their hindquarters and swayed back and forth on their front feet, or trotted out of our way when we got too near. Some of the young ones darted out from behind their mothers to get a closer look, but all those jerky movements on spindly calf-legs didn't seem to bother Samson. He just plodded on after Alexander. Before I knew it, we were at the far gate.

"*Bubbe*, you think Nathan's serious?" she asked, jumping down to help us through.

"Who knows what's in a man's mind? He's coming to see me. So we'll have breakfast, do some touring. That's all I know."

Susan looked disappointed. "You do like him, though, right?"

"To like is one thing; to marry is something else altogether different." Susan latched the gate and we went on. I could tell my *Susa-le* was thinking, but about what I didn't know. I hoped it was about my warning against hasty marriages. "So, you're seeing a lot of this Geoffrey?"

"Not enough to worry you, *Bubbe*, especially now that I'm restricted. Let's trot a little bit," she said.

Against my better judgment, I agreed. Sorry I was, almost

41

immediately. My brains and *kishkes*, insides, felt like they were riding a blender set on "chop." We stopped under a tree, and not too soon for my stomach, which, I don't mind saying, was back with the cows.

I looked over my shoulder. The school was out of sight. "How far are we, *Susa-le?*" It seemed like we'd ridden forever. My legs were a little tired. I felt like a wishbone being pulled for luck.

"Halfway. We'll stop here for a bit, *Bubbe*. I brought a Thermos of coffee and some croissants. We can eat before starting back."

"But if I get off, how do I get back on? You brought that big block of wood, maybe, in your backpack?"

Susan laughed. "The mounting block? No, *Bubbe*. But there's a nice rock over there and I'll help you."

I squinted my eyes looking for the rock. A pebble it was next to Samson. "But he's so tall," I protested.

Susan jumped down and came to help me. She eased me to the ground. Thank heavens she was holding my arms. I felt so funny, like that cartoon my grandson watches with the little rubber Gumby and his horse. I walked around under the tree until my legs stopped shaking like an aspic out of the mold. Well, rubber legs I needed to straddle that wide horse, and rubber legs I now had.

Susan spread out a blanket and poured two cups of hot coffee. The steam from the cups curled into the air. "Just walk around some more, *Bubbe*. You'll be fine for the ride back."

I did what my granddaughter suggested and before long my legs felt like they belonged to me again. Soon I was munching a flaky roll drizzled with honey and sipping strong, black coffee. So good it tasted in the cool morning. "I'm glad you suggested this," I told my granddaughter, as she poured some more coffee from the Thermos. "I think maybe I'll see if I can talk Sadie into some riding lessons when I get home."

Susan nodded her encouragement and bit into her croissant. "Doesn't food taste much better out here?"

I had to admit that if it always tasted this good, I would have a weight problem, tennis or no tennis. Then I told Susan all about my tournament win over Amanda Klarner.

42

Susan laughed and applauded, congratulating me on my sixth victory. "When we get back from riding, remind me to show you the bulletin on tonight's movie. Maybe you'll come. It's Rock Hudson and Doris Day."

"*Pillow Talk?*" I guessed.

"That's the one, *Bubbe.*"

"You bet I'll come." I poured more coffee.

"So, how are the cats?" she asked. "My Edgar Poe and Sasha and Charlie Dickens. Do they miss me?"

"Miss you? Of course they miss you. But I think they're getting to like me. Especially when I pick up the can opener.

"Such a *schnorrer* your Charlie, a mooch. Do you know what he does to get his breakfast if I don't get up early enough to suit him? He *klops* his paws all over my dressing table, knocking down the perfume and picture frames until I get up and feed him!"

Susan laughed. "That used to make Mom so furious!"

"He's done this before? You could have warned me to earthquake-proof my dresser for Charlie-cat," I said, trying to use my frail voice on her for sympathy, but I had to smile at the thought of anything that got Judith's goat. No wonder Judith insisted the cats come to stay with me.

"Don't try your tricks on me, *Bubbe*, you're not frail; I know all about your two years as an actress. Besides, you know you think Charlie's just precious when he—" Suddenly, Susan stiffened and stared over my shoulder at something. Then she jumped up and said a word I wished she didn't even know, much less use!

"Susan!"

"Oh, dammit, *Bubbe*, it's Joshua. Damn that Mary Louise all to hell! She's not supposed to ride him yet."

I looked around in time to see a blond streak on a large, coppery horse come flying across the meadow at top speed.

"I'm going to stop her!" she yelled, and ran for Alexander.

"Susan, no! Mind your own business. Enough trouble you've had with that one!"

She was already up on Alexander's back and turning him for the chase. "It's my business that she's going to cripple a helpless animal for life!"

Susan raced off after Mary Louise. Half stumbling, I hurried to Samson and tried to get up on him, cursing first my arthritis and then his height, then my arthritis again. I found the rock and lined Samson up next to it. It was a pebble—no, a mere grain of sand—next to that ox.

Susan was closing the distance between Alexander and Joshua. I held Samson near the rock and balanced myself on it. Wobbling, sweating even in the chill, and cursing, I finally pulled myself half into the saddle. Then he moved. I was almost on the ground again. My shoulders stretched and creaked. I grabbed his mane and yanked my body upright at last.

I set off after Susan, but I knew I'd be too late. They were already to the fence at the far edge of the pasture. I couldn't get my foot into the other stirrup. I kicked Samson into a jolting trot and nearly lost my balance, again. I jerked on the reins and fell forward onto his neck trying to hold on. What a mess. The Lone Ranger I wasn't.

By the time I got going again, I saw Mary Louise hurtling straight at the fence. With shock, I realized she must be going over it. I could hear Susan shouting at Mary Louise to stop.

Up into the air Mary Louise sailed. My Susan was right behind her. Alexander's powerful stride carried them both into the air. I held my breath until she cleared, watching as they vanished into the trees beyond the fence.

Frantic, I urged Samson forward. He seemed to know I was in a hurry and he broke into whatever they break into after a trot. Terrifying. Then I noticed it was smoother. Faster, but smooth like my rocker on the porch at home.

I was closing the distance and feeling quite good about my riding, despite my fear for my granddaughter, when across the clear morning air, I heard a horn blasting and the unmistakable, sickening squeal of tires on pavement.

Then nothing.

Four

STOPPING at the fence, I stood up as tall as I could in my stirrups. Even with Samson's height I couldn't see over the bushes and small trees. My heart in my mouth, I leaned forward on Samson's neck and swung my right foot over his back. Then I hung for a moment, facedown like a sack of potatoes, before dropping to the ground.

If my legs were rubbery this time, I was too worried to notice. I hurried to the fence, leaned down, and squeezed between the rails. On the far side of the road, I could see Alexander, head down as he munched grass. But where was my Susan? I felt sweat running down my forehead, and I began shivering as I searched the bushes.

I heard a soft moan and went toward it.

Susan lay on her back, half under a small tree. Even I could tell that its low branches had swept her from Alexander's back. Pulling my hankie from my pocket, I dabbed at the blood on her brow and slowly, she came around.

"Bubbe!" Susan struggled to sit up. I pushed her back gently.

"You lie still a moment. Such a lump you have, I could put it under a hen to hatch."

Susan smiled but reached to feel her forehead. "I couldn't duck fast enough; a branch knocked me off Alexander." She started up again. Again I pushed her back.

"He's fine. Across the road eating his head off in the green grass."

Susan smiled and lay back. "Did you see what happened to Mary Louise and Joshua?"

I shook my head. "No one is here but you and Alexander," I said.

"That's not possible!" She sat up. This time I couldn't hold her. She scrambled to her feet and hobbled around for a moment, whistling and calling, but there was no sign of the other horse, or of Mary Louise Malbys. "She jumped the fence right ahead of me, *Bubbe*. Look, here are the skid marks in the road where the lorry had to slam on its brakes."

"There was a truck?" My heart sank into my shoes. "You could have been killed." I hugged her hard. "I want to get your head looked at. Do you think you can ride back?"

Susan started to nod and then held her head still with both hands. "But I don't know how much help I can give you getting back on Samson."

"For you is not to worry about me. I'm getting good at this anyway. I'll use that fence and we'll be at the school before you know it."

Back at the barn, I wanted to take Susan to see the doctor immediately, but she shook her head. "*Bubbe*, you tell me all the time: Torah says we have to take care of the animals first," she reminded, smiling at me. I shook my head and sighed. She was right. We couldn't just leave them and I didn't see the stableboy around.

Once we put the horses away, I insisted on taking Susan to see a doctor in York. Susan agreed it would be a good idea, since the nurse had already left school for the day. Before we could leave the barn, we were greeted by Miss Kentworth.

"So here you are, you little ruffian."

Susan and I stopped in our tracks. I didn't like the tone of the lady's voice and I was about to tell her so when she continued.

"Miss Malbys tells me that you asked her for the answers to the math exam," the headmistress accused. "You're restricted for the rest of the month, Miss Zindel."

"Me?" Susan's eyes went wide. "I wouldn't even ask that girl for a used tissue. She tried every way to see my paper except a periscope. Ask? Never. If my answers were the same as hers, it's because *she* took them from *me*."

"That is complicity, then. You know you're supposed to go immediately to the proctor should someone try to cheat from your work."

Susan rolled her eyes. "Sure, and Mary Louise and her gang would be after me for the rest of my life in revenge."

Susan became flustered. I knew it was my turn to step in. I smiled my best Nancy Reagan smile at Miss Kentworth. "If my granddaughter is cheating, you can ground her all you want. I'll even ground her for you." I glanced at Susan, letting her know that I was sure she would never do such a thing. "You'll have them both take the test over again in front of you and that will prove who cheated from who. Now, I'm taking Susan with me to the doctor," I said, pointing to the bump on her head. Purple it was already. "I'll bring her back after dinner, *if* the doctor agrees she's all right."

I marched us out the door, past the scowling Miss Kentworth. So shocked we were at the accusation of cheating that neither of us thought to tell her about Joshua. A pity, but there would be time for that. First, a doctor for Susan.

The rest of the morning we spent at National Health.

Once the doctor had assured me that my *Susa-le* was fine we had a nice afternoon. A little bump. It would be black-and-blue for a few days, a week maybe, and then it would heal. He told me to watch her at first, just in case.

By dinnertime I could tell she was fine. A healthy appetite. Always a good sign. We ate at a lovely Tudor restaurant on Goodramgate. The fire blazed in one corner of the room and we took a table quite close to the hearth. Such atmosphere. It was done up like an old house, and I was not surprised to

47

learn that it was a conversion. Upstairs, on the way to the ladies' room, you could see one of the original bedrooms complete with authentic furnishings. The window from the bath looked down on an enclosed courtyard with flower boxes and tables, both waiting for better weather.

It was while we were on our way back in the cab that Susan began to complain that she hadn't said anything about Mary Louise's taking Joshua for a run.

"Is it so bad what she did?"

"*Bubbe,* she could kill him. Running Joshua on an injured leg like she did could lame him for life. Then they'd probably put him down."

"You mean . . . dead? They'd kill him for that?"

"Yes, it's horrid. But at least he wouldn't keep suffering."

I shook my head. "Such a beautiful animal. You mean somebody wouldn't keep him, just for a pet? Even if they couldn't ride him?"

"*Bubbe,* number one, not everyone feels about animals like we do. Number two, even if we didn't ride him, a horse like Joshua weighs well over a thousand pounds. He has to be able to carry his own weight, at least."

So sad, I thought, as the cab turned into the school drive.

"Are you sure you feel well enough to go to this movie?"

Susan nodded. "Yes, especially if you're going with me." She tugged on my arm and gave me that look, the one grandchildren give their grandparents when they know they can wrap them around their pinkies. I climbed out and sent the cab away.

Too warm for my jacket, but a little cool yet. I asked Susan if I could borrow a sweater. "A California evening in March this isn't."

Susan laughed. "I know. But I just love being able to wear all those wonderful things you crochet for me without getting heatstroke." She ran ahead of me to her room.

Before I could make it up all the stairs, Susan was back, a shocked look on her face. "*Susa-le,* what's the matter?"

She flew into my arms and, shaking like a tea towel drying in a wind tunnel, she shoved a letter at me. "It's so awful!"

48

I read the words. More awful it was to see them on such pretty paper and written in such a fancy hand. What it was, was ugly. Pure hatred put down on paper. I wanted to tear the note into a million pieces. "Who would do such a thing?"

"I think that's Mary Louise's handwriting."

"Oh, *Susa-le.* Where would children get such ideas?"

"From her father, that's who! That damn vicar is as anti-Semitic as Hitler."

I was shocked. "He's a churchman, Susan. He couldn't."

"I believe there were a few churchmen in Hitler's Germany who went right along without being exactly defrocked for their feelings toward Jews! What makes you think things are so different, *Bubbe?*" Susan started to cry.

I knew in my heart that she was right. Not enough had changed despite the lesson we all should have learned from that war. I hugged her tightly and rubbed little circles on her back with the flat of my hand, like I used to do to all my kids when they were upset or ill.

"*Susan,*" I said softly. "You'll make yourself sick." Gradually, she stopped crying so hard. "Now, we'll take this note to Miss Kentworth and—"

"No!" Susan lunged from my arms and grabbed the paper. "Mary Louise'd kill me!"

"*Feh!* Susan, this will get her grounded, maybe expelled. There are laws. Antidefamation leagues—"

"No!" She started to tear the paper, but I put my hands over hers.

"Now I am the one to say no, Susan. This you do not destroy. It's evidence. I'll keep it for you."

Susan pulled it from my grasp. "No. You'll call Mom and Dad."

"I won't unless you agree to it."

Susan shook her head. "You don't know what you're up against, *Bubbe.* Mary Louise and her gang practically run this place. Miss K is too friendly with the vicar to ever take anyone's side against his daughter. I'll keep it. Maybe it'll give me a little leverage over Mary Louise."

I gave her my Clint Eastwood look, the one where you

know he's going to clean up the whole town single-handed. "If it's that bad, I'm going to get your parents to take you back home right away."

Susan looked really scared. *"Bubbe,* you wouldn't. You can't. Promise me? I have some good friends here and the classes are just what I need for vet school. The teachers are great and I love Alexander. I can't lose him. Please."

I wasn't completely convinced. *"Susa-le—"*

"I can take Mary Louise down a peg by reporting her for mistreating Joshua. He's one of the school's best hunter-jumpers and worth a lot of money. No one was supposed to take him out but the stable lads."

"Well, I won't promise further ahead than just a day or two," I said. "We have to see how this works out." Susan threw herself into my arms and hugged me almost as hard as I was hugging her.

"Thanks, *Bubbe,* I knew I could count on you."

We decided against seeing the movie in the school library and I phoned for a cab as soon as I tucked Susan into her bed, like I used to do when she was little and would stay overnight with me.

As I waited in front of the dorms for my cab, I saw Mary Louise hurrying toward the stables with a young man. Remembering my granddaughter's accusation, I decided to take a closer look.

Keeping to the shadows, I walked to the side of the barn and tried to see something through the windows. They were *schmutsig,* so dirty I couldn't have recognized my own dear Morris if he had been inside with the horses.

Such a commotion. I didn't need to see, I could hear. But not clearly enough to know what it was about.

Suddenly, the door banged back, almost squashing me against the wall. I flattened; a blintz couldn't lie closer to the pan than I was to the wall, I can tell you.

The young man rushed toward the gates. He looked as if he'd been crying. The only thing I could think was that Mary Louise had given him the big heave-ho and he was taking it badly. I didn't have a lot of time to wonder, because she was next through the door. I flattened again.

50

Mary Louise waved to two girls across the quad. They joined her. Both quite pretty from what I could see in the poor light, and they all hurried toward the entrance to one of the classroom buildings, giggling. Hardhearted these girls, to be laughing on the heels of that young man's pain. I started to follow, but saw my cab pulling up the drive. I would have to run if I hoped to keep the driver from honking and drawing attention to me.

I ducked low, as if going for a drop shot, and darted through the shrubs toward the dorms.

The cab was coming to a stop. My back ached from the hunched position and I straightened a little to relieve it. Glancing over my shoulder to make sure I hadn't been noticed, I saw Mary Louise, now alone, going up the steps.

Someone else joined her. A large, male someone. Perhaps Susan was not just being spiteful when she spoke of Mary Louise seeing not only boys her own age. I stood straight and waved to the cab, then I hastily looked back. Strange, it seemed as if the shape who put an arm around the girl was somehow . . . familiar.

The cab pulled closer to me and I got in, craning around to look out the back window. "The Royal York Hotel, please, on Station Road," I said, watching as Mary Louise and whomever she was meeting climbed toward the lighted doorway. I wanted to see if I could recognize the man, at least enough to see if Susan's suspicions were fact.

As the cab pulled away from the buildings, I twisted in my seat and tried to stare a hole in the blackness.

Five

THEY were just about to step into the lighted doorway, and I was determined to see who she was with. "Slow down," I told the driver.

Mary Louise's blond curls caught the light. The driver slowed, but not soon enough. The cab coasted around the bend in the driveway. I lost sight of the entrance and the mysterious pair just a second before the light could reveal the man's face. It was enough to make even me curse. Frustrated, I sank deeper into my seat and chewed my lip. I forced myself to stop. A bad habit at my age I didn't need. Especially one that could irritate me into a lip cancer.

Maybe it *is* natural to want to know the worst about a potential enemy, but I tried to remind myself that Mary Louise was just a child, a high school girl. Besides, if the favoritism Susan spoke of was real, then no amount of scandal about Mary Louise would sway Miss Kentworth anyway.

Suddenly, I thought it might be an omen. I was ashamed. I was behaving like the teenager I had been when Sharon Feferman and I had tried to spy on Rachel's date with Harvey.

Later, I should have only known how much better it would have been to know whom Mary Louise was seeing.

I was still upset when I got back to my room. Janet was just making some tea. Unfortunately, she wasn't too busy to notice my worries.

"Fanny, you look exhausted. I hope riding wasn't too much for you."

"The riding was fine. It was the rest of the day that took the starch out of my hat feathers."

Janet made comforting clucking sounds and fixed me a cup of tea from the electric kettle. Then we sat at the little table by the french window that overlooked the garden and I told her everything. The ride, the injured horse, the accusation of cheating, right up to the anti-Semitic note. "I think maybe I should go over tomorrow and have a talk with Miss Kentworth. Maybe she can speak to Mary Louise's father. A man of the cloth should be able to do something about his daughter having such thoughts."

Patting my hand, Janet shook her head sadly. "I think that would be a mistake, Fanny. I had five years' teaching experience before I went for my M.F.C.C. I did a lot of my practice hours as a high school counselor."

"Then you know how cruel some girls—"

Janet squeezed my hand and stopped me. "*And* I know how much young people need to work out their own problems. Problems are part of life and life is what they are learning. Susan can't mature if her grandmother always intercedes for her."

"You think I meddle."

Janet put her arm around me. "No. I think maybe you care a little too much."

"Janet, anti-Semitism is not a children's squabble."

"No, of course not. But teasing is," she said gently. "I was the only Christian in Kenneth's family until he converted. You should have heard what they called me. But his converting didn't help. It made things worse. We broke up our marriage over it." She looked as if she was about to cry.

It was my turn to put an arm around her. The minute I did,

her eyes filled and she gripped my shoulders with hands that were surprisingly strong. "Fanny," she said, "Life includes some things that are quite ugly; you can't protect Susan from life. You can only make sure she's strong enough to survive it."

We hugged and dried our eyes. After we cleaned up the tea things, I began to pace in front of the garden windows.

"You're nervous as a cat, Fanny," Janet said, picking up the tourist guide and thumbing through it. "Ah-ha," she said, thrusting the book under my nose, "Here's what you need."

"A ghost walk?" I gave her a look. "This you suggest for nerves?"

"Sure. It'll be fun. Scary enough to take your mind off everything else."

I stared at the flyer. It did look interesting.

"Come on, Fanny. I'll treat us to a late dessert after the walk."

We grabbed our coats and I plopped my tam back on my head, sticking in one of my extralong hatpins to make it stay—just in case. Then I scooped the handles of my everything bag over my arm, checking inside to make sure I still had a bagel and the packet of lox from lunch.

On the elevator, Janet read from the guidebook. "It says that on some nights Clifford's Tower is supposed to glow red with the blood of the slain Jews."

"Pish-posh. I'll believe it when I see it," I said, stepping out into the lobby and darting around a slow-moving couple in front of me.

"What's the rush, Fanny?"

"If we're taking this tour, we have to get to the York Minster by eight. We don't want to miss the group," I said, hurrying out the door of the hotel.

Janet ran to catch up. "For someone who wanted to sit home and mope," she panted, "you—"

"Mope?" I cut her off. "Worry, maybe, about such a thing as my granddaughter and anti-Semitism in her school, where I never wanted her parents to send her in the first place. But I never mope."

Janet smiled. "All right. But you won't have time to 'worry' on this tour, either."

The lights of the minster made such wonderful patterns against the stonework. Little gargoyles grinned from almost every corner and the floodlit spires reached up into the black night sky. It took my breath to look at it. Soon the tour crowd gathered around us.

Our guide, a professor of history at one of the local colleges, had a real flair for the dramatic. I didn't have to be on the stage myself for two years to notice. He wore a black cape and spoke in a hollow, deep voice as we followed him through the winding streets to the Shambles. Hans Conried couldn't have done it better.

As old as the rebuilt Clifford's Tower itself, the narrow rows of houses with overhanging second floors were as fit for a ghost story as anything I had ever seen. A stage set it was, all ready for Banquo's ghost or the witches from *Macbeth*.

I shivered as the guide began to tell us about young Margaret Clitherow, a butcher's wife who had hidden a Jesuit priest. For her great sin, she was placed under a door, and it was slowly heaped with stone after stone—*heavy* stones—until she was pressed to death.

A saint she was now, and her house was a shrine for healing. Maybe I should come here tomorrow and see what St. Margaret could do for my arthritis.

Janet leaned close to my ear and asked if I wanted to come back the next day and see if Margaret could heal her migraines. I had to laugh at the way we each thought immediately of our own aches and pains.

We went on through Spen Lane and saw the foundation of the house of Baruch, one of the Jews murdered just before the massacre. The rebuilt house was said to glow as if on fire and have ghostly figures walking endlessly up and down the smoldering outside staircase.

"Such a lot of glowing going on," I said to Janet as we walked. "It's a wonder anyone in York can get any sleep." She laughed and squeezed my elbow.

I saw a shadow flit into a doorway and heard a soft cry.

"Come here, puss-puss," I said, stooping down to scratch the ears of a small gray kitten. He purred and rubbed his head hard against my hand. "A little something you'd like, maybe?" I dug in my everything bag for the lox. I fed him a piece from the end of my finger. His tongue, rough as my grandmother's hands after washday, licked the food and one small paw came up to beg for more.

"Such a mooch," Janet said, watching the little *schnorrer*, but I could tell she wasn't being critical.

"And hungry. So glad I could help, Mr. Cat," I said, dumping a portion of the lox from the baggie onto the stoop in front of him and hurrying to catch up with the ghost walk.

"Are you always a one-woman humane society, Fanny?"

"Always," I said, nodding and grabbing her elbow to speed her toward the other people.

The guide pointed ahead to the Black Swan Inn. As we caught up and stood with the rest, he told tales of Dick Turpin, the famous highwayman who was caught, sentenced, and finally hung in the city of York in 1739. One of the young people asked if Dick Turpin had really ridden a horse nonstop from London to York. The guide said probably not, that that had really been done by another highwayman, Swift Nicks Nevison, who'd first needed to set up a relay of fresh horses all along the route.

Thank goodness, I thought, recalling how long it had taken me to get to York from London even with a connecting flight to Manchester. Of course we hadn't been galloping, but I thought of how long Susan and I had ridden this morning to get across a pasture!

Exhausted by now, I took Janet up on her idea of a late dessert. Maybe something sweet would give me the energy I needed to get back to the hotel. Some apple pie and thick cream, just enough calories to keep me going through a tennis match. A match? This would carry me through all three days at Wimbledon. Nevertheless, I enjoyed.

On the way home, I had to admit Janet was right. I wasn't nervous, I was tired.

A note in our hotel box told me that Nathan had arrived safely and would see me tomorrow morning as planned.

Exhausted or not, I lay in bed a long time thinking about Nathan, picturing his spaniel brown eyes, his smile, the way the strands of sandy hair were brushed across the balding spot that was most of the top of his head by now. Would he have grown chubby with not working in the field for Mossad anymore? I didn't think so. After all, hadn't he written me about his workouts and his walks? The Nathan I'd known was trim, but he could have had a pudgy middle if he allowed it. I wondered if he would ever grow back the moustache I had seen in the photo he'd shown me. I secretly hoped so.

I had to admit that I was excited about seeing him again. So close we had become during our adventure in Israel. Many letters he had written and I had answered in the months since we had saved Susan's life as well as our own.

Nathan was a charmer, and a strong but loving man. Hadn't he helped me learn about my brother, Albert, at no little cost of his own time and effort? He was a dear, and he certainly did things to my heart rate with his kisses. But was it really thoughts of romance that set me tossing on my pillow tonight? After all, it wasn't every day I had a man travel thousands of miles for a date. Flattering, especially for a sixty-five-year-old widow who hadn't ever thought to have any romance in her life again.

"Good morning," Nathan said, and gave me a kiss. Such a kiss. And in the lobby in front of so many people! I know I was blushing when he pulled away. "I'm glad to see you, Fanny."

Another kiss like that and neither of us would ever get to breakfast. I felt a tear on my cheek and grabbed for my hankie. A silly old woman I was becoming. Such emotion over a kiss. Then I realized that it had tickled! The moustache from the picture; he had grown it back. "I like the moustache as much as I thought I would," I said, reaching out a finger and touching it to make sure I wasn't dreaming.

Nathan smiled, his teeth showing white beneath the tidy moustache. "Well, you said you thought it looked nice in that photo, so . . ."

I smiled to know he had thought of me when he'd grown it back. "It's very handsome."

"So have you missed me, Fanny?"

I hugged him, just so he would know, in case he didn't already. "We'd better go before breakfast turns into lunch."

Nathan laughed and took my hand. I was like a young girl again. He tucked my hand into the crook of his elbow and we started down the street toward Betty's Café.

Soon I heard a soft meow and felt a furry body rub my legs.

"I might have known," Nathan said, laughing. He leaned down and scooped up the kitten in one hand. "You picked a winner, cat." He couldn't hold the kitten; it lunged from his arms and toppled headfirst into my everything bag. "And he knows from whence all blessings flow, eh, Fanny?"

I laughed. Nathan held the struggling kitten again so that I could get the cream cheese off the bagel I'd fixed this morning for my everything bag. I fed the cat some from my finger to quiet him. So much for keeping up my supply of *noshing* stuffs—just in case. Well, I could refill my bag later. We set him on the cobbles and watched for a moment while he wolfed the cream cheese I'd scraped off my bread.

"Come on, Fanny, he's making me hungry." Nathan smoothed his new moustache with a quick gesture of thumb and forefinger and took my arm.

We hurried on to Betty's on St. Helen's Square.

So posh. Soft music, dark wood panels halfway up around the walls, waiters in starched black and white, snowy table-cloths, and silver trays to match the silver service. Everyone talked in whispers. The prices were to whisper, too.

"So," I asked, as soon as the waiter took our order, "you working on any interesting cases?"

"Some." His eyes sparkled, but he said nothing more.

"So, tell me."

"Fanny, you know I can't talk shop with an outsider."

"Me? An outsider? After what we went through in Israel? Why I'm practically a member."

"Practically, maybe. In reality, you never accepted the offer to join us."

I shrugged. "Being a spy I don't have time for."

"Think about it, Fanny. Meanwhile, let's drop the subject. I came here to be with you." The gesture again at the moustache.

The waiter brought my almond croissants on a silver tray and a small pot of steaming coffee for each of us. Such an omelette as he set in front of Nathan I never saw in a restaurant before. No flat scrambled egg folded over a filling, but a high, fluffy mound out of an omelette pan. "You might have to help me with this," Nathan said.

I edged my bread-and-butter plate closer and he lifted a section of cheese-and-mushroom omelette onto it.

"You want to take a tour today?" Nathan asked. "Maybe we'll take Susan?"

At the mention of my granddaughter, I felt my interest in the food fade. Frowning, I told him about the trouble and about the letter Mary Louise had pushed under Susan's door. "So, what do you think I should do? Janet, my roommate, thinks I should let the children work out their own squabbles."

"Fanny, anti-Semitism isn't just a squabble."

"Exactly what I told her myself. You think I should talk to the headmistress, Nathan?"

"Yes, and I'll come with you, if you want?"

I shook my head. "I don't want to threaten the woman with outsiders. Let me talk to her alone first."

"At least let me drive you, Fanny. Cabs are expensive."

I smiled. A man after my own heart. "I'd appreciate a ride, but I wouldn't like Susan to see us there. She'll think I'm meddling."

"You, Fanny?" He laughed and smoothed his moustache. "Don't worry. I'll be careful. I spy for a living, remember?"

I laughed, too. He reached across the table and took my hand and squeezed it. That made breakfast go down a little easier. After all, if I wanted to see Miss Kentworth, I'd have to keep my strength up. I reached for another croissant and put a bun into my bag for later.

* * *

I have to admit my hands shook a little as I opened the door
to Miss Kentworth's office. Her secretary announced me and
Miss K came out from behind her desk to greet me.

A coal fire burned on the hearth and the room seemed too
warm and cozy for the talk we were about to have. I almost
hated to ruin the friendly feeling.

"Mrs. Zindel," she said, pumping my hand. "How may I
help you? Have you decided to take our gamesmistress up on
her offer of a match? Ms. Westenbury is looking forward to
it, I know."

I shook my head and took a deep breath. Might as well
plunge right in. "I'm afraid it's a little more serious than
tennis."

"If you're still concerned about that cheating episode, I can
assure you we will take every precaution when we retest the
girls." She gave me a toothy smile. "Good idea, yours."

"Thank you, I appreciate that. But Susan's math grade isn't
what I'm here about."

"Oh?" Miss Kentworth motioned me into a soft wing chair
by the fire and called her secretary to bring in tea. Then she
sat on the loveseat across from me and set out two cups,
waiting patiently. Sara brought the pot and poured before she
left again.

"I'm afraid I am much more concerned about the anti-
Semitism problem." I didn't pick up my cup until I got that
out so my hand shouldn't shake and chip her china.

"Anti-Semitism?"

I had to give it to her, she looked shocked right to the toes
of her very British shoes. I nodded.

"What makes you think we raise our girls in such a climate
here at Taddington?"

I told her about the note Susan found shoved under her
door. I quoted it as best I remembered, such a thing I could
hardly forget.

"Well," Miss Kentworth whispered when I finished.
"Well. I certainly want to assure you that if I find out who did
this she shall be severely reprimanded."

60

"I know who did it."

Miss Kentworth seemed uncomfortable. "Yes?"

"Yes. Susan believes the handwriting is Mary Louise's."

She looked as if I had hit her with a rock. Her hand trembled and her china cup gave one more clink than necessary as she set it on the tray. "I hardly think that I can take action without seeing the note—"

"Susan has it. I told her to keep it for evidence."

"Of course, it would have to be proved to be her handwriting. Schoolgirls all have a similar round and childish hand, and they will play the occasional prank on one another."

"This was no prank. This is what started World War Two." I said it more sharply than I intended and got to my feet. "And for your information, Mary Louise was traipsing around in the dark last night with a man who looked old enough to be her father. But it was no vicar she was cuddling with in the doorways!"

Miss K got up, too. "That is a vicious accusation."

"That is no accusation. It's fact. I saw with my own two eyes. My cab was just pulling out or I'd have the identity of the man as well." I started for the door. "If I were you, I would call a meeting with the vicar about the behavior of his daughter. It is most . . ."—I thought a moment—"un-Christian!"

Miss Kentworth gave me a stare so cold I could have got pneumonia. "I trust you will find your way out, Mrs. Zindel. If not, my secretary will show you the way."

She turned her back on me and I left. No help was going to come from her direction. Now my only worry was that I had made things worse for my granddaughter.

Nathan was waiting for me outside the administration building in his car, just as he'd said he would. "Did Susan see you?"

"Don't worry, Fanny. I was careful." He held up a pamphlet he'd been reading and three tickets to a lecture at the Borthwick Institute at St. Anthony's Hall scheduled in a half hour.

"But Susan can't get off—"

61

"Fanny, you mentioned you have a roommate here. I thought your Janet might like to come. In fact, I left a message at your hotel for her to meet us."

I smiled. "Such a nice thing to do—and for a stranger, a woman you haven't even met yet."

"Any friend of yours, Fanny . . ."

I kissed his cheek.

"So, tell me. What happened?"

I told him. He wasn't happy either. "Maybe you should suggest to Larry and Judith that they take her out of school."

"Oy, Susan would kill me. That's the one thing she made me promise not to do. I said I wouldn't talk to her parents without asking her first." I shrugged. "To tell you the truth, Nathan, I think Susan assumed I included Miss Kentworth in that promise, as well."

"You feeling guilty, Fanny? You shouldn't. I would have done the same thing. After all, sentiments like that gave Hitler his tool for controlling the masses."

I looked at him. "That's almost exactly what I told Miss Kentworth."

He smiled, and I felt a lot better that we were of the same mind.

As we drove in silence, I thought about how good it felt to have Nathan's support in this. Living alone might have its advantages, eating what and when you wanted, doing what and when you wanted, but sometimes, I had to admit, that two people made a stronger launch pad for all this going and doing than one person alone. Compromise was hard sometimes, but his companionship was easy to take.

We parked the car in the lot for the Black Swan Inn. Nathan assured me we would make it legal by having lunch there later. We walked across Aldwark to the main entrance of Borthwick Institute and found it locked. We were puzzled, but we circled the building and found a charming little garden area and the door to the museum.

Waiting by the door was Janet. I waved, and introduced her to Nathan. They seemed to hit it off right away. And why not? What was not to like on either side?

Nathan showed our tickets and we went in. Upstairs was the Guild of St. Anthony. The hall appeared exactly as it must have looked back in the 1400s. Fascinating, I thought, looking up at the high-timbered ceiling and whitewashed walls. It seemed odd seeing metal folding chairs in this setting. Logs lashed together would be what I expected.

We took our seats and a tall, thin man wearing a doctoral robe entered. He stood before us, shuffling his papers and clearing his throat like a beginner, but when he started to speak, I knew him for the performer he obviously was. Years on stage couldn't give that much presence. A gift it was to open your mouth and capture a hundred or more people with your words.

Almost before we knew it, it was over and I was wanting more. As we filed out of the building, my mind was still full of the troubles caused by Richard the Lionhearted and his selling of offices to the nobility of the time. The Baron Malabestia and his friends, having borrowed heavily from the Jewish moneylenders of York to buy their titles, later hated the Jews for the stranglehold they had on finances. This hatred finally flared into the 1190 massacre.

Janet and Nathan must have been as spellbound as I, because we walked to the pub without speaking.

Nathan held the door of the Black Swan for us. Already it was smoky in here. I coughed a bit as we walked past the bar. Someone cheered as a dart hit the bull's-eye. The thrower slapped his partner on the back and shoved a pint of dark, foamy ale into his hand. Thank goodness the smoke cleared a little over toward the eating area.

We found a table in a corner where the roof slanted down as if it was an attic. Janet and I had to duck when we took our seats. Nathan, being taller, sat across from us.

His voice cut into my thoughts, "Powerful speaker, wasn't he?" He turned his chair sideways to the table. Janet didn't seem to notice, but I knew. Nathan would never sit with his back to a door. No Mossad agent would, not even a semiretired one. Old habits.

Janet looked over. "Oh, yes. I could almost see the baron's

men breaking into Baruch's house to reclaim Malabestia's collateral and take revenge."

"Me," I said, "I can still hear Baruch's wife screaming as the baron murdered her sons and raped her."

"I'm sure King Richard never imagined his coronation would lead to all that," Nathan said, shaking his head.

The waiter came to get our orders: steak-and-kidney pie for Janet, Welsh rarebit for me, and fish and chips for Nathan.

"It wasn't his coronation," Janet said, as soon as the waiter left, "it was the news of the curse from the archbishop of Canterbury."

"I guess if someone told me my entire reign would be doomed if I allowed Jews, women, or gypsies into my hall, I might keep them out, too," Nathan said, sipping from a pint of dark ale.

I frowned. "So superstitious they were in those days." The waiter put shandies—beer and lemonade—in front of Janet and me.

"Everyone has something they're superstitious about." Janet smiled and tasted her shandy. "I like this." She daintily licked her upper lip. "For instance, I love Friday the thirteenth, but I won't walk under a ladder."

"As a girl, I almost fractured an ankle trying not to step on cracks to save my mother's back," I added, remembering Rachel, Sharon, and me, hopping down sidewalks when we were young.

Our food arrived and for the next few minutes everyone was too busy enjoying the wonderful lunch to say much. My rarebit was smooth and creamy, cheese running deliciously over the edges of the toasted muffin. Nathan's chips were also delicious; he slid a few onto my plate before I could even ask.

I excused myself to go to the rest room. Nathan stood as I left. Such a gentleman he always was.

That was what caused all the trouble, my leaving.

I hadn't even gotten back to the table when seemingly out of nowhere the accusation came. "So! He's the reason you needed all our money!" Kenneth roared, gesturing angrily with his pipe.

Janet looked up in shock. Nathan stood, his fingertips

braced against the tabletop. He may have looked to others as if he were about to sit; I knew he was ready to defend.

I stepped closer and watched Nathan's face. I didn't have to look a second time to recognize Janet's ex-husband, the one who had made such a scene at the check-in only three days ago. From a corner of my eye, I saw Kenneth reach toward Nathan. A mistake, I thought.

He clapped his large hand over Nathan's shoulder. "Without interference from hangers-on like you," he shouted, "she'd never have had the guts to leave me!" He put the pipe to his mouth. There was a wet slurping sound as he puffed angrily, the smoke making him look even more like a demon out of hell.

Janet turned an unbecoming shade of rose. "Other men have nothing to do with this, Kenneth. I wouldn't be married to you after the way you humiliated me with all those students. I'm surprised you weren't fired for fraternizing."

"If you had your way, I would have been. And if I had my way, you'd be in jail for grand theft. I want my money back."

Everyone in the room was staring at us. Like statues they were, in that children's game, forks halfway to their mouths, glasses raised but not yet to lips. Janet glared at her ex-husband. "This is ugly. You have no right to take this up in public. I said I'd speak to you *alone*."

At her words, Kenneth stepped past Nathan, pushing him aside with that big hand, and grabbed Janet by the arm. "You're coming with me. Now!"

Janet cried out. It was all Nathan needed. His neat hand, well manicured I noticed, closed in a deadly grip over Kenneth's wrist, his thumb finding some delicate nerve point or other, and without even changing his expression, he brought Kenneth almost to his knees. The pipe fell from his fingers as if Nathan had squeezed them numb. His wide shoulders slumped and he bent at the waist in an effort to lessen the pain Nathan was causing.

Looking mildly into Kenneth's face, Nathan said, "If you don't leave now, and quietly, I'll have the barman call the police."

Kenneth didn't look ready to give up. It was a tiny move,

but I caught it. Nathan dug his thumb in and pressed harder. Now, Kenneth's expression changed from anger to despair. He knew it was a lost cause with Nathan here.

"Are you going to leave quietly?"

Kenneth's eyes began to water. I knew it wasn't from the smoke from his fallen pipe. He dropped to one knee.

"Fine, you win this one."

Nathan eased the pressure a little. Kenneth scooped up his pipe as he got to his feet. He yanked his wrist free of Nathan's grip and turned to Janet. "You'll keep your word about that meeting or I'll be back." He spat on the floor near Nathan's shoes and walked out.

The silence in the room continued for a moment more and then the general restaurant clatter of silverware and china returned. Everything was back to normal—almost. My heart was still pounding.

"Thank you, Nathan. I'm sorry this had to spoil our lunch," Janet said, as I hurriedly took my seat again. The flame in her cheeks still clashed with her fair coloring and her expression was pitiful to see. I looked away.

Nathan smiled. "Well, maybe not spoiled but it's probably too late to ask how you're enjoying your steak-and-kidney pie."

Janet laughed. It wasn't really a laugh-out-loud kind of joke, but I knew how she felt. Anything to relieve that awful humiliation.

Eventually things eased and we all decided to splurge on apple pie with thick Devonshire-type cream on top for dessert.

No sooner had the waiter brought our sweets than I heard Nathan's name being paged over the loudspeaker. "Who knows you're here?" I asked.

"I left our itinerary at the hotel in case the office called." He left the table and returned a moment later. "Fanny, it's for you. It's Susan."

"*Oy vey*, what now?" I tried to read his face. Was that worry? I hurried to the phone.

Moments later I was back. My face was probably as white as the cream on the pie. Nathan jumped up and took my elbow. "She's all right?"

I shook my head. "Susan's been expelled."

Six

OH, my God. That poor child. You two go help her. I can take care of myself." Janet started to reach for the check, but Nathan put his hand over hers.

"I wouldn't think of it," he said. "Are you sure you're going to be all right? We can walk you back; I wouldn't want you to have to deal with that man alone."

Janet shook her head. "I dealt with him for five years. I can handle another day." She gave me a hug. "Don't worry, Fanny. I promised to speak with him and I will. But I'll wait until he's calmed down."

"From your mouth to God's ear!" I said, hugging her in return.

I watched her walk bravely from the restaurant, but while Nathan paid the bill, I also saw her looking nervously up and down the street. Poor Janet.

"Let's go, Fanny."

I hurried into Miss Kentworth's office, Nathan at my heels. Susan bolted at me like a frightened colt. As soon as my arms were around her, the tears began.

I fixed the headmistresss with a look that would have done Joan Crawford proud. "Just what is going on here, Miss Kentworth?"

"Your granddaughter is responsible for the death of one of our prize hunter-jumpers. Her father will have to reimburse us for the animal and the vet fees. She has been expelled for life-endangering misconduct."

Suddenly, I felt as if she was Joan Crawford and I was helpless Betty Davis. I felt my knees trembling and I sank back onto a seat. "Explain."

Susan cut in, still choking through her sobs. "I came in to report Mary Louise for abusing Joshua, *Bubbe*. Mary Louise claimed I rode straight at her and hit Joshua with a crop, making him jump the fence and run into a truck." She looked at the floor, her voice cracking. "He was injured and they . . . had to . . . to destroy him." Her shoulders shook and she was in tears again.

I stood and put my arm around my granddaughter. "Susan, you go to the car with Nathan. I want to speak with Miss Kentworth."

Nathan nodded and led Susan out.

I stepped closer to the big desk. "You get that Mary Louise girl in here. I saw the whole incident. I was riding a horse called Samson."

Miss Kentworth pushed a button on her phone and asked her secretary to bring Mary Louise to her office. It was an uncomfortable few minutes marked with silence that nearly made me deaf.

At last the pretty blonde came in, looking tragic but still beautiful, and curtsied to the headmistress.

"Miss Malbys, Mrs. Zindel says that she was on the scene yesterday morning. Did you see her there?"

"No, ma'am. I was just so scared," Mary Louise quavered. An academy award this one should get, I thought. "When Susan rode at me—and hit Joshua—I was busy hanging on for dear life." She lowered her lids, displaying a damp fringe of long lashes. "I'm not the rider Susan is. When Joshua jumped the fence to escape her beating on him, I nearly fell myself."

She sank into the blue wing chair and put a dramatic hand to her forehead. Sarah Bernhardt, yet.

"My granddaughter would no more hit a horse than she would cheat on a test. For Susan, both are unnecessary."

Miss Kentworth cut in. "Mrs. Zindel, every rider hits a horse at some time."

"Not Susan. And neither do I. In California we have a group—Foxfield—that rides with neither saddle nor bridle. Susan was in that group for three years. They use carrots as a reward and never punish their horses, never, ever hit them." I made myself as tall as I could and glared at Miss Kentworth.

"I say she both yelled and hit him." Mary Louise's eyes flashed anger and I could see the kind of emotion that had probably written that hateful anti-Semitic note. It was no longer hard to imagine.

"Mary Louise, I was there. I saw you riding Joshua, hell-bent for the fence, and I saw my Susan ride after you at great risk to her own safety as she tried to stop you from ruining that horse's legs."

Miss Kentworth cut in. "Then you admit you watched Susan riding down on Mary Louise?"

"Susan saw Mary Louise riding a sick horse too fast. She only rode after them to stop her."

Miss Kentworth held a hand up to quiet Mary Louise. "Mrs. Zindel, how well do you ride?"

"I haven't ridden in years. But by the time we had stopped for coffee, it was coming back to me."

"Do you know what a riding crop is?"

"Of course, I know." I was indignant.

"Was Susan carrying a crop yesterday?"

In my mind, I could see her tapping it to make a noise to get Samson across the stream. "Yes, she did," I admitted. "But she used it only against the palm of her hand. The noise alone made Samson move." Miss K looked surprised. "Pain to an animal she would never cause."

Miss Kentworth took a riding crop from her desk drawer. "Mrs. Zindel, you say you saw everything; Miss Malbys says she did not see you on the scene. If you were too far away for

Miss Malbys to see you, can you explain how you managed to spot the absence or presence of a crop this size"—she held the whip aloft—"and exactly what was being done with it?" She smiled at Mary Louise. "You must have exceedingly good vision—"

"I said my Susan would never strike an animal in anger, let alone for personal revenge! And, yes, my distance vision is as good as anyone's. Farsightedness is an advantage for women of our years." As old as I she wasn't, but I felt like being a little nasty.

"The crop wasn't like that." I pointed. "My Susan carried a flat leather type that just made a little slapping noise with the large, loose leather paddles at the end."

"Mrs. Zindel, I don't think the type of crop is at question here. You're not a good rider, are you?" The headmistress showed me her teeth for a moment. "In fact, Susan said you had trouble even getting up on Samson by yourself. Could it be that you saw nothing because you were too busy trying to mount and control your own horse?"

I hoped my face was already too red with anger to show that I could still blush at my age. "Yes, I had some trouble, but I also rode after them and saw what I saw. Mary Louise went over that fence on her own, Susan only followed. I know. I had my heart in my mouth for both of them."

"Could you or could you not see the crop, Mrs. Zindel?"

"I couldn't, but the one you're holding is meant to hurt, Susan's was for making a little noise only, and—"

She cut me off. "Then you can't say what was done with it. And for your information, a snapping noise is as good as a blow if you want to make a horse bolt. Miss Malbys?"

Mary Louise looked up at the headmistress, her eyes wide. "Thank you, Miss Kentworth." She turned to face me, blue eyes wide with fake innocence. "Mrs. Zindel, I'm sorry that your granddaughter has such trouble getting along with me. I've tried to be friends with her, honestly." She looked over at the headmistress. "But every time I've tried to extend the hand of friendship, she just nearly snaps it off!"

The eyes filled with tears. The head drooped. "I loved that

horse, I did, honestly. But suddenly Susan was just riding at me and screaming horrible things and then she struck Josh on the rump. I mean, maybe it was an accident and she didn't mean to hit him; maybe she lost control and bumped us—" Her voice cracked convincingly. "But it scared him. He's high strung."

"So why did you leave the scene if you had nothing to hide?" I said, thinking of Susan lying in the dirt unconscious.

"The lorryman and I were going to try to help Susan, even though he said her falling off was only her 'just desserts' after what she did to Joshua. But the horse needed to be taken to the vet's immediately and he said we could send someone back for her."

I glared at her. She was good, very good. What makes a child into such a liar, such an actress? I had a twinge of pity for her, having come from the type of background that had shaped her into a liar to survive. But just a twinge. It passed. "Mary Louise, I saw you go over that fence while Susan was still shouting for you to stop. Then she followed you over. She couldn't have been close enough to hit your horse."

Miss Kentworth held up her hand. "This is getting us nowhere, Mrs. Zindel. I have the report from the lorry driver. I'll make you a copy. I'm sure Mr. Lawrence Zindel will want it for his counsel."

"My son is an attorney, Mrs. Kentworth. He'll provide his own counsel, I'm sure. And you'll be hearing from him."

"Not in England, Mrs. Zindel. He's not licensed to practice over here." She looked at Mary Louise. "You can return to class, dear." Mary Louise dipped a curtsy and hurried out the door.

I felt my heart sink. I had forgotten for a moment that we were the strangers in a foreign country and at their mercy for now. "The report?" I said, holding out my hand.

"I'll give you copies of that and the statement from the groom saying Miss Malbys had permission to take Joshua. As well as our bill for the horse and my write-up of Miss Malbys's report to me. That's everything. Exactly as I'm sending it to her parents in the next post." Miss Kentworth shuffled some papers on her desk top, put a packet together, and then rang her secretary. "Make a copy of all these for Mrs. Zindel before she leaves, Sara."

There was nothing for me to do but go. My poor Susan. I would have to help pack her things. I hurried out of the office and waited just long enough to collect the copies. Defeat left an unpleasant taste in my mouth and the lunch Nathan had bought me churned in my stomach. I felt ill.

Susan sat sobbing in Nathan's car. When she saw me, she flung herself into my arms. "Did you fix it, *Bubbe?*" She gripped my shoulders so hard I thought they would break. "Is it all right now?"

It nearly killed me to shake my head no. I handed her the papers.

Susan's eyes raked the pages as she read, frantic as she quoted from it. "Nathan, the truck driver says I chased Mary Louise and Joshua into the truck and the accident ruined his front fender. I didn't even know they'd been hit. By then I was unconscious." Her fingers went to the purple mark on her forehead. "He says Daddy owes him several hundred pounds for fixing his truck!"

Nathan put an arm around both of us. "That's just his side, Susan. Please, don't cry."

Susan pulled away, waving the papers at us. "It's all lies! Everything here is a lie."

Nathan patted her shoulder. "Susan, your grandmother can help pack your things. I want you to sit down at your desk and type out your version of the story while it's still fresh. Every detail."

"Good idea," I said, taking Susan's elbow. "Let's get started." As I walked her to her room, I saw Nathan nod slightly and knew he would nose around while we worked.

Susan lifted her electric typewriter—the one I had given her for a going-away present when she came here—from beside the desk and plugged it into the converter. "Should I type first, before I pack?" Her voice wavered on the last word.

"You type," I said with just enough firmness to push her tears back. "I'll start getting your things together."

"Thanks *Bubbe*," she said, and sat at her desk, rolling a sheet of paper into the machine.

I pulled open the armoire and began to fold her slacks, jeans, and sweaters into her steamer trunk. The clothes I knew were her favorites I left out for the suitcase.

Occasionally, I would ask her about this sweater or that skirt. But Susan didn't seem to care. She just sat typing, tears running down her face.

So it went, the next hour, her fingers flying and tapping, mine busy folding and sorting. From the corner of my eye I could see it was hard on her to remember it all, she swiped at tears with one sleeve or the other and typed on. Those cuffs were soggy by the time the writing slowed and Susan came to the end of her story, if not her sorrow.

"*Bubbe!*" she said, a new edge to her voice. "I'll never see Alexander again!"

I put out my arms and she flew into them like the little bird of the pet name I used to call her. She would always be my *Faygele*. I stroked her back. "Now, now, don't jump to conclusions—"

"I'm not. He belongs to the school and I'm expelled. No Taddington, no Alexander!" She seemed frantic. I wondered if a doctor would give her a sedative, maybe, before she made herself sick.

"Come, we'll talk to Nathan. He'll know what to do." I led her toward the door. "Besides, only he's strong enough to lift your trunk." I smiled so she should know it was a joke, but she didn't even notice.

Outside, Nathan started toward her immediately, but I stopped him with a hand on his arm and a look. "Nathan," I said, urging my granddaughter into the backseat. "Can you help with the trunk?" I led the way back to the room.

"Fanny, is she going to be all right?"

"I don't think so, Nathan. I want a doctor to give her something to quiet her. She's frantic over not seeing Alexander—her horse—ever again." I opened the door to Susan's room and looked at the report she had made of the accident. So neat, even in her state she was a beautiful writer and a

74

perfect typist. I gathered the pages and folded them into my everything bag before putting the lid on the machine.

"You'll want me to come back for that, Fanny, it's heavy," Nathan said, as I hefted the typewriter with one hand and Susan's suitcase with the other.

"I think I can manage," I said, sliding the handles of my everything bag farther up my arm and trying again for the suitcase.

"I said *I'll* come back for it. I don't want you hurting yourself, Fanny." Nathan gave me a look and I had to admit that it was very nice to have someone caring for me for a change. I left the suitcase on the floor. Nathan: one, Fanny: zero. Except his care really made me a winner, score or no score.

I was so used to doing for myself since Morris, bless him, had his first heart attack, but before that he had pampered me shamefully. Nothing heavier than cook pots or a sack of flour did I lift in my married life. When we were a young couple, it was my Morris who carried the children when they were too tired to walk. Me, I carried them the first nine months, as we used to joke.

I took only my everything bag so that I could help Nathan with the doors.

Two trips later, Susan's room was empty and Nathan's car was full to bursting. The trunk wouldn't even close and Nathan had to tie the lid down with twine. Thank goodness I had some in my everything bag, just in case.

Susan cried all the way from the school to the doctor's office. Fortunately, the same doctor who had treated her for her head injury was in. He agreed that she should have a mild tranquilizer.

"My stars!" Janet cried, when we walked into the hotel room with Susan looking like a war refugee. Her green eyes were puffy and her dark hair lay tangled and damp against her neck and shoulders. So upset she was that she didn't even greet Janet before collapsing on my bed. "You poor things." Janet plugged in the kettle and set out cups. "I think I should get another room."

I stopped her as she reached for the phone. "No. I'll get a cot sent up, if you don't mind."

"Not at all, I just thought that you and Susan might need some privacy."

I waved a hand at her. "Privacy-shmivacy. When there's trouble, you need your friends. And Susan and I aren't the only ones with a problem. Your Kenneth wasn't exactly pleasant today at lunch."

"Please, Fanny. You mustn't think about me at a time like this. I'll be—"

"There's safety in numbers, Janet. And I need your help." Right away, Janet looked supportive. I knew it would work. My granddaughter I could stay up all night to watch by myself, but if Janet needed to feel useful so that she would stay where she was safe from Kenneth's anger, then useful I would make her.

"Can you stay with Susan for a few moments? I want to get another copy of all this." When Janet nodded, I took the papers and left the room, only just catching Nathan in the gift shop before he left on errands.

"Nathan, why would anyone want to murder a beautiful horse like Joshua?"

"An accident is not murder." He was giving me his you're-jumping-the-gun look, which I knew so well from Israel. "You know children are willful, Fanny. She probably just thought his leg was all right because she wanted to ride him so badly."

"You didn't see how vicious Mary Louise was in Miss K's office. I'll bet there's more to this than we know yet. You should have seen them. A regular road show, Miss K and Mary Louise. Like they had it all rehearsed."

Nathan patted my shoulder. "I know you love your granddaughter. I love her, too. We went through Israel together, remember? But I also know you get so defensive that you lose all your perspective. You have no balance where family's concerned.

"You have to at least consider that Susan might have meant

well riding after Mary Louise, but overplayed her hand in her anger. It is possible that she really did scare the animal into the injury?"

I gave him my Spencer Tracy look; I don't have to tell you which movie; Nathan should only be dead from it. "Susan did not cause this."

Nathan tried to calm me but I pulled away, angry at his betrayal. "Fanny, I didn't mean intentionally, but children misjudge sometimes, try too hard with good motive but sad consequence. And children aren't the only ones."

"Now you're blaming *me* for something, I suppose?"

Nathan shook his head. "No, just in general."

"Well, you can keep your 'in-generals' to yourself, Mr. Nathan Weiss. Mary Louise jumping the fence and the accident with the truck were just the nuts on the strudel."

Nathan shook his head. "Kids are careless, Fanny. You always have to look hard at both sides because even the best of them can make mistakes. Maybe Mary Louise didn't realize how hard she was riding and then once the accident happened, it was too late to do anything but try to cover up."

"Cover-up. That's just what I think this is." I wanted very much to slap Nathan's face. There he was, excusing Mary Louise, that horrible girl. "If there's an excuse for Mary Louise, then it means Susan's to blame. Just leave." I turned on my heel and headed for the elevator.

"Fanny! I'm not placing blame. But you have to consider all sides; you know how kids—"

He had started after me, but I turned on him. "Susan did nothing wrong. *I* was there. *I* saw it. *You*, Mr. Weiss, were still on your plane. I suggest you get back on it. And go home!" I marched away, leaving him standing near the hotel doors.

Why was Nathan, my dear Nathan, doing this? I could feel something in my heart freeze over against him and it didn't feel good, I can tell you. How glad I had been to see him only this morning! The elevator arrived and I got in and punched the button for our floor. So hard I punched that I broke a nail. Right back into the quick. I held it with my other hand and cursed the pain.

77

By the time the slow old thing creaked to a stop, I was in even more pain in my heart and my head. But I had to admit that there seemed to be no reason for Mary Louise to deliberately try to cripple Joshua.

Could she possibly not have known? Susan said she was a poor student at every subject. My Susan couldn't have made things even worse by trying to stop her. Could she? For the moment, I hated Nathan for suggesting it.

Seven

*I*WAS glad Susan was asleep when I got to the room. She looked so small and helpless in her drugged sleep. I was ashamed for even thinking she could be at fault. But maybe I had been too hard on Nathan. A devil's advocate can have his uses. Perhaps I owed him an apology, but I would think about it.

Janet looked up with a finger to her lips. I nodded. Without making a sound, I took my everything bag and carefully emptied it on the cot. I threw out the bagel I hadn't eaten. A shame, but it was like a rock by now. Then I replaced all my emergency items and swept some crumbs off the spread into my hand.

Janet caught my eye and motioned me out into the hall.

"Fanny, what happened to that child?"

I told her. All of it. Then she sided with Nathan. Well, maybe not sided, but she asked the same things. I was shocked, a little hurt, but when two people, each so different, each a friend, asks you the same embarrassing questions, maybe it is time to realize that there could be two sides.

"Look, Fanny, let's go down to the dining room and get a

bite to eat. I haven't had supper and lunch seems forever ago."
Janet took my arm. "Susan will be fine. She's resting. The best
thing for what ails her. I'll just get my purse. You won't need
your bag, dinner is my treat."

A moment later she stepped back into the hall. "I left a note
telling Susan to page us if she wakes. But she'll probably sleep
till morning."

I looked at my watch. It was only about six-fifteen, but it
had been a long, hard day and I felt as if I could sleep till
tomorrow myself. "I'm not very hungry, to tell you the
truth," I said, half hoping to call off dinner despite Janet's
kindness. Besides, I felt a little naked without my purse or my
everything bag.

"Nonsense. If I know you, Frances Zindel, you'll only go lie
down and toss and turn for hours with all this on your mind.
Besides, you'll need your strength to help your granddaughter." She slipped her arm through mine and we went downstairs.

A nice restaurant. Elegant. We got a table in the corner near
a window and Janet ordered us each a glass of white wine. As
we sipped and looked over the menu, Janet kept the conversation afloat. Me? I wasn't even up to a dog paddle.

"You must have the Scottish salmon," she insisted. "It's
heaven. If you don't want to eat it, you can lure every cat in
York to your everything bag by tomorrow at breakfast."

I had to laugh, Janet was getting to know me. "All right, I
don't mind if I do."

I sipped my wine. "How are you doing, Janet? With all my
troubles I nearly forgot what a scene your ex made at lunch."

Janet didn't look as if she minded my asking. "I'm fine,
Fanny. We had our talk, Kenneth and I."

I raised my eyebrows at her but didn't speak.

She went on. "He really has nothing to complain about. He
accuses me of taking 'our' money from the joint account, but
I only took what was mine. I withdrew it before he could
squander any more of it on teeneyboppers."

I nodded. "A younger woman can be such an expense.
Made of money she thinks an older man always is. If he isn't
a big spender, she's quick to go somewhere else."

"Exactly, Fanny." She gave a shudder as if her wine suddenly tasted bitter in her mouth. "He spent endlessly on them while I worked along, nose to the grindstone, oblivious, and then he wondered why our savings account wasn't growing. He still seems to think that he should have been able to spend all he wanted and then still get half of what was left! Can you believe it?"

I shook my head. "I'm sure you were fair about it, Janet. Men with young women on their minds don't have much else up there."

She laughed bitterly and gulped her wine. The waiter came with our dinner, and I changed the topic. Just so it shouldn't be too gloomy, I talked about my cousin, Lady Doris Bond, and her fabulous estate and gardens.

Janet seemed to know such a lot about all the sights near York. She had even seen the gardens around Doris's estate, although that was back before Doris and her husband, Sir Bernard Bond, the magician, had purchased it.

"So Doris's husband was knighted for his expertise in entertainment?" Janet asked.

"Yes, he performed for the queen and the Queen Mother. Many times Doris has met the royal family. You should hear the stories she can tell."

The salmon was wonderful and I was a little hungrier than I thought, but I still had plenty to take up to my everything bag. Janet gave me her leftovers also. "What with all the strays in town, you'll need extra," she said, smiling.

We had agreed that I would contact my cousin, Lady Doris Bond, in the morning. Janet suggested that if anyone could help with a legal problem such as Susan's, Lady Bond would certainly know who it would be.

It was a great idea. I liked Janet. She was pretty and smart. A real head on her shoulders, that one, and not just for smiling nice and holding her hair in place and her ears apart.

We tiptoed past Susan and took turns in the bathroom getting ready for bed.

Sleeping I can tell you, wasn't easy. First I tossed one way and then the other. Could I ask Susan if Nathan and Janet could possibly have a small point without making her think I was accusing her? Personally, I didn't think so. But I must have finally dozed off because when I woke, I saw Susan standing at the window, staring down into the winter-gray gardens. A zombie. Her skin was an unhealthy gray in the pale light of dawn.

Quietly, I got up from my cot, my joints aching with the dampness from the river. For a moment I remembered my night in Amsterdam. That bed-and-breakfast had been right over a canal.

"*Susa-le*," I said, putting a hand on her shoulder. If I had been worried that I would startle her, I could have saved myself the effort. She didn't even blink.

"I thought you were asleep, *Bubbe*."

I hated the way her voice sounded, so flat and hopeless.

"Can you dress quietly?" I asked.

She nodded and moved toward her suitcase.

In the near dark, we both put on our slacks and walking shoes. Susan took a jacket and me, a heavy sweater. What else for a *bubbe* who crochets? We slipped out the door, careful not to wake Janet, and locked it behind us.

"You should see the river with the mist rising in the early morning, Susan. Beautiful."

Susan didn't even answer, just followed like a whipped dog at my heels.

As soon as we were outside the hotel, I made her stand and take some deep breaths. A few stretches, a little exercise, my joints would loosen and maybe her spirits would lift. A walk through town with one from the dead I didn't need.

Stubborn like me, like her father, like her Aunt Deborah. So, it ran in the family. But I insisted, and she was still my good granddaughter.

"I feel silly, *Bubbe*," Susan said, lifting her arms over her head and leaning to touch her toes.

"Again," I said. "Never mind, silly."

Susan gave me the start of a smile and leaned forward, almost placing her palms on the ground. Such a thing youth could do. Me? I was lucky to make it to midcalf; this early, maybe to my knees only.

A few leg lunges like Errol Flynn in a sword fight and we started out. Well, Susan's lunges were like Flynn's, mine were more like Julia Child getting a pot from a bottom cupboard. I trotted from the hotel doorway, missing the weight of my Sony recorder strapped to my waist, but now was no time for music and thinking, now was time for my granddaughter.

Station Road was deserted as we walked briskly up the grade to Lendal Bridge. The stone bridge house looked almost haunted in the fog, like a castle and a moat out of the movies. I half expected Katharine Hepburn to come sweeping down to a waiting boat like she did at the end of *The Lion in Winter*. It gave me a shiver to think that horrid Miss Kentworth had sent my Susan away from what she loved, also.

At the middle of the bridge, Susan stopped, rested her elbows on the old stones, and looked out over the river Ouse. The glassy water reflected the lamplights that had not yet been turned off. On some of the occupied boats, people were obviously getting up and ready for their day. I always thought it looked cozy, the yellow glow shining out from the small round windows.

I looked at Susan and thought that perhaps I might tackle the difficult problem of her sharing in some of the guilt. "*Susa-le*, Nathan thought the report you wrote out was very good."

She nodded but didn't say anything. She just kept staring out at the water.

I tried again, "He thinks it needs a diagram, though. Maybe something to scale?"

Susan turned. "Scale?"

"You know, like where one inch equals one mile and it shows how far things were from other things."

"*Bubbe*, if you want to know, did I ride into Joshua, and was I close enough to hit him, why don't you and Nathan just ask me?" She glared, turned quickly, and walked on over the bridge.

Too smart she was. I hurried after my granddaughter. Such a *shmendrik*, a fool, I had been. Now she was angry with me as well as with the world.

I was puffing, like after a hard set of tennis, when I finally caught up with her, halfway down Lendal Street. I hooked my elbow through hers. It didn't stop her, but at least it kept us together. By the time we reached Mansion House, the oldest residence for the lord mayor of any in England, I felt a few centuries older myself. But at least I had convinced Susan that I didn't mean any harm. Now I would have to phone Nathan and convince him of the same thing. He deserved my apology.

"I just don't understand why everyone thinks I could be to blame. I was trying to stop her, you know?"

"I know, *Susa-le*, but you were also very angry. You can't blame people if they think maybe a young person might get a little overenthusiastic. It's not uncommon, you know. I'm sure kids at rock concerts don't go there planning to trample their friends or rip the performers limb from limb."

"*Bubbe*, nobody knew Joshua better than I did. I was with him almost as much as I was with Alexander. Maybe more, since he got hurt. I knew exactly how nervous he was, and I would never ride up fast and screaming at him. That could hurt him, too."

"So, what happened?"

"I did scream and ride toward Mary Louise, but I made sure that I only got close enough for her to hear me. I know she did, because she looked straight at me and kicked Joshua until he broke from his canter into an uncontrolled run. That was when she really pulled away from me. I won't even run Alexander—who's healthy—over unfamiliar ground. There might be a hole or a burrow."

Well, she was making sense now. I only hoped she had thought about all this at the time. "So how far away were you when she went over the fence?"

"Maybe half the length of this building, *Bubbe*."

I looked up at the arches in the light-colored stone of the Mansion House. Sixty feet or more it stretched, its elegant cream columns dividing the red brick face of the top two floors. Surely that was far enough for safety, I thought.

I tried to remember if Susan had still been shouting when she seemed so close to Mary Louise. I looked down Stonegate toward St. Helen's Church. At least as far away I had been from Susan and Mary Louise. And from here, the front of the church looked flat, nothing forward of anything else. Eyes like a hawk my contacts gave me, but depth perception at that distance I had to admit wasn't so good.

We walked up Stonegate toward St. Helen's, then turned down Davygate. Not far, but we were nearly to Parliament Street and the start of St. Sampson's Market Square by the time she spoke again.

"I'm sorry, *Bubbe*. I guess it's really a sore point, everyone thinking I might have done something stupid where animals are concerned, just because I was angry. I'm going to be a vet. I'm more professional than that."

I put an arm around her shoulders, hugging her against my side. "I'm glad to hear you put it that way, about the professional part, I mean. But you know, I had to ask."

She nodded. "But it hurt."

I sighed. "Yes. I'm sure a lot of things will hurt before this is over. You know what Rabbi Nachman of Bratslav, said: 'Where there is no compassion, crime increases.' "

"Yes, *Bubbe*, and he also said, 'Toothaches afflict those who have no compassion for animals.' "

"So you listen when your Aunt Deborah speaks?"

"Aunt Deborah says that, too?"

"Only every minute she was growing up. Sayings like that she would always use on me every time she came home with another stray and reached for another of my kosher bowls to make *trayf*, unclean, with animal food."

Susan laughed. It was good to hear it. "Actually, Geoffrey's father always reads from the scholars before we have lunch on Saturday. He likes me to come over because I listen and Geoff doesn't."

I raised my eyebrows at her. "Over *there* you listen? Maybe I should have Geoffrey come over to give *your* father an audience on holidays."

Susan grinned. I was happy to see her smile. She ran ahead of me toward the market stalls. It was nearly seven and most of the merchants had their wares displayed.

They called to us as we passed. One smart cookie was selling cups of coffee or tea. Susan looked his way and I had to admit it smelled good.

"Let's get some."

She nodded.

The vendor, a cap pulled low over his eyebrows, his fleshy nose red with the morning chill, greeted us with a gap-toothed smile. In his heavy English accent, he wished us a good day and sold us steaming cups of coffee with cream, begging us to see the vendor next to him for some muffins to go with it.

The town was beginning to come to life around us. While we were walking, there had only been the milk delivery van on the streets. Now, cars were lining up to get into the city. Here in the marketplace, the rag merchants hung brightly colored shirts and dresses on cheap waterpipe racks, such *shmattes* as I had thought to find only in the garment district, set out by my Uncle Ernest, Lady Doris Bond's father, he should only rest in peace. Like a state fair it looked, with its open stalls and the men and women bundled against the cold as they called to everyone who passed. "Come. Buy!"

"You know, *Susa-le,*" I said, as we sipped our coffee and strolled through the stalls, "I hate to bring up an unpleasant subject, but have you any idea why Mary Louise would want to hurt an innocent animal?"

Susan put an emerald green blouse back on the rack and frowned. At first I thought I'd upset her again.

"I really don't know, *Bubbe.* But she must have wanted to, mustn't she?"

Good. It hadn't been me she was mad at. She was frowning because she was as puzzled as I was. I breathed a sigh of relief. "You said she was a bad student. Is it possible she didn't know she was riding hard enough to hurt him?"

"She knows the difference between a walk and a canter. Joshua was only supposed to be ridden at the walk. He could only trot on a longe line, no weight on him. Cantering or running were forbidden."

"So, we're back to my question."

"As pretty as she is, *Bubbe,* she still can't be that dumb."

86

I shook my head. "Such a stereotype, Susan? You think smart and pretty can't go together? Have you looked in your mirror lately?"

Susan shook her head, gave me her sheepish grin, and I went on.

"Pretty she may be, but a little hard looking. How you live shows in your face," I insisted. "She ignores the rules all the time?"

Susan shrugged. "One of the girls who left last semester said Mary Louise had had an abortion."

"Was this girl in a position to know, or is it more *Lashon Hara?*"

"Gossip? No. She was friendly with Mary Louise and her whole group. Then the rumor started. About the same time, she went away suddenly, even though she loved it here. I always wondered if they forced her out. Mary Louise and her group could be mean enough to make a horse stay away from sweet feed."

"The school would allow such persecution?"

"I told you that Mary Louise is a favorite. Miss K wouldn't do anything to harm a hair on her blond head. Or to upset the vicar."

Susan fell silent. Her eyes got so dark they looked almost brown instead of green. "What's the matter, *Susa-le?*" I had thought she was feeling better.

"Miss K. What if she calls Mom and Dad?"

I patted her arm. "A phone call that one would make? When everything has to be in writing anyway? Never. Besides, she mentioned mailing it. By mail it'll take a week or more. There's time."

"Time for what, *Bubbe?* It's hopeless!"

"No. I have an idea. You'll help by being a good girl and staying at the hotel this morning. I have an errand."

"What errand?"

"If it works, I'll tell you. Not to worry."

As soon as we reached the hotel, I called Nathan's room to patch things up. Lucky for me, he was an understanding man, although he did slip in that he was waiting for me to come to my senses. I had to admit to him that it took longer for that to happen when something involved my family.

Doris was so glad to hear from me that getting time with her was not a problem. She simply cleared her morning calendar. Even transportation was provided. Because Janet decided Susan shouldn't be alone, she would stay in and let me take her car. I wondered if she was glad not to risk seeing Kenneth again on her own.

Janet assured me that the car was easy to drive and the road to Easingwold—A19—was clearly marked. All I had to do was get out of town. Which wasn't so easy as it sounded, given the English fondness for something called a "roundabout." *Vey is mir,* those things were straight from hell! Two or more lanes circled around and *HaShem,* God himself, couldn't have taken a turnoff from the inside track.

Staying to the left wasn't hard as long as I was just going straight down the road looking at the sheep and cows grazing in the green fields. But when it came to turning, or those *meshuge* roundabouts, everything seemed backwards to me.

A wreck nearly. And all because I tried to stop for a small calico bundle I saw struggling toward the highway. I held my breath as a car whizzed around Janet's rental. Thanks to God that the way I had parked—half on the road and half off—had sheltered the little animal from that maniac. Looking to make sure no other crazies were coming at top speed, I got out and hurried to help.

Half-dead the kitten was, and shivering. In this wind, so was I. Hoping it would live long enough for me to ask my cousin where I could take it for care, I tucked it under my coat and returned to the car.

Now driving was even more difficult. The kitten, as it grew warmer, began to wriggle and squirm within my clothes. Finally, I had to pull over again. I took the kitten from the folds of my coat and plopped it on the seat next to me. "You're going to make me wreck the car," I scolded, grabbing her from the floorboards under my feet. She nosed my everything bag, straining with her back legs to push her front end inside.

"All right!" I dug out some of last night's salmon and

placed it, wrapper and all, on the seat near Miss Hyperactive. She lunged into the fish, small front paws kneading the foil.

I pulled out into traffic again, hoping that the food would keep her busy until I reached Doris's. No such luck. A wolf would have taken more time with the food. I hadn't driven a mile before the kitten, now fed and warm, was on my shoulders, under my feet, and bouncing gratefully all over the car.

When I finally found the sign to Easley House, I can tell you, it was the first time I stopped praying. Twice I had turned and ended up nose to nose with another car. Lucky for me, they must have been used to Americans trying to learn about keeping to the left.

I promised myself that if *HaShem* would only get me back to York without an accident, I would leave driving to those who knew how to do it backwards.

Such a house. All gray stone it was, but not gloomy. And huge.

As soon as I stepped from the car, like *Jaws* from the movie, the wind nearly bit me in half. "You stay here, Miss Hyper-cat. I'm going to ask Doris if she knows a home for you." The kitten bounced toward the open door. I pushed her back and shut her inside. She squealed in protest. It took all my willpower to leave her behind.

I cranked one window down enough for her to get air and locked the car. Pulling my head down into my collar, I hurried toward the front door. My skin felt brittle. The wind stung my eyes. It was hard to believe that the withered-looking gray stalks and shrubs would turn into a famous garden within a few months. Dirty patches of snow still lay in the shadowy areas beneath trees and along the foundation on the north side of the mansion. I ran for the porch.

Just as I was about to become a Popsicle, the oak door opened. Cousin Doris pulled me inside and hugged me.

Doris was as I remembered. Maybe a few gray hairs more, but tall and robust just like her father, Uncle Ernie, had been. I could still remember him picking us up and swinging us almost to the ceiling in his strong arms.

"Come by the fire. These old places are hard enough to

keep warm. I don't want you to catch your death." She rang a silver bell while I huddled close to the huge stone hearth.

Within moments, a housemaid in a starched white apron and a black dress entered with a tea cart.

How good it felt to warm my insides with her tea and her friendship. "Shocking!" she said, when I told her of Susan's trouble. Immediately she was ready to do what she could to help. Robbie Patterson, a friend of hers, would be able to provide Susan with legal help, should it come to that. In the meantime, she offered to check with others and see if anything strange was going on with either the Vicar Malbys or Taddington itself. She mentioned that she had known one of Taddington's important officials.

Doris said she felt quite guilty for ever putting Taddington on the list of suggested schools for Judith and Larry to consider. I assured her that that was silly. She had given no special recommendation for Taddington over the rest. There had been five or six schools on Doris's list. Hadn't the family traveled here the summer before to check them all out and make their own decision? That seemed to put her at ease.

"Not to impose," I said, "but I have another favor."

"Ask."

"A little visitor I picked up on the way here. A sweet little calico darling. Half-dead from cold and staggering onto the road. Do you know of someone who would want a kitten?"

Doris shook her head. "Our Tom would kill a kitten. But I know just the place. Mrs. Johnson at the Four Pause Cattery is a darling. I've done charity work for them."

"Is it close?"

"It's on your way back. Just a little off the beaten track."

"I'm not very good at driving over here," I said, hesitantly.

Doris smiled at me. "Don't bother yourself. Leave her with me. I can have my gardener drive her down later today."

"It's no trouble to keep her away from your Tom?"

"I'll shut her in the kitchen. Tom's an outdoor cat unless we get more snow."

I nodded. "Miss Hyper-cat will like that better than the rental car."

The tea grew cold and the scones vanished as we visited. Doris pushed a paper bag with a dozen fresh scones into my hands. I paused only long enough to get her the kitten from the car. Then I hurried back to town for the Clifford's Tower services.

"Love to Susan!" Doris called from the door as I ran for the warmth of the car. "Be sure to bring her back with you on Sunday afternoon."

I was uneasy all the way back to York. My mind kept churning like noodles about to boil over. Until Doris mentioned how odd it was for a headmistress to play favorites, one girl over another, it hadn't occurred to me to wonder about the school itself. All the way back to York, it was so much on my mind that driving was even more of a nightmare.

I should have been thinking about how nice it was that Doris and Bernie had had such a full life before he passed away. She had started as his magician's assistant and traveled the world with him. Then they had returned to his home country and had many prosperous years. It was topped off by his receiving his knighthood, just before they bought the grand estate, Easley House.

Bernie had left my cousin more than just comfortable in her later years. Although she had lost Bernie, he'd died quickly, without pain, and had not lingered. Such blessings!

Instead of these thoughts, my mind whirled with Susan and the trouble at Taddington. Some things Doris had said kept coming back to me.

I swerved back onto my own side of the road as a huge truck honked viciously and the driver yelled out his window something I'm sure I was glad I hadn't understood.

If there was anything wrong at the school, what could Miss Kentworth be trying to hide? Why would she favor such an obvious liar as Mary Louise? And why persecute my granddaughter?

Eight

WHEN I returned to the hotel, I had a welcoming committee. All three, Nathan, Janet, and Susan, were in the parking lot waiting for me. Something told me Nathan had probably been scandalizing them with tales of my driving in Israel. I was so glad to see him again I didn't even care. As soon as I got out of the car, he gave me a big hug. I knew all was really forgiven.

"So, I was a little late," I said, handing the keys to Janet. "From driving in England, I don't need. I thank you for the loan, but next time I'll leave the driving to someone else."

Janet grinned. "Was it keeping to the left or the roundabouts?" she asked, wickedly.

I waved a hand at her. "You knew and you didn't warn me?"

She shrugged. "What could I say? Roundabouts have to be experienced to be believed."

Nathan cleared his throat and looked at his watch. "Ladies, we're going to be late for the opening ceremonies."

"Oh," I said, "I'm so sorry. I meant to get a picnic lunch packed—"

Janet cut me off in mid-apology. "I had the hotel kitchen pack one for four while you were visiting with your cousin. It's all dairy so you and Nathan don't have to worry." Janet pointed to the wicker basket sitting by her side.

I threw my arms around her. "Such a good friend. I wouldn't have been late, but I found this kitten by the road and—"

Janet burst into laughter. It wasn't long before Nathan and Susan joined her. They all knew me.

Nathan carried the lunch and we all hurried toward Clifford's Tower.

On the way, I told them about the kitten, how I rescued it (Janet rolled her eyes and sighed), and finally, Doris's thoughts on Susan's problem.

I know it made Susan feel a lot better to know help was standing by. At least, she felt better until we reached the tower and found that Vicar Malbys had already begun speaking. Quiet as snow falling, we crept to our seats. Unfortunately, it didn't keep the vicar from pausing a moment and staring, making notes on who came late.

Susan blushed beet red. I could almost feel the heat in my own face as the vicar glared at us. Then finally he went on. I saw Susan look over at Master Barr and her history class. I knew she wondered if they'd noticed. Mary Louise and two of her friends glanced over, obviously pleased at Susan's trouble. I felt guilty because I was the one who had made us late.

I'm sure I don't have to say the vicar's was the longest speech of the bunch. I was glad it was winter or we'd all have had heatstroke before he finished. As it was, the wind had picked up sometime after the third speaker. I had to put my crocheting away because my fingers got numb. With nothing to occupy my hands, my mind wandered a bit, I have to confess.

I kept looking up at the huge circular tower of stone that had replaced the wooden original after the fire. At least if such a thing happened nowadays, God forbid, the Jews would have a fireproof fortress in exchange for puffing up all those steep stairs with their worldly goods.

At last the opening ceremonies ended. While most of the delegates joined a tour of the city, we four set off to find the warmest side of Clifford's Tower that was out of the wind.

We settled for the park side below the hill. Eagerly, I poured hot coffee and bowls of vegetarian vegetable soup. Susan spent most of her time ignoring her food and walking around the carousel on the grassy area near York Castle.

Even in the cold, the park's gaily painted animals reminded me of summers when we'd gone to Navy Pier in Chicago. Right off Lake Shore Drive, it was. My father would load us all into the old Lincoln and we three children would bounce up and down in the backseat until he parked and let us out. Such festivals they used to have on that pier: the Fourth of July celebration, with all sorts of foods, rides, fireworks, live music; every time I saw a carousel or a Ferris wheel I thought of those happy times with Esther and Albert.

I leaned over and kissed Nathan on the cheek. He smiled. "What was that for?"

"I was remembering the good times I used to have with my brother and sister." I didn't have to tell him any more. He smiled and squeezed my hand.

Once we had finished lunch, and the basket was lighter, Nathan agreed to hike up to the tower with us. As we climbed the zillion stairs, I tried to imagine what the original wooden tower must have looked like when the Jews had decided to burn down their own shelter rather than have the mob kill them to steal their possessions. The same method the Russians used to defeat Hitler: run and leave nothing behind that the enemy could use, no food, no possessions, no shelter. It had just worked better in Russia.

After we toured the main floor of the fortress, Susan wanted to climb to the top of the walls. Nathan and I went with her, but Janet said she had been up before and wasn't crazy enough to risk the narrow passages and rocky steps a second time.

Right she was about narrow and rocky, but such a view. I was glad to see it. I took half a roll of pictures while I was up there. All York spread at my feet.

Back outside, Susan wanted to walk around the base of the tower.

"Come with me, Janet. There's as good a view here as there was from the top and it's not as precarious as the tower wall."

"Such a steep, grassy hill isn't my idea of safety."

"Come on, Janet. I'll hold your hand. The path is really quite wide. And look"—she stamped her foot on the grass—"good solid ground."

Janet sighed. "All right. I guess it looks wide enough."

Wide maybe it was, I thought. But it still made me nervous to see them out there. I would have felt better if the water from the original moats and fish ponds still surrounded the tower. A softer landing for anyone who might roll down the hill.

"Nathan, maybe you should go with them? Make sure they don't fall," I said. I raised my camera and called to Susan to pose a moment. It would give Nathan time to catch up.

As Janet and Susan made funny faces for my camera, I clicked away.

Suddenly, like a moving picture I couldn't stop or close my eyes to avoid, I saw Nathan lunging toward the women. Susan screamed. Janet shrieked. I dropped my camera and stood frozen to the spot as a rock crashed down from the upper walls and fell toward them.

Nathan pushed both Janet and Susan out of the way. Either the rock struck Susan a glancing blow or she lost her balance trying to avoid it. I screamed as I saw her falling, turning over and over in a tumble of arms and legs, down the steep hill from the tower's base clear to the bottom and the chairs still set up for the conference.

Nine

I WAS headed for the stairs even before Susan stopped roll-ing and lay still. Nathan didn't bother with stairs. He plunged down the grassy steepness, half on his feet and half on his *tuchis*, the seat of his pants. He was the first to reach her.

Janet and I could hardly keep our balance as we pushed gaping people aside and hurried down every one of those zillion stairs with our hearts in our mouths.

I could hardly believe my ears when Nathan shouted to us that Susan was alive. I made it to the bottom faster than I'd ever crossed a court in tournament tennis.

"Please," I cried to the people who had gathered around her. "That's my granddaughter!"

They parted to let me through.

"*Faygele?*" I bent down.

"Don't move her, Fanny. I think her arm's broken."

I gasped and drew back, hearing the sound of the ambu-lance siren. Someone had already phoned for help.

Susan looked up at me and reached out with her uninjured hand. Tears ran from her eyes. I gripped her fingers in mine. She held on as if for dear life. What more could go wrong for my poor *Susa-le?*

96

I rode in the back of the ambulance with Susan. Nathan and Janet returned to the hotel for the car. By the time they arrived at the hospital, I was pacing and Susan was in the casualty ward. Nathan was right. Her arm was broken, so was her spirit. First the trouble with Mary Louise and the death of Joshua, then the anti-Semitism, the expulsion, and now this.

I ran into Nathan's open arms even before he was all the way through the waiting-room door. I couldn't help myself. Tears came and I sobbed out my fright and anger. "How much trouble could *HaShem* give a young girl like my Susan?"

"I'm not sure *HaShem* had anything to do with this," Nathan said.

"What do you mean?" I pulled back a little and looked at him.

He shrugged. "It may not have been an accident. The police questioned us before we left. I went up to the top of the tower with them. That rock was really a bit of the masonry. It appeared to have been loosened and pushed off deliberately."

"But who would do such a thing?"

"The police are checking into it now. How's she doing?"

"Not so good," I said, tears in my eyes again. "The doctor says she is so depressed about all this that she's a poor surgical risk."

"Surgery?"

"Well, they have to knock her out to set the break. You think maybe they give her a stick to bite on like in the Old West?"

Nathan smiled at me and shook his head. His arm came around my shoulders, comforting me. "So defensive, Fanny."

"Sorry. I'm worried. Tomorrow's her birthday and look where she's spending it. Expelled and in a hospital bed."

"Is there something special she'd want? Something to cheer her?"

"Two somethings—and both she can't have."

"Nothing's impossible," he said, stuffing change into the coffee machine. He handed me a cup with extra cream and sugar, just like I liked.

"Alexander would cheer her up, and he belongs to the

school. I would think next she would want to see her boy-friend, Geoff. But he's going to London with his parents this weekend." I sipped the coffee and walked back to the waiting room.

Nathan took the chair next to mine. I settled back in the ugly green plastic couch. "It's a shame her boyfriend didn't know she was going to be laid up. I bet he would come to see her."

I looked at Nathan in surprise. Such good ideas he had. "We'll call," I said. "He's not leaving until tomorrow. Noon, I think she said." I started up from my couch.

"You have the number?"

I plopped back down. "No. I don't even know his last name."

"Susan's already in surgery?"

I nodded. "Even so, it would be better as a surprise."

Nathan was silent for a moment. Then he got that twinkle in his eye. "So? You have all her things at the hotel. She must have his name and number."

"But Nathan, that's private."

"I seem to remember that didn't bother you when you searched *my* room in Israel."

I blushed. "That was different. This is family. I never read any of my kids' private things. Not diaries, not letters, not even the envelopes."

"Don't think of it as snooping, Fanny. Think of it as a good deed. That kid up there will need something to cheer her when she comes out of surgery."

I raised my eyebrows at him. "The doctor did say she would heal better if she wasn't so depressed."

"That's right, Fanny. You're just giving her what the doctor ordered."

"You think?"

He nodded.

I smiled.

We headed for the hotel.

It took hours, but at last I found what I needed.

* * *

When Susan was ready to leave the hospital the next morning, we had a surprise for her. Geoffrey was waiting in the hall with a big bunch of flowers. Hothouse, this time of year. Also a nice card from his parents, who it turned out liked her quite a lot, and who approved of Geoff's staying with us for the weekend and maybe spring break instead of going with them.

Susan cried, but I could tell she was happy. At least I had done one good thing. Now, if I could only find out why everyone from the truck driver to the stableboy had a story that went against my granddaughter.

Geoff had arranged, asking me politely, to take Susan to his midmorning soccer practice and then to lunch. Such a nice young gentleman my Susan had found. We had chatted a lot while we waited for her release. At least I could rest my mind now that Susan had someone who seemed to deserve and return her care and affection.

I asked Janet if she could attend the Friday morning lectures at the conference and make my apologies for me. She was sure everyone would understand that Susan's welfare came first. Nathan warned her to be careful of trouble with Kenneth. She put on a brave face, I could tell, and laughed it off. I'd have rested easier if she had taken my advice about the knitting needles and maybe a few lessons.

Nathan and I were now free to get on with the business of finding out what was going on at Susan's school.

Now that Susan was taken care of, Nathan was anxious to share with me all he had learned. As we pulled away from the Royal York, he was talking almost nonstop.

"So, this stableboy," I said, when he paused, "you think he was bribed to say Mary Louise had permission to ride Joshua?"

"More than likely. From what I could find out about local wages, that lad had more money this week than his position should pay. His friends at the pub were well pleased with his generous buying of rounds. That was Tuesday, the night before Susan was expelled."

I shifted in my seat so that I could see Nathan's face. "You think there's a connection?"

He nodded, one hand reaching to smooth his moustache.

"Not only that, but I had a friend run a make on that truck driver. He keeps some pretty rough company. Twice he's been arrested for disturbing the peace. Once for burglary, but they couldn't make it stick. His friends all keep coming up in 'known associate' files."

"What's that?"

"It means he's a crook and he hangs out with other crooks."

My eyes widened. "A girls' school would associate with someone like that?"

"Fanny, the lorry driver was one of the victims of that accident. There's nothing to really tie him to Taddington. As far as anyone knows, he was just Mr. Good Samaritan."

"Oh." Disappointed, I sank back into my seat. I looked around. "Nathan, this isn't the road to Taddington."

"I know, Fanny. We're going to have all our facts straight before we see Miss Kentworth."

"So, where?"

"Gresham."

"Is it animal, vegetable, or mineral, Mr. Twenty Questions?" Sometimes Nathan's having been a spy for so many years irritated me to pieces. Him and his "just the facts, ma'am" attitude. More you could get out of Joe Friday!

"Fanny, don't get angry. I found out that there's something fishy with some of Mary Louise's friends. One in particular."

"Why didn't you say so?"

"You didn't give me a chance."

"You've got it." I tapped my foot against the floorboards and waited.

"Mary Louise is an exceedingly popular girl."

"Tell me something I don't know. Like why?"

"Take it easy. She dates a lot of boys but not, it seems, for love alone. Some of the guys at the pub think she's running a ring, she and her friends. And it's not around the rosy!"

I kept quiet and waited.

"Prostitution, Fanny. Sex for money."

"I know what prostitution is, Nathan. That sheltered I'm not, but children?"

"Seventeen, and from what I hear the men are older. Some of them a lot older. One of the men in that pub who had a lot to say about it when he was in his cups looked nearly forty."

I gasped. "You're sure?"

Nathan blushed. "The men, some of them, were pretty explicit. Nothing I'd repeat to you, Fanny, but, yes, I'm sure. One even offered to introduce me. Said there was a cute little redhead who was a 'hot number I might fancy.' "

I put my hands over my mouth. So sick I felt all of a sudden, I thought I might lose my breakfast. I remembered the girls I had seen with Mary Louise that night by the barn. One had been a redhead. But they had looked so young, so carefree, giggling in the dark together.

"Sorry, but you asked."

"And I accused my granddaughter of *Lashon Hara.*"

"Well, she wasn't gossiping. I doubt she knew as much as I heard. At least I would hope she didn't. But whatever she did hear was probably true. I have names and numbers if Miss K wants to get hard-nosed about it."

"So who's this Gresham we're seeing?"

"Not who. Gresham is a boys' prep school. They have dances with the girls at Taddington. Apparently that's where a lot of the deals are made. The boys have to pay for the room. Or provide one. The fee seems to be rather small for the actual service."

I drew in my breath. So callous. And so young! I thought of the man I had seen with Mary Louise that night. I had thought he looked older. Had that been one of her dates for money? Such a thing at a respected English school? Wasn't anyone watching these girls?

"My Susan gets restricted for just kissing Geoff at the gates and this is going on? Something is more than fishy, Nathan."

I swayed as the car swerved into the iron-gated drive of Gresham Preparatory School. Prepping for what? I thought to myself as Nathan parked.

"You'd better let me talk to him, Fanny. Given the subject, I'm sure it would be easier without a lady around."

I nodded. There were things I didn't need or want to hear.

I wished him luck and pulled my crocheting from my everything bag. My fingers flew through the lime green wool, my hook flashing faster the angrier I got. How could such a thing be happening? And how could it even begin to involve a girl like my granddaughter?

When Nathan came out of Gresham, he looked grim but satisfied. "The boy confirmed that Mary Louise led him on sexually. Then she dumped him. Hard. There's a lot of anger in that young man, and I know he's holding something back, but I'll talk to him again later. Right now I want to get to Miss Kentworth."

It wasn't far from Gresham to Taddington. Nathan had both barrels loaded by the time we asked Miss K's secretary if she was in.

"Miss Kentworth is extremely busy this morning."

I noticed she ignored me. That was fine. Men were good for strong-arming.

"Miss Hovely?" Nathan smiled, glancing at the brass plate on her desk. "My name is Nathan Weiss. I'm a close family friend of Mrs. Zindel's. I think Miss Kentworth will make time for me. Unless she'd rather talk directly to the police."

Sara Hovely straightened her spine and stared at Nathan. I could have told her he didn't bluff. At last she said, "One moment," and whisked into the inner office.

I smiled. Nathan: one, Taddington: zero.

From the inner office we could hear Miss Kentworth, her voice loud and unpleasant. "I'll not donate any money, Miss Johnson! You and your absurd organization have had all you're getting from Taddington."

"We'll see about that," said a high-pitched voice I didn't recognize. The door opened and Miss Kentworth's opponent, a painfully thin woman about my age, came hurrying out, a terrible scowl on her sharp-featured face. She whirled out the door, cape flapping like the dark wings of a hunting hawk, and slammed it behind her.

Barely a second it was before Sara came back and showed us in.

Miss Kentworth stood behind her desk. "What's the meaning of threatening my secretary with the police, Mr. Weiss?" She had obviously decided to attack first.

"No empty threat. I am fully prepared to call them." Nathan was so cool. A regular cucumber he was.

"On what pretext?" Miss K looked only furious, not frightened. I began to wonder if we had made an error.

"Several counts. You know a boy from Gresham named Harry Parker?"

Miss Kentworth looked uneasy. "Never heard of him."

"Seems he's heard of you. Mary Louise Malbys was dating him, to put it nicely. You threw him off the grounds."

"Of course. My girls are not allowed dates on campus unless it is a school-arranged function. Like our dances with Gresham, which are *thoroughly* supervised. But that doesn't mean I remember every randy little twerp by name."

So haughty she looked. Nathan: one, Taddington: one.

Maybe she didn't know what was going on. I almost felt sorry for her.

"Mr. Parker's father is going to see about pressing charges against Miss Malbys. Soliciting, I believe?"

Miss K gasped and started to reach for her intercom.

"I'd wait, if I were you. There's more. The men at the local pub say it's easy to get a bit. Mary Louise will arrange everything but the room." Nathan: two, Taddington: one. I looked back and forth between them. The ball was in her court.

"I believe that would be slander, Mr. Weiss."

"Only when it's not true. We have a number of witnesses. Also, it seems that your stable lad had an excess of money to throw around the pub the night before you expelled Susan Zindel. Would you care to explain how that happens to be?"

Hooray, Nathan, I thought, cheering him in my heart. Let her explain that one. He was scoring so fast, I was almost losing count.

"I'm sure I don't know," Miss Kentworth said, glaring and sitting down in her chair. She groped for the inlaid box on her desk and came up with a cigarette. Her free hand reached for the sterling silver lighter. She didn't offer Nathan a cigarette.

Good, he didn't smoke. Well, a pipe now and then, but not much.

"Maybe you would venture a comment on the fact that the lorryman who turned in a report against Susan has a criminal record and a number of very unsavory friends." Another point for Nathan.

"Why should I comment on a perfect stranger? I'm only grateful that he had enough decency remaining, despite such a background, to save that poor tortured animal extra pain and suffering."

Did she have a point there? I was afraid so.

Nathan stroked his moustache. I hoped it wasn't nerves. "His employer said he makes regular deliveries to Taddington. Hay and feed and such. Occasionally he transports furniture or delivers loads of schoolbooks. How is it you call him a stranger?"

Now I was sure he had her on the run. My ears perked up. This he hadn't told me. Miss K knew the lorry driver? I leaned forward in my seat, wondering who would score the game point.

"Mr. Weiss. I am not in the habit of introducing myself to every Tom, Dick, and Harry who happens by the school with a delivery." She lifted her chin and drew heavily on her cigarette. She casually removed a bit of tobacco from the tip of her tongue with a tissue. Not even a filter, I thought. Lung cancer she'd have before she knew it.

"Are you sure there isn't something more you want to tell us about the incident that got Susan expelled? I think, you see, that a lawsuit is already out of the question," Nathan said.

"Even if what you are suggesting about Miss Malbys's behavior has a grain of truth, Mr. Weiss, the private actions of Miss Malbys would have no bearing on the fatal accident caused by your granddaughter, Mrs. Zindel."

A point. A definite point. And maybe the game.

She glared at me for the first time. I couldn't keep still any longer. "Miss Kentworth, when I was a girl there was a saying, 'If you'll lie, you'll steal.' I say that if Mary Louise could keep you in the dark about this prostitution ring in your own

104

school, she's certainly not above lying about the death of a valuable animal."

Nathan glanced at me. I saw pride in that look. One for our side.

Miss Kentworth stood and turned to face me. She ground her cigarette in the Waterford crystal ashtray before she spoke. "Mrs. Zindel, you seem bent on believing that Mary Louise is certainly guilty of one crime because she may be guilty of another. I won't have that."

"Perhaps we should confront the young lady directly," Nathan suggested.

"Not without legal representation," Miss Kentworth said, and lit up another cigarette. "You'll remember, Mr. Weiss, she is a minor."

"So is my Susan," I said, probably louder than I should have. "And she's already been punished without even a trial." The game was going steadily downhill.

"We have written testimony of her life-endangering behavior; from not just one, but two sources." She had more than evened the score.

Nathan took a step closer to the desk. "Testimony that, indeed, may be fraudulent." Good for Nathan.

"Then court is the place to prove it so." She stood, rang for her secretary, and asked Sara to show us out. So sudden? A slap in the face.

I walked out, not really sure anymore as to who had won what. Games with stakes as high as my granddaughter's whole future and reputation weren't much fun to play. Suddenly, I didn't care what the score was anymore. I just wanted to get my hands on Mary Louise Malbys. Preferably around her lying little throat.

No sooner were we in the hall when I tugged at Nathan's sleeve. "I still want to talk to that girl."

Sara Hovely darted from the office and hurried from the building. She hardly glanced at us as she practically ran through the halls.

Nathan looked uncertain. "Could be trouble, Fanny."

We stood for a few minutes, arguing about our next course

105

of action. We were still discussing it when we got to the car. Nathan wanted to talk to the stableboy in person. I wanted to see Mary Louise.

While we argued, the secretary came lurching back across the grounds and bolted into the administration building. We were still looking after her when the voice of Miss Kentworth came over the public address system.

"Security, restrict everyone. Close the campus gates."

Suddenly people were scurrying everywhere. The heavy, wrought-iron gates of the school clanged shut and in less time than I could think, we heard sirens. A minute more and the gates were opened to admit a police car.

Oy vey, what was happening?

Naturally, Nathan hurried forward and introduced himself to the chief officer. The police must have accepted Nathan's offer of assistance because Nathan began walking with the bobbies toward the girls' dorms. I started to follow, but Nathan waved me back and told me to wait in the car.

A short time only they were gone. Nathan's face was white when he came up to me. Like a piece of paper he looked, pale and flat. Even his voice was toneless.

"What's wrong?" I whispered.

Nathan shook his head. "They want us back in Miss Kentworth's office. Mary Louise is dead."

I started to say something.

"Murdered." He took me by the arm. So stunned I could only follow, my mouth yawned open like the Grand Canyon.

Before I could find out anything, the police had us all lined up for questioning. The officer asked us if we had been anywhere before we went in to see the headmistress. We told him that we had come straight from Gresham. Nathan gave him the time and the names of the people he had spoken to there.

The officer wanted our names and how we could be reached later. I mentioned that as a delegate to the conference, I would be at the representatives' dinner at the Viking Hotel that evening. The police took my information and made me wait in the hall. Nathan, as usual, was quickly released.

We were about to leave when the front doors banged open

106

and the security guards frog-marched two youngsters toward us and toward Miss K's office.

My heart sank into my shoes and pinched as if I'd stepped on it. My Susan and her Geoff!

Ten

I WASN'T the only one to turn to ashes at the sight of Susan and Geoff here when they should have been almost anywhere else. Nathan looked sick, really as if he would have to excuse himself to the men's room for a moment.

"Nathan?" I said, clutching his arm.

He grabbed my sleeve and tried to drag me to the door.

I pulled back. "Susan! What are you doing here?" I said, glaring at her in my hurt and anger.

"Fanny! Shut up." Nathan grabbed me quite roughly and practically shoved me from the building.

"Nathan, what do you think you're doing?" I said, yanking at my arm to free myself. What had come over the man?

"You could only make things worse."

"What worse? Susan is where she isn't supposed to be and—"

"Exactly. And better that the police shouldn't have you to point it out to them. Susan will be suspect enough."

"Susan?" Nathan was making me really angry. And frightened.

"Mary Louise wasn't just dead."

"Dead isn't enough?"

"It was a ritual killing. The thirteen stab wounds, Fanny. Like Passover. The medieval ritual blood letting. The Jews always got blamed."

That did it. I clamped my lips together as visions of the horrible killings the Jews had been accused of for centuries flashed through my mind. Babies drained of blood and Jews blamed for the crimes by anti-Semites who said they used the blood for the making of matzo, the Passover bread. Sometimes a crown of thorns would even have been pressed into the young scalps. Before the original Clifford's Tower Massacre, there had been at least five blood libels in towns not far from York. Now there was the memorial, and it was happening again.

I felt nauseated. I leaned against the fender of the car.

"And that's not all," Nathan said, taking my hand. "Half under the body was a gold Jewish star on a thin chain. It looked like Mary Louise yanked it off her attacker in the struggle."

Now I gasped and leaned forward over the fender. I was sick. Nathan supported me as I vomited. Then he offered his hankie.

"Fanny? I'm sorry. I shouldn't have. . . ."

His words faded and I saw only a black curtain coming down over my eyes. I could hear Nathan's voice, but not his words. I felt his arms grab me around the waist. Then nothing.

"Fanny? Fanny, I thought you would want to know the facts. Fanny?" His fingers tapped me softly on the cheek, first one side then the other. His hands rubbed my wrists, but I fought coming back to this ugly world. For just a moment, I wished I was dead.

"Please, Fanny. Are you all right?"

Tears flowed down my cheeks and I couldn't answer him right away. "That star . . . on the chain. It sounds like one Geoff gave to Susan."

It was Nathan's turn to be struck silent. "We've got to get her a lawyer. Call her parents."

"No! It's the only thing Susan . . ." I hesitated. "You're

109

right. I'll have to phone." I shook my head. "I hate to betray her like that."

"Fanny, it's not betrayal. If the necklace is hers, they'll find out. Either they'll know right away or Susan will tell them, or I will. It would look better for her if we bring it up first. Then she'll surely be arrested for murder."

"What nonsense. She was—"

"She was here. On the grounds. Where she had no right to be. She had the best motive in the world. A favorite horse was killed and she was expelled in disgrace because of that girl."

"Susan couldn't kill anyone!"

"I know that. But think of how it looks, Fanny."

"But . . ." I couldn't think of anything to say.

"We have one hope."

I looked at him like a starving man looks at a meal.

"If only the time of death is wrong. If only Mary Louise wasn't killed while Susan had no alibi." He helped me into the car and went back inside.

I don't know how he did it, but in spite of them knowing it was Susan's necklace, Nathan talked the police into waiting to arrest Susan—leaving her in our custody—until the coroner made a decision. We returned to the hotel to wait.

"I'm not going to the banquet tonight," I said, slumping in my chair by the french doors. Nathan paced a hole in my carpet as the scent of fresh-turned earth sailed up from the rose garden. The groundsman was evidently trying to coax the plants into an early recovery from winter. Susan, sedated again, lay on the cot. A pain-killer and a shot from the doctor; she would be out for hours.

"You are going. It's the safest place. Lots of witnesses."

"What else could happen?"

"How will it look if you don't go? Like you have something to hide?" Nathan answered my question with two good ones.

"All right. But you'll stay with Susan. I'll be back as soon as the presentation is over."

"I'll escort you. Janet can stay with Susan."

"Janet is a delegate. We'll be fine. We'll walk over together."

110

Nathan gave in without much grace. "What if Kenneth gives you a problem? You forget he's here at the conference, too?"

"She already talked to him. Besides—" I took my knitting needle from my everything bag and thrust it at the air. "You think I can't handle myself with that one?"

Nathan laughed. "All right, all right." He came over and put his arms around me.

I had to admit it felt good to have him to lean on. What I would have done without him, I couldn't even think.

Nathan looked at me for a long moment. "I love you, Fanny." Then he pressed his lips against mine and gave me such a kiss. Kisses like that could get a woman in a lot of trouble. "Nathan! Geoff will be back any moment." He just kissed me again.

"I love you, too, Nathan," I said, when he stopped kissing me for a moment. I think I blushed when Geoff came back to sit with Susan. I left with Nathan, his arm around my waist.

When I got back to my room later, I was troubled, and not just over Susan's problems. I hated to argue with Nathan.

Many months I had known him. Many times, I know, we had said what we felt for each other, in person, in letters. But still, when it came to thoughts of an affair, I hesitated.

Maybe I was being silly about it all. After all, times had changed. Nathan was a man of the world, handsome, a Mossad agent, for heaven's sake. People were more free these days. Certainly I shouldn't be angry if he found me attractive enough to want more. But a mistress I wasn't cut out for, and Nathan still lived very far away.

Thoughts stormed in my head while I lay in a hot tub later that afternoon. Me, a widow of four years, and all my married life never a thought for any man except my husband. By the time I got out of the water, I had washed away my indecision. For now.

Susan was still asleep and Geoff had gone for a walk. Janet wasn't back from the conference lecture on historical York yet. No one to face. Good.

Janet would probably check out of my room, Kenneth or

111

no Kenneth. Suspected murderers she wouldn't want as roommates.

What with the strain of being police suspects, concern over what Janet would think of us now, and my poor bandaged Susan sleeping like the dead, it was a very long afternoon.

Finally, the police called to say that Mary Louise had been dead for at least five hours before she was found. She must, therefore, have been killed in the predawn hours or very late last night. Susan couldn't have done it. She was only checked out of the hospital an hour before Geoff's soccer match.

Still, the police were very firm about us all not going anywhere while the investigation was in progress. Not only didn't they have an answer for Susan's Star of David being in the room and under the body, but it seemed they thought I might have just as good a reason to want Mary Louise dead. And of course, once I had arranged for Geoffrey to stay with Nathan in his room for the weekend and I was sure that Susan was out of any danger, I had been back at my hotel room during the suspected time of death with only a sleeping Janet for a witness.

The Sabbath candles were already lit when Janet and I arrived at the banquet hall. Late as usual. The Gresham boys' choir was already singing part of the Friday evening service as we searched for our seats. I craned my neck looking for table twelve, seats G and H. The boys sang on.

Apparently, a boys' choir had been selected to pacify the Orthodox rabbis in attendance. Orthodox law forbade women singing in front of men. It was supposed to incite some sort of lust in the men and keep them from being as holy as they needed to be for their prayers. *Feh!* Such a weak lot they thought men were to be drawn into lust by everything to do with a woman. Well, to each his own. I was glad I had moved away from such rigidity, glad for the egalitarian temple I had at home.

Oh, goody. I saw my seat. It was just to the left of Reverend Malbys. On my other side, Janet squeezed my hand under the table to give me courage. "Last person I expected to see here," she whispered to me.

The vicar glared at us. Like John Carradine he looked for a moment.

Every bite of the meal nearly choked me with Reverend Malbys there. I wondered if he knew I had no alibi for the time of his daughter's death.

At least, he didn't have much of an appetite. That would have been carrying his responsibility to the conference too far.

I'm sure I don't have to say that after I presented York's mayor with a charter *B'nai Brith* membership and said a few words, I couldn't get out of the hall fast enough.

While I was at the dinner carrying the banner for the United States Jewish community, Nathan had not been napping. Susan slept, but he'd been busy on the phone. He had contacted a fellow Mossad agent. What with the ritual killing, I can tell you, Mossad was interested, even though Nathan was no longer officially active. It would give them someone to help check out all the clues that were coming like the plagues at Passover.

It felt wrong for Nathan to return to his room for the night. I needed him to hold me. I thought about our night in the kibbutz in Israel where he had stayed awake and brushed my hair out for me before I went to sleep. That was the sort of attention I needed from him.

It was a restless night for all of us. Susan tossed around and moaned and mumbled a lot. I was awake to hear her.

Out on the little balcony before the sun even thought about getting up, I heard a soft step behind me. Susan stood shivering in the chill night air. Cold. With frost glittering on everything in the garden, but the wind had stopped.

"Put something on, *Susa-le!*" I urged.

She got a sweater and came back out. "I miss him more than ever, *Bubbe*."

113

"Didn't I arrange for him to spend your birthday with you?"

"Not Geoff. Alexander!"

"Oh." I put my arms around her. "He's fine at the school. He has his stall and his hay, a nice pasture to run in."

"He doesn't have anyone to love him."

"He's beautiful. Lots of the girls must take good care of him."

Susan began to cry. "They can't love him like I do, *Bubbe!*"

"All right, all right," I said, patting her back as I held her. So typical of teenagers. So melodramatic. Of course no one could love her horse as she did. "You'll be able to see him again soon."

"You think so?"

"You didn't do anything wrong, did you?"

Susan shook her head.

"Then there's no reason you can't go back after this is all over."

"But Mom and Dad will never let me stay now. Not after all this."

My heart almost stopped beating. I would have to tell her. "Susan, I had to break my promise to you. I called them. When it was only about Joshua, I agreed that you and I could take care of it. But now it's murder."

"*Bubbe!*" she squealed. "You've ruined everything."

I put my arms around her. "Susan, I had no choice. Nathan and I decided it would be for the best."

"But they know I couldn't have murdered anyone. I was in the hospital." Susan held up her broken arm. The cast gleamed whitely in the dim light.

"I know, baby. But this could get worse. Anti-Semitism in your school was one thing. Even getting expelled we might have dealt with alone. But now it's linked to murder."

Susan hung her head. Big tears rolled down her cheeks. She didn't like it, but she knew I was right. She gave a heavy sigh. "When are they coming, *Bubbe?*"

"They should be in London by early Sunday morning and be in York by lunch. They'll stay with Doris. Nice of her to offer with the hotels being filled with conference members."

Susan nodded. "So soon?"

"Nathan and I called yesterday, as soon as the police finished questioning us about Mary Louise's murder. They said they'd get the first plane.

"Your father was very supportive, Susan. You should only thank God that you have such a family. What did Mary Louise have?"

Susan shuddered. "What did Mom say?"

I shrugged. To tell the truth, I'd rather she hadn't asked. "Well, you know your mother, the hysteric."

Susan looked frightened. "She wanted me back home, didn't she? Away from Alexander. Away from Geoff. Away from everything I love!" She started to weep, huge, gulping sobs.

"Now, Susan. Your mother was only worried out of her mind. We all are. I'm sure when things settle down, she will, too."

"She won't!"

I took Susan's face in my hands. "All right. Such a prophet you are now? You want to make yourself miserable, go ahead. Me, I'd wait to see."

To myself I wondered, What was it with me and trips overseas and promises? Keeping the one I had made on my vacation to Israel had nearly cost both Susan's life and my own. I had hoped to do better this time.

"You'll go to the *Shabbos* service this morning. The conference has arranged to hold it at Clifford's Tower. You'll pray about it all. *HaShem* will hear you."

I helped her back to bed, gave her one of her pills, and tucked her in. She seemed so small beneath the covers, so hurt with that huge cast on her arm. My heart gave a wrench so hard I thought it would break then and there.

At breakfast, the sight of Nathan and Geoffrey, all slicked up and smiling, made me feel much better. I could tell by the look on my granddaughter's face that she was feeling better, also.

115

She gave Geoff a hug and he kissed her cheek and then looked sheepishly at me.

"You want to kiss my Susan, you better work on your aim, young man," I said, trying to keep from smiling as Nathan showed him how it should be done.

Geoffrey grinned and he and Susan took their plates to the buffet table. Having raised two sons myself, I can tell you, I wasn't surprised to see Geoff come back with enough food on his plate to stop world hunger. Nothing has an appetite like a teenage boy.

Nathan looked at the portion and smiled. "I remember when I could eat like that," he said, eyeing all the sweet rolls and pancakes Geoff had taken.

"I used to be able to eat anything and never gain a pound," I said. "The only model Crawford's Department Store ever had who didn't need to diet. Then I had three children, turned thirty, and bingo! I have to watch every bite."

Still, I looked with disapproval at the skimpy breakfast Susan brought back to the table. "A rail you'll be if you keep eating like that."

She just smiled at me. I knew what it was like to not want to look like a piggy in front of a boy, but Susan was carrying it too far.

"Susan," Nathan said, as soon as he got back with his food. "What's the drug situation at school?"

Susan looked at her plate, stirred the yogurt into her stewed fruit, and didn't say anything.

"*Susa-le*, Nathan asked you a question." My heart almost stopped beating completely while I waited for her answer.

"I know kids can get them if they want to. Just like anywhere."

"Yes, but what do you know about it at Taddington?" Nathan wasn't letting her off that easy.

"Well, I think maybe Mary Louise knew where a person could get them. That's what I heard, but it was just a rumor. I mean, I never checked it out or anything. It doesn't interest me."

Nathan nodded. "That sounds right. I don't know where

they're coming from, but my man called this morning. That lad at Gresham, Harry . . ." Nathan started to dig in his pocket for the missing last name.

"Parker," Susan said, stirring her food furiously.

"Tell me what you heard." Nathan looked at his notebook and then at Susan.

She looked uncomfortable. "Not much. Just that she turned Harry on to drugs. She got him hooked on being with her and getting blasted. When she dumped him, he was really angry. Gossips said they wondered which he missed more, his sex or his highs." The last words came out so softly, I had to lean forward to hear her. Then she jumped up and ran from the table.

Geoff was up in a second, but Nathan stopped him and went after her himself. They stood talking for a moment in the lobby and then he brought Susan back.

If I thought she ate like a bird before, now she just dabbled with her breakfast. I tucked extra into my bag. Yesterday's nervous waiting for the police to prove Susan innocent and a very nervous night had just about finished all my supplies. The banquet at the Viking hadn't offered anything of interest. Like at most public functions, the food was only fair.

Maybe Susan would be hungry later, I hoped, tucking an apple and two bran muffins into my bag. Or maybe Geoff could get her to eat something. I wondered what Nathan had said to her in the lobby.

We walked to the service, Geoff on one side of Susan and me on the other. Nathan and Janet walked a little behind.

A beautiful morning. Cold but clear, with a blue sky like you hardly ever see back in Los Angeles. The rabbi opened the portable ark and we all stood. As he led the alternate reading, I thought about how perfect it felt to worship *Ha-Shem* out here in the open. Better even than in my own synagogue at home. In the old times, all Jews must have felt this way when they sang to Him in the silence of the desert.

Scarcely halfway into the service, Nathan got up and hurried in the direction of the hotel. What now? I thought. I lasted only another minute myself. Then, asking Janet to make

117

sure the children got safely back to the hotel, I followed him.

At the car park, he finally noticed. Why not? Me puffing like a steam engine to catch up.

"You're not at the service?"

I shook my head. "From praying about this *tsuris*, this trouble, I'm doing all the time anyway. Even the Torah says a life comes before praying."

"But Fanny," he said, obviously unhappy that I had come. "You'll miss all your Saturday afternoon conference lectures and dramas."

I sniffed. "No. From all the history of the massacre, I already know like the recipe for *kugel*," I said. "Where are we going?" I walked to the passenger's side.

"You going to try driving again?" Nathan said, smiling at me.

I had forgotten. Here, the passenger's side was the *left* side of the car.

Nathan sat behind the wheel for a moment. "I really wish you'd stay with the kids, Fanny."

"I have an offer from Mossad and *you're* turning me down?" I asked, giving him my offended look, like Katharine Hepburn in *Adam's Rib*.

"Fanny, I'm going to try to track this drug connection. I think I should go alone. I found out the same thing Susan just mentioned. The sex was used to lure the boys into a drug habit. These people won't talk in front of you."

Hurt, but understanding, I nodded and walked from the car without a word.

I headed to the front of the hotel. Cab fare wasn't so much when my granddaughter's reputation was at stake, I thought.

"Taddington School," I said to the driver of one of the shiny, black, boxy cars that waited near the hotel.

I only hoped that the teacher I wanted to talk to would be there on Saturday. Mr. MacMurray had been kind without pouring on some phony charm act. Besides, he had seemed completely in tune with Susan's relationship to Alexander. I always tended to trust people with that kind of sensitivity.

* * *

118

"I don't think I can help you, much as I'd like to see this cleared up," MacMurray said, stroking his red beard and looking sadly at me. "I wouldn't know if she had a steady beau, but that certainly wasn't the sort of thing that was ever attributed to her. She being known as more of a loose end, y' know. But Miss Malbys was only in my class for a few weeks before she was sent down."

"Sent down where?" I asked, puzzled.

He'd made us tea in the masters' lounge and now set a cup in front of me. I took the bran muffins from my bag, un-wrapped them, and put them on a plate.

"She couldn't do the work, poor lass. I heard she was into parties, fun, and some sort of substance abuse, not her sums. If it was true, it was no surprise she couldn't keep up. I sent her back to remedial class, so I'm not able to give you much help." He poured, nudged the sugar bowl my way, and took one of the muffins.

Substance abuse, there it was again. I wished Nathan more luck than I was having. "I'm not asking you to betray any-one," I assured him. "But a child's whole future is at stake. One child has no future left at all and others may be in trouble."

"Y' don't understand," he said, his accent thickening his words so that I had to listen even harder. "I'm not usually around on the weekends or holidays. My mother isn't well and I usually go home t' take care of her. Anything I know is only hearsay." He broke off a bit of muffin and chewed slowly. "Very good, these. Thanks."

I nodded. "I'm sorry your mother's ill," I said, meaning it. "Will she recover soon?"

"Ach, no recoverin' from the arthritis she's got. Rheuma-toid. Had it for years now, I'm afraid."

I shook my head. "I have friends who suffer from that. Such a pity. My kind of arthritis I can ease with the proper exercise."

We sat quietly for a few moments, enjoying our tea and the muffins.

"Perhaps one of the masters who's here full time would

119

know more details. Though I'm not sure they'd tell you." He smiled. "I could check around."

I thanked Mr. MacMurray and gave him my number at the hotel before seeking the pay phone on the side of the main building.

Before I was halfway to the administration hall I saw the redheaded girl I had been watching that night with Mary Louise when she had been with the older man. I hurried toward her. Could she have been the one recommended to Nathan in the bar?

"Excuse me," I said, catching hold of the sweater that flapped from her shoulders.

"Yes?" She turned and I saw a hardness that made me ache for her. I was almost willing to believe she was the subject for bar talk.

"May I speak with you a moment?"

"I'm really busy, Mrs. Zindel."

News traveled fast, I thought, surprised that she knew me by name. "You were a close friend of Mary Louise, weren't you?"

"We were . . . chums, I guess you'd say." The girl got a smug look on her face that did nothing to make her attractive.

"I'm a delegate to the conference. Her father's a friend of mine. He asked me to see if there was anyone special he should inform of the memorial service," I said, making it up as I went along.

The girl hesitated. "I don't think she cared about anyone very much. She was sort of all out for Mary Louise, y' know? That's what got her in dutch with Fang."

"Who?"

"Miss K. The headmistress. You don't get a favor from someone and then try to screw them."

"Favors? They must have been quite close."

"Naw. That's one thing they weren't. Miss K has a crush on the vicar. We all know it. That would've served her right, though."

"I beg your pardon?"

"Getting Fang as a stepmother." She laughed, a sound like ice cubes in a disposal. "What a kick!"

"Such a thing as Miss K helped her with and she was ungrateful?" I said, pretending I knew what she was referring to.

"Yeah, I guess it isn't everyone who'll help you get a bun out of the oven. And then Mary Louise wanted to hold out on her. Fancy that!" Her voice held amazement and I played along.

"Was she angry about that? Miss K?"

"Angry? She was through the effing roof." She laughed. "Hell of a packet."

"Packet?"

"Eh, what is this? I thought you knew it all." She stared at me with all the anger of youth. "You're playin' me." The girl's blue eyes turned gray like Lake Michigan in a midwinter Chicago blizzard. "I gotta go."

She walked briskly toward the stables and left me with my next question still on my tongue.

The stables. Maybe I could find someone else who could tell me more about Mary Louise and that "packet."

So far my fishing trip had netted me some interesting information, but I needed to find out what could have been in this package Mary Louise had kept from Miss K.

As soon as the stableboy got the redhead off on a horse, I approached him. "Hello," I said, stepping from behind a hay bale.

He looked around. "What can I do fer y'?" he said, taking the cap off his carroty hair with one hand. His other gripped a horse halter. Skinny, with bony hands, an expression that was hard to read behind all the freckles, and pants too short for his long legs.

"I wondered if Samson was in today?"

He looked toward the back of the barn. "Yeah. Last stall on the left." He pointed and crammed his hat back on his head. "But y' need more than permission from Jock here"—he jerked a thumb at his chest—"to take 'im out. I can't say yea or nay."

"Just a social call, Jock," I said, starting down the hay-littered aisle. The barn looked large and rather empty. More room than need for it. Joshua's stall stood empty, of course.

121

His brass nameplate could have done with polishing, but I guessed they'd be changing it now.

I came to Samson and dug an apple from my everything bag. Greedy. His soft nose in my hand made me smile. "I wish you could talk to me," I whispered. He just crunched apple bites, juice running off his sagging lower lip as he chewed.

When I walked back, I waited until I was sure the stableboy would see and then faked a stumble and a little cry of pain. What with my arthritis and my stage experience, it wasn't hard to make it look real.

In a flash he was at my side and helping me into the tack room. "You just sit down a bit. Can I get you anything?"

I dug in my purse. "Damn!" I said, looking up with my best Bernhardt quiver. "I forgot my arthritis medication!"

He looked embarrassed. "Got a little horse liniment here," he offered.

"That might be too strong for a woman of my years, young man." I gave him my frail look.

"I'll thin it out a bit. Or maybe some freeze-gel. I've used that m'self for muscle strains." He reached down a bottle and unscrewed the lid, held the blue goop out to me. "Just rub a little on what ails."

I tried to look alarmed. Actually, it looked just like the mineral ice I used at home before a tennis tournament. I dipped a fingerful from the jar and rubbed it around my knee. Nippy. *Freeze*-gel it was!

"You wouldn't have anything a little more general for pain, would, you? Aspirin?" I put on my sweet granny look.

He shifted from foot to foot. " 'Fraid not, ma'am."

I groaned and grabbed my knee as if it were the most painful thing known to man. "I don't think I can walk at all."

He shifted some more. "The school nurse is off for the holiday. Clifford's Tower, you know."

I nodded. "That's always how it is. Never help around when you desperately need it." I rocked and groaned a little more. "You wouldn't have a little medicinal spirit, would you?"

He grinned. "Old Kentworth don't allow booze on the

grounds. Not even to keep warm in this effing—'scuse me, ma'am—place at night." He shook his head.

I went on a bit about how awful it was for him to be so put upon by girls'-school rules. He agreed and then went to tack up a horse. "You give that freeze-gel time to work."

When he came back a few moments later, I tried to get him on the subject of the horses. "Such a big place you have to take care of here," I said, letting my expression show him I thought him a miracle worker. "All by yourself, are you?"

He puffed up a bit, stuffed his hands in his pockets, and rocked forward on his toes. "Yeah. Few less horses now, though, than there's been."

I made a sad face. "I heard you just lost one."

He looked angry for an instant and I was afraid I had gone too quickly. Then he shrugged. "He weren't no good for work anymore, anyway. Sent 'im off to the knacker's."

"Knacker's?"

"Rag-and-bone man. Y'know. Hoof glue and such."

I'm afraid I gasped. "Such a shame. To think he looked so healthy racing across the field only last week. Was it a sudden illness?"

The boy shook his head. "Naw. He was lame as a crutch."

I gave him my puzzled look. "But he seemed so fit."

"Bute."

"Pardon?"

"Anti-inflammatory. He was chock full. Let's 'em move without the pain, but doesn't fix anything. He was a goner. Should be able to replace him soon as the insurance comes through."

"Oh," I said, digging in my bag as I changed the subject. I decided my own "pain" was worsening. "I could use some of that sort of thing myself about now."

"Yeah. I got a bum shoulder. Came near to trying it myself once. Vet said don't take it."

I dug some more in my purse. "I haven't anything with me I can take for this pain, I guess." I sank down a bit and groaned. "I don't think I can stand it," I whimpered. "My cab won't be here for another twenty minutes." Then I sagged

123

some more. "I think . . . I'm going to faint," I said, slowly leaning as far as I dared without falling off my tack-box seat.

He lunged to catch me and looked just about as worried as I'd hoped. "Maybe I can find something that would get you through," he said. "You hold on, mum."

He rummaged in his locker while I watched him through half-closed eyes. Sure enough, he got out a bottle of prescription drugs.

"Would this help?" he said, holding out the bottle.

I acted like it was a heroic effort to fight the pain as I read the label. "Sounds like something I've had before," I said. I thanked him and took one from the container. "Some water?" I asked. I palmed the white pill and mumbled, as if I had put it in my mouth already.

He smiled and handed me a cup. "That should fix you up before your cabby can set his brakes. Just sit here till he comes."

I relaxed back against a saddle. "Thank you so very much." Digging a pound piece from my purse and pressing it into his hand, I smiled my best at him.

He grinned. "Many thanks, ma'am."

"The least I can do for your kindness." I let my eyelids droop a bit.

"If you'd be needing some of that stuff while yer here . . . I could probably let you have the rest of that bottle. I can get a refill at the chemist's on Monday, if you'd be willing to pay me some." He had sly look on his face.

"I'm afraid I don't have much on me. Just my cab fare and lunch money. But I think this works better than the medication I brought from home. I can feel the relief starting already." I gave him a look of bliss. "Could I come back tomorrow for some?"

He smiled. "Sure thing."

"How much?"

"Ma'am?"

"How much should I bring for the rest of that bottle?" I tried to act as if I'd done this sort of thing before.

He pried it open again and counted the pills into his palm. Ten tablets like the one I had just put in my bag. Pills from

124

such a dirty hand as his, I would die first, but I tried to look just a little eager.

"Two pound apiece for nine?" He said. "I gotta keep one for m' shoulder."

I tried to look a little surprised, but not so much that I scared him off. Certainly it was cheap by U.S. prices, but I wouldn't tell him that.

He stood on one foot for a bit and then shifted his weight. "It'll give me some for my trouble. Y'know. Getting into town, the refill and all."

"Of course," I said, quickly. "You've been so kind."

I looked at my watch. "I'm really feeling so much better," I said. I stood up and took a trial step on my supposedly injured leg. "Not too painful, now." I thanked him again and limped from the barn.

"Anytime. I can probably get you whatever you need."

"You are so kind," I called, batting my lashes over my shoulder at him and trying to look a lot like Jean Seberg in *Saint Joan* thanking her God for her calling.

He grinned. "Lucky you came to me. I get only the best. Not like some."

I felt my heart thump against my ribs. There it was. He was *used* to getting drugs for people. I wondered, if I came back when he wasn't here, would I find a "packet" like the one that Mary Louise's friend had mentioned? I would have to find the time to try.

I waved to Jock and kept limping on through the barn door.

I could hardly wait for the cab to get here and take me to my hotel. I wondered if Nathan had done as well with *his* snooping. Not only had I found a drug dealer at Taddington, I had discovered much more. I also knew that it was no rumor that Mary Louise had been pregnant. And as a bonus, I'd found out that it was Miss Kentworth who had helped her get an abortion. I wondered how she had helped. Maybe, since Mary Louise was under eighteen, she had pretended to be her mother. The redhead had seemed to find it quite funny that Mary Louise might really have ended up with Miss K as a stepmother.

By the time I got back to the hotel, my knee really did hurt

125

a bit. I must have strained it faking my injury. Fair payment for lying, I thought guiltily.

Would I never learn to recognize an omen when it walks up and tips its hat?

Eleven

GOTTENYU! Nathan was already waiting for me when I got back to the hotel lobby. I quivered as he stalked up to me.

"Where have you been, Fanny? As if I couldn't guess."

"The school," I confessed. It was easier. He'd find out soon enough.

"I begged you to stay with the kids." He looked hurt.

"What begged? You asked me. I decided I could do better at the school."

"Such a risk. I hope you haven't made yourself more of a suspect. I hope it was worth it." He pushed the elevator button.

He was so angry. I hoped it was just concern. I reached out and put my hand on his arm. "I think it was," I said, as I stretched my legs to keep pace with him into the elevator. My knee twinged. I balanced against him. "I learned that Mary Louise was pregnant. 'A bun in the oven' was how one of her friends put it. She also told me that Miss Kentworth helped Mary Louise get an illegal abortion."

"How do you know it was illegal?" He held me and looked down at my leg. "You hurt?"

"Just a little stiff." I waved his worry away. "She was under-age. You think she would maybe tell her father, the vicar, to give his consent? I bet Miss Kentworth helped by signing as Mary Louise's mother."

Nathan looked thoughtful. "An interesting prospect, Fanny." We got off on our floor. Through the door of my room, I could hear Geoff and Susan talking. Nathan waved me past toward his room.

He let us in.

"And I know the drug pusher, though he admitted he had some competition," I said, grinning triumphantly at him as I produced the little wad of tissue from the bottom of my everything bag and handed over the pill. "It's the stableboy. The same one, I'll bet, who lied about giving Mary Louise permission to ride Joshua," I added.

"How do you know he's the same one?" Nathan asked, turning the white tablet over and over in his hand. "And what makes you think he has competition?"

I sat down on the edge of the bed. Nathan took a chair across from me and switched on the desk light to examine the pill more closely. "He said he got the best, not like some others around there sold. I know he's the main stable lad because he has his room there in the barn. One bed. One nightstand. No sign of anyone else to help him full time. Besides, I sympathized with his work load and he agreed it was quite a job for one person."

"He must learn a lot if he lives in there."

I nodded. "Well, he certainly seemed to know all about Joshua. He told me the horse was incurable. 'Lame as a crutch,' he said, and he said the horse was all doped up. That's why Mary Louise could run him so hard that day; he couldn't feel the pain."

Nathan's attention came from the pill back to me again. "Was he sure the horse was destroyed?"

"The 'knacker's,' Jock called it. For hoof glue," I said, my stomach turning. "And the stall with Joshua's name on it was still empty."

Nathan jotted in his notebook.

128

"What are you writing?" I asked.

"Well, I think if your son is going to be sued for the price of the horse, we ought to verify that he was really destroyed. We should get the name of the vet who put him down."

"He must have been destroyed. The boy said they would probably be getting a new horse as soon as the insurance paid Taddington."

Nathan frowned and drew a line through his note, scribbled something else. Then he asked: "Did he tell you what this pill is?"

I shook my head. "He showed me the bottle, but the name wasn't familiar. I couldn't write it down. He said he took them for a bum shoulder. Then he offered to *sell* me the rest. He had ten pills and said he would keep one, in case, and I could have the others for two pounds a piece."

He whistled. "At the current rate of exchange, that's about four dollars a tablet. If it's a real prescription, and he's getting it through the National Health, he's only paying about forty pence for the lot. No way to know how many that included originally. Quite a profit margin."

"You think it's a legal drug?" I asked.

"Well, Fanny, it may be a real prescription, but it's still illegal for Jock to sell it to anyone else."

I nodded. "So, you did any better with your fancy-shmancy contact? Or maybe with your Mossad friends?"

Nathan shrugged. "I found out that Mary Louise's death was an overdose."

"An overdose? But you said it was a ritual murder."

"Apparently that was done after the fact. I suspected as much when I saw so little blood around the wounds. My friend confirmed it. But keep it quiet, Fanny. No one else is supposed to know. She was dead of the overdose before she was stabbed by someone who tried to make it look like the ancient blood libel."

I found myself shivering. "Who could do that to a poor dead girl? A child?"

"Maybe a murderer who wanted to throw suspicion on someone else."

"A Jewish someone else!" I said, suddenly furious.

"It looks that way, Fanny."

"So, if she was involved with drugs, the death was, maybe, an accident. Or suicide?"

Nathan shook his head. "I'm afraid those are the things we don't know yet. But if she died by her own hand, then who made the stab wounds, the blood libel act? And why?" He pulled one of those cheap tabloid papers from his briefcase and hesitated before handing it to me.

I gasped as I read the more lurid details of Mary Louise's death. They showed not only a sketch of her body and its mutilations, but also ancient pictures of historical ritual murders. It was disgusting.

I shook my head. "To do such a thing, a person would have to be something other than Jewish or completely crazy. Probably both."

Nathan rang room service and ordered a pot of coffee and some scones. "At least they didn't mention Susan in connection with the star that was found. They also don't know about the overdose. I'm sure the police held that back to check false confessions. This is bound to bring out more crazies."

"Nathan, are these papers everywhere?"

He nodded. "You know. Just like these rags in the States. They have them at every supermarket check-out stand. I'm sure it's no different here."

I looked at him. "You think Judith and Larry will see them at the airport when they arrive? They'll have such a fit."

Nathan shrugged. "It can't be helped, Fanny. I hope you prepared them."

"Who could prepare them for something like this?"

I tucked the tabloid back into his briefcase. It made me feel dirty just to handle the paper.

The food arrived and we waited until we were alone again. I poured coffee and waited some more.

"Much of what I learned doesn't seem to mesh with what you found out," Nathan said, at last.

"*Nu?*"

"Apparently there's been more of a drug problem with

schoolchildren in this area than your stableboy could possibly be serving with his little prescription scam."

"Really?"

He nodded. "I think he's just the garnish on the main course. The most he could do is refill at intervals that would correspond to his using them all himself. That's not a lot of stock for a thriving business."

I took another scone and spread it with jelly. "So where does it come from?"

"If I could solve that, I'd be a local hero."

"Back to the beginning again," I said, sighing.

"Well, not quite." He smiled. "I did have a bit of luck about that lorry driver."

"Yes?"

"He won't be so anxious to lie about Susan anymore."

"Why? Tell me?" I hated it when Nathan dribbled out information like he was feeding a baby bird with an eyedropper.

"He's part of the supply line. I did confirm that. The police have arrested him, but I think he doesn't know any more than the people under him in the chain."

"Like you said about Jock?"

He nodded. "The small fry never know who's in charge. It doesn't make for a successful business. But at least he'll be out of the way. He'll get a few years just for his part in the drug ring and his charge against Susan will be discredited."

"Small fry or not," I said, "I'd like to look through Jock's things."

"Why, Fanny?"

"Well, Mary Louise's friend, the one who told me about the abortion, also mentioned that Mary Louise was holding out a packet on Miss K. I'd like to find it."

Nathan shook his head. "Fanny, that's an expression over here. 'Holding out a packet' probably meant Mary Louise kept back a lot of money. They use 'bundle' the same way."

"I don't know. So you say. What if she did mean a real packet? A package."

Nathan gave me a look, but he didn't argue. "Let's take this tablet to the chemist's and see what it is."

"As soon as I check on Susan." I hurried down the hall.

I found her snuggled up in front of the television with Geoff. Janet had gone back to the conference. "We're making progress, *Susa-le*. You just stay put."

"Can't Geoff and I go over to the Viking Museum? I want to see the reconstructed village tour."

I hesitated. "Two years you're in York and you haven't seen it?"

Susan shrugged. "I don't get into the city that often. And you know how it is with sights that are local. When was the last time you went to Disneyland, *Bubbe?*"

I laughed. She had me on that one. Even with the grandchildren, so much standing in lines in the hot California sun was not for me. "All right, but there only, then back home. Now is no time to be wandering around. And stop by the conference suite in the hotel. Janet may want to go with you."

Her smile faded. "Oh, *Bubbe!*"

"A witness would be nice. Just in case someone else gets bumped off, so you shouldn't be accused again."

It was almost noon by the time we found out the pill was Temgesic, a prescription drug for pain that the kids used as downers.

As we came out of the chemist's, Nathan looked depressed. "What's wrong? You found out the pills are commonly used for what they call recreation drugs."

Nathan shook his head. "It doesn't really get us anywhere, Fanny. As I said, the amounts this fellow could deal in are too small." We kept walking. Such a crowd on the sidewalks. I could hardly stay by Nathan's side. It had been like this last summer. Packed like sardines, but I had thought at this time of year, there might be room to breathe. No such luck. Summer or no summer, a city as old as York always drew the tourists. And now the conference crowds.

"You know," I said, "it's not just the pills. That's a big

barn. You think maybe he's hiding marijuana in all those bales?"

Nathan laughed. "Fanny, Mary Louise didn't die from an overdose of pot. She didn't even die from an overdose of pills like these." He held up my white pill. "She died of too much heroin, injected directly into her system. Either self-injected or otherwise."

"Heroin?"

"Why so surprised, Fanny? That's one of the most common causes of deaths among drug users—heroin, cocaine, and now crack."

I shrugged. "Drugs like that I expect in big cities, Los Angeles, New York, and London, even. Here is the country. Here I expect cows, sheep, a few horses, maybe."

"I admit that I was a little surprised to find such a drug problem around here. Both Gresham and Taddington are well established and steeped in tradition."

"Nathan, just because a hog is big doesn't mean he's kosher."

Nathan laughed.

"I still think I should go back to the stable for the rest of the drugs. Maybe we could watch Jock and see how soon he gets more. Maybe he has a Mr. Big who supplies him instead of the National Health."

"I think we should discuss that over lunch." Nathan took my arm and escorted me into a small restaurant. We were shown to a table and he ordered iced teas while we looked at the menus.

"So?" I said, adding sugar and squeezing my lemon wedge into the glass. I cupped my other hand over it, it shouldn't squirt in someone's eye.

"I think it's too dangerous for what we're apt to get out of it."

"Even if it leads to a Mr. Big?"

He shook his head and stirred his own tea. "These things usually never lead to anyone at the top, Fanny. Big drug business keeps its head down, so to speak. Even if we could arrest that stable lad for selling to you, it's not likely he'd even

133

know anyone but other small fry. I'm waiting for the lorry driver to put the finger on him."

"You think they were in it together?"

"Perhaps. It's not very likely that the lorry driver would supply Jock and his competition. He'll finger one or the other."

"Then I hope he wasn't supplying Jock. Then we'll know who Jock's competition is." I sighed and decided on a nice artichoke with vinaigrette and some braised mushrooms with garlic. "You have something with garlic, too, Nathan. Then it won't matter."

"What won't matter?" he said, a teasing look in his eyes. I blushed.

I was only half-finished with my meal when Nathan excused himself to make a phone call. His contact, I didn't doubt.

Sure enough, when he came back he had more news.

"What did you find out?"

Nathan gave me an odd look. "The school is in a little financial difficulty. At least they were up until the middle of last year. Then things picked up for them. They called it a private donation, but my source is questioning that. Most of Taddington's girls are from middle-income families. No one who would be likely to make a donation of that size."

"How much was it?"

"Well, enough that they held off the legal firm that was going to move to give the school grounds and property to the contingent beneficiary."

"Beneficiary?"

"Yes. Seems Taddington is part of a probate struggle. He's going to try to find out who is involved."

"And?"

"What 'and'?"

"And I know there's more, Mr. Nathan Weiss. I didn't go through all of Israel with you not to know when you're keeping something back." I patted his hand across the table so he should know I meant it in a nice way.

He shrugged. "Mossad has learned that Reverend Malbys had been involved in a number of anti-Semitic actions in the past. I think you should steer clear of him."

"So why would he get so involved in the Clifford's Tower Memorial service—something that honors Jews—when he's so prejudiced?"

Nathan raised his eyebrows. "Community pressure. That could draw him into it for appearance's sake. And an appearance is apparently as far as it goes with that one."

I made a face. "That tells me nothing I didn't know by the note his daughter sent Susan. A shame to raise his child with such hatred." I finished my iced tea.

"You should see the film clips we have access to on how the KKK raises their kids in the South." Nathan paid the check and we walked some more through the town. "My Mossad contact is arranging to have someone keep track of Reverend Malbys' activities in the future. We think he's been involved in a lot of underground defamation groups. We'll catch him sooner or later."

I got back to my room to see that Geoff and Susan were still out. A shame. Obviously, Janet wasn't with them. She lay in bed, as if asleep, a washcloth over her eyes.

I tiptoed to the bathroom.

By the time I had finished a nice soak in the big claw-footed tub, I heard sounds from the room. Good, I thought, Janet was awake. Maybe she was getting ready for the choral drama at the tower this evening. I put my hand on the knob and had almost pulled the door open when I heard Janet's angry voice. I opened the door just a crack.

She had the phone to her ear and her tensed jaw formed a tight line. "It's no longer a legal issue. The court's made its decision. I want you to abide by it."

I stepped out so she could see me in case she wanted to talk privately. But I was the one who got the shock. Janet's cheekbone had a purplish bruise and her eye was swollen half-shut. I gasped, my hand flying to my mouth. If Janet hadn't noticed me before, she saw me now.

"I'll talk to you later about this," she said, and hung up the phone.

"Your face."

Janet raised a hand as if to hide her injury, then looked away, embarrassed.

135

"Such a monster they shouldn't allow in a school," I said.

Janet lurched around, her eyes wide, and stared at me. "What do you mean by that?" she snapped, her good eye as squinty now as the hurt one.

I drew back. So fierce. Not like my Janet, at all. "Only that a *meshuge*, so crazy like your ex, shouldn't be allowed to teach. That's who you were shouting at, wasn't it? That's who hurt your face."

"Oh." She sank down onto the bed like an inflatable pool toy with a puncture. "Yes."

I sat down on the bed next to her and put my arm around her shoulders. "Did he do that at the conference? Were there any witnesses? Have you called the police?"

Janet buried her face in her hands. "I feel so foolish," she said. Her words were muffled.

"He hit you?"

Janet shook her head. "It was my fault, really. I fell trying to run from the nasty scene he was creating."

I frowned and wondered if she was telling me the truth. "In the streets of York you must have a million witnesses. You sure you don't want me to call the police?"

"Thanks, Fanny, but no. I'll have to deal with this myself." She got a strange look on her face, thoughtful. Then she said: "You know what I told you about our joint account? He still believes I owe him something. The whole thing makes him so angry that he becomes unhinged. It gives him very poor impulse control."

"Explain, please. What impulse?"

"It means, Fanny, that what most people see as the proper way to behave or as accepted social convention, he recognizes, but can't make himself act accordingly."

"Maybe you could give me an example?" I asked, still not understanding.

"You know. Poor impulse control is 'I see it, I want it, and I don't care what the law says.'" She shrugged. "It's the category that shoplifters, and even relatives who commit incest, fall into, as well as explosive tempers, like Kenneth's."

I nodded. A brave front she was putting on. "I would

136

suggest that the police could maybe get a restraining order, bar Kenneth from the rest of the conference."

"No. I'll stay away. The conference ends tomorrow, anyway."

"Why should you have to miss out? He's the villain, the *momzer*."

Janet reached out her hand to touch mine. "You are wonderful, Fanny, but really I'm not going to go out with my face like this."

"Nonsense, cold compresses, icy tea bags for the swelling, then a little makeup. You'd be surprised what a good foundation can do."

Janet gave a little laugh. "I love your pluck, Fanny, but this time we'll do it my way. I need a good rest before going on with my business over here."

"You're behaving like a typical battered woman. Always excuses, but they work in his favor. I know. Sadie and I, my best friend back home, we volunteer at the women's shelter. I don't want to see you start like that."

Janet shook her head. "Don't worry, Fanny. I'm a professional, remember? I'm not on the fence about this. I don't owe him any money. And I don't owe him any free shots at me. I really did fall."

I could see she was trying to find a polite way to tell me to butt out. Maybe she was right.

"Thanks for caring, Fanny. Just so you don't have to worry, I'll call room service for Susan, Geoff, and myself tonight. That way, you and Nathan can have a romantic dinner alone." She winked at me with her good eye.

Nathan and I ate that evening in a pub. Just a few tables and very close together. We could hardly squeeze into the chairs at the one nearest the front window.

The effort was worth it for the garlic mushrooms alone. Not mushy like this afternoon's, but toasted, almost crispy. I asked Nathan to order me a second helping to go with my vegetables and rice.

Good that England had such an influence from India, a kosher Jew could find a meal. Almost every city I had been in in Great Britain had several vegetarian restaurants to choose from. Of course, a *glatt* kosher Jew has trouble wherever he goes. Restaurants that follow the dietary laws *that* religiously are hard to find.

Nathan had his fish and chips with extra chips on the side so I could sample. Such a darling. Always thinking of me. Considerate. I let him eat in silence for a bit. He'd need his strength to answer all my questions.

"Fanny, are you ill?"

I looked up. "Me? No."

"I've eaten half my dinner and not a question yet. Does that mean you're giving up? Or does it mean you think I'm going to need my strength?"

I couldn't help but smile. Reading my mind, now. That was dangerous, a man knowing what you were thinking.

"That's it. I guessed it." His hand reached for mine across the small table.

"So smart you think you are, Mr. Nathan Weiss," I said, holding my hand back for a moment. "I shouldn't be curious about the outcome of my granddaughter's whole future?"

"I was only teasing you, Fanny." He gave me such a look with those spaniel brown eyes that my fingers touched his before I could stop them. So I couldn't stay mad at him.

"Where do you want me to begin?" He held out his glass for the waiter to bring him another shandy.

Me, I would stick with straight lemonade. "Tell me everything."

"Well, I checked out 'Jock.' He's an ex-jockey who grew a little too tall to keep his weight within limits. Most of his track action is with the bettors now. He seems to regularly drop more money there than his stable job could be netting him."

"Ah-ha, you see? I told you he was at the bottom of it." The waiter came with our dessert, warm cherry cobbler and cream.

"Fanny," Nathan shook his head, "bottom is right. He's probably one of the lowest rungs."

"And what makes you say that?"

"He lives too far on the edge to be trustworthy."

"The edge? Of what?"

"He gambles, he drinks, he sold drugs to you without a qualm. No one would trust him with any important information. He'd be too easy to put the pressure on."

I sighed. I could see what Nathan meant. "Such a young man, and so many weaknesses." Again, we ate in silence for a while. The cobbler was too good to allow it to get cold.

We finished our coffee and Nathan paid the check. By the time we were nearing the hotel, I felt ready to ask him more questions.

"Did you check into anything besides the stableboy? From him we have a biography, already."

Nathan took his arm from my waist long enough to hold the hotel door for me. "The insurance company is reluctant to pay the claim for Joshua's death on the grounds of negligence."

"You mean I was right? They hurt the horse on purpose?" I gave the elevator button such a punch that Nathan jumped a little.

It came almost immediately. Nathan pulled the gate shut with a clang. "Don't start crocheting anyone a noose, yet. I don't know that that's the case."

We got off on two. Nathan took my hand and walked me to my door.

"Oh, no you don't, Mr. Pulling Teeth. I want to know what makes you so sure no one deserves hanging."

"Fanny, you'll wake Janet and the children," he said, making a show of looking at his watch.

"Fine," I said. "We'll talk in your room." I led the way farther down the hall.

Nathan turned on the bedside lamp and took two sodas from his room's bar refrigerator. He handed me one and we sat on the edge of his bed. "Explain," I said.

"Well, I found out that Joshua was a gift from wealthy alums and heavily insured. If he hadn't been donated, a school would never have a horse of that quality for young ladies to learn on."

139

"So, if the insurance investigator rules that Joshua's death was unavoidable, the school will make a little money on the side?"

"Probably, since they will replace him with a horse more suited to schoolgirls in both price and ability."

I set my soda can down on the nightstand. Hard. Some of it splashed up out of the opening. "Money from murder. That poor horse!"

The french doors to Nathan's balcony burst open and Susan and Geoff charged into the room.

"*Bubbe*, what were you saying about Joshua being murdered?" Her eyes were wild.

"What were you doing eavesdropping?" I said, answering her with a question to cover my surprise.

"Janet wanted to go to bed early, so we came in here to watch TV, but there wasn't anything on."

"I was practicing my aim on the balcony like you suggested, Mrs. Zindel," Geoff said, grinning at me.

Susan blushed and slapped his shoulder in mock anger. "Please, *Bubbe*, if you know something about Joshua, tell me?"

I glanced at Nathan. He stepped in smoothly, just when I needed him.

"Everything we found out you probably already know, Susan. Joshua was a more valuable horse than a school like Taddington could afford. The insurance is still investigating his death. They haven't paid up, yet."

She looked from him to me as if she wasn't sure he was telling her the truth. "That's exactly what he said."

"I wasn't eavesdropping. But I did hear you say 'murder,' *Bubbe*."

"Yes, you know what we said, you and I, about Mary Louise maybe causing his death with rough riding. To us, that's murder. You and I already agreed. That's how I meant it."

Susan didn't look convinced, but she took Geoff by the hand. "We're going to go down for coffee. We won't be long."

140

"Stay in the hotel." I waited until the kids were out of the room before I looked at Nathan again. I didn't like lying to Susan. "If you're worried about anyone crocheting a noose, it should be Susan."

"Well, at least we have some time until she gets her arm out of the cast."

"She's injured and you're making jokes."

Nathan looked at the floor. "I'm sorry, Fanny. I didn't mean it that way. But I have to admit, I'd like to count on a set space of time during which neither one of you would get yourselves into more trouble."

"Trouble? You won't know what trouble is until I have to meet with Larry and Judith tomorrow. Do you know what a scene Judith will make? And in front of Doris? I'm sure my cousin isn't used to such conniptions. She never had any children of her own. A daughter-in-law like Judith I *know* she never saw before." I put my hands to my head. Already I was having tomorrow's headache.

Nathan put his arm around me. "Maybe I should drive you, Fanny. Give you some moral support?"

I sighed. "If only you could. But if there is anything Judith would have a bigger conniption about, it would be having this sort of *shandeh* discussed in front of anyone who isn't family."

"I'm sorry I can't help, Fanny. I hate to have you driving when you're upset."

It struck me then, like a punch to my stomach. "*Oy Gott*, Nathan, I'd almost forgotten. Roundabouts. Driving on the left, *vey is mir.*"

"Fanny, maybe I should drive you out there and drop you off. I can find something to do."

I looked at him for a moment. So tempting. "No, Nathan," I said, at last, "this I'd better do myself. It's family."

Nathan followed me to the door and gave me a kiss before I went to my room.

Susan was back in the room and sound asleep while I lay staring at the ceiling. I couldn't sleep. For one thing, my arthritis was paining me.

141

Unfortunately for Nathan's peace of mind, that gave me an idea. With all the *tsuris* tomorrow because of Judith and Larry, I might not have another chance.

Dressing quietly, I picked up my things and let myself out into the hall. While I waited for a cab, I did a few stretches so my joints shouldn't creak when I needed them to be quiet later. One of the moves loosened the pain in my knee, thank God.

I glanced at my watch. Late. Good, if everyone was asleep, my job would be easier.

Twelve

THE cab coasted to a stop. "You sure you want me to let you out here, ma'am?"

"Yes," I said, paying him and stepping from the car.

Dark. Especially after he pulled away. I followed the line of trees until I reached the gate. Locked. "Well, Mrs. Smarty," I said to myself, "now what?"

My feet were freezing. Such a winter Los Angeles didn't have. I wished I had thought about the gate being locked, but I hadn't. There was nothing to do but hike around the edges until I found a way in. Susan had taken us through the hedges when we'd ridden the horses, so it couldn't all be fenced.

In the heavy frost my shoes crunched and slipped as I leaned through the shrubs to feel for a wall. At last, when I was almost frozen, I reached between two little trees and felt only air. Cold branches slapped my face as I pushed between them. Such a night I wouldn't wish on a dog, but at last I could see a building, dark even against the midnight sky. A little moonlight I could have used, but the sky was full of clouds, which only let a faint glow through.

Inside the barn was warmer, even though many of the stalls

were empty. I groped along one wall and then another, being careful not to trip on the occasional bale of hay or rattle the halters that hung on the walls.

I stopped and held my breath each time one of the horses snorted or shifted as I passed.

Finally, I saw a thin ribbon of light underneath the tack-room door. I breathed a sigh of relief and hoped the stableboy was alone. I paused outside the door and pressed my ear against the wood. At first I froze. Voices. Then I realized it was the radio. I knocked.

The door was yanked open so suddenly I almost fell into the small room.

"What the bloody 'ell!" He paused and squinted at me. "Oh, it's you. How'd you get in?" One bony hand raked through his carroty hair.

"I . . . I came across the fields." It wasn't much of a lie. "I didn't have enough for the cab and your money, too." So sympathy couldn't hurt.

"My money?"

"Oh, please. I know you didn't expect me until morning, but the pain was so awful. I couldn't even sleep." I put a hand on my hip and hobbled to a stool. A little cry I gave as I sat, just to prove the point. "I know I could sleep the night through with one of those pills you gave me."

Jock stared at me for a long moment. Then he shrugged. "Right." He turned his back to me and rummaged in a small chest of drawers next to his cot. Within moments, he was dumping pills into his hand and counting them out. "Now at three pound apiece . . ."

I drew in my breath. "You said two earlier, I only brought twenty pounds with me."

"Two pound? I never. You got twenty? Then all I can give you is . . . six."

"The extra two dollars? Er, pounds?" I corrected.

"Got no change. I'll slip you one extra, all right? Then I'm out the extra quid. You can owe me 'cause you're a nice old girl." He smiled. It wasn't a pretty sight.

I blinked back my tears, hoping they would soften him. "But I need to have them. My pain."

"Sorry. Three pounds each. Seven for twenty is a bargain for you. That's me price. You want more, you pay more. After all, this is the real thing—full strength—not that diluted stuff the local competition sells."

"What do you mean?" I asked, digging in my purse and reluctantly taking out the money. I held the notes where he could see them but not reach them and asked him again.

"They don't mess with Jocko no more. Used to have a little competition. Damn amateurs thought they could undercut my business. Better'n them 'as tried." He laughed. "And failed."

My blood thickened in my veins like good soup stock. If he meant Mary Louise, maybe he had eliminated his competition. "Well, I can see you're a professional," I said, hoping to flatter him. "How could amateurs cause you any concern? A good businessman like you?" I smiled at him and handed over the bills to distract him from my curiosity.

"Bloody right! My people know they get all they pay for with Jock."

I reached into my everything bag as if I was putting away the medication. I took out the bottle of scotch and two glasses I had borrowed from the hotel. I poured him a shot and handed it over. "For being so helpful," I said, smiling at him. "It'll warm you." I glanced around the drafty barn and gave a little shudder to show him I knew it must be hard for him to live like this.

He grinned and downed the liquor in one gulp. Then he counted my bills. "Here now, you tryin' to cheat ol' Jock?" He waved the money at me. "First a drink then y' short me a quid?"

His being so nasty about this made what I was going to have to do a lot easier. "I'm sure you've miscounted. I wouldn't think of cheating anyone as clever as you," I said, forcing my voice to sound sincere. I recounted the money into his hand and took his empty glass.

145

He grunted and nodded. "All right then, sorry." As he turned away from me to tuck the money into the nightstand drawer, I dropped some of the powder from my sleeping pills—already removed from the capsules—in the bottom of his tumbler. By the time the boy had turned back, I had his portion all ready for him. The scotch and a little something extra, just in case.

"Thank you for letting me buy my medication a little early." I pushed the drink at him and he took it.

He raised the glass at me as I poured some for myself. "Not so much early as late, ma'am," he said, looking at the clock and laughing at his joke.

I laughed, too. Then I sipped a little so he shouldn't think I was letting him drink alone.

I sipped. He swallowed. Soon I was adding more to his glass.

"Nice idea, this, mum."

"Please, call me Fanny. We're friends now."

"Fanny?" His grin nearly split his face. "Your name is the same as the part you put against the horse?" He howled, holding his sides. "No offense, ma'am—Fanny."

I smiled, used to this reaction. "Well, it's better than Frances, which I never liked much. And my middle name we don't talk about."

"And you can call me Jock, on account of I wanted to be one, 'til I grew so bloody large." He was looking too drunk for such a small amount of liquor, so I assumed the sleeping powder was working. I hoped he hadn't been into something else that evening. I felt panicky. If he had, what I gave him plus the drink as well might kill him. I chatted on and took little nervous sips. He looked more and more under the influence.

Soon he was slumped on the bed and nodding.

I looked at my watch. Another few minutes and I ought to be able to search his room from top to bottom without a peep from him.

When Jock began to snore, I started. His dresser had only three shallow drawers. I found more of the pills he'd sold me.

Another bottle, almost full. I tucked them in my bag, wondering if they were the same 'full-strength' kind he'd sold me. There was no label on this bottle.

Then I lifted the lid of a large tack box. A saddle, nicely polished. Some riding boots and breeches, from a much smaller, more slender man than Jock. If this was the size he was *supposed* to be to ride as a jockey, I could see why he now worked for Taddington instead. I set everything to one side and then lifted out a tray with brushes and saddle soap and rags. Nothing.

Suddenly he stopped snoring. I had a moment of pure hell while I worried that he had stopped breathing permanently. I leaned over him with a mirror and saw that his breath would fog it. It was all right. I went back to my task.

After thirty minutes of searching, I had found nothing more than those pills. If something was hidden here, it must be out in the barn itself. I nudged Jock. Only a groan and a loud snore. He'd sleep for a while yet. No matter what Nathan said, there could still be some sort of a packet hidden in the barn. If there was, I'd find it.

Helping myself to his flashlight—it was bigger than my own—I started on the barn. Where, I asked myself, would I hide something in here? I let the beam pick out first one stall, then another. The horses stamped and moved uneasily. That reminded me. If anyone caught me snooping, I needed to do something to make the excuse I had planned seem real.

I found Alexander's stall. "Hello, boy. It's just me, Fanny. Susan's grandmother."

I patted him and he seemed to know me. I gave him a bit of carrot from my everything bag. While I chatted, I pulled out a small jar of harmless white salve. "You're not going to mind this a bit, I promise." I took a bit of the salve on my fingertip and drew wet, whitish streaks from his nostrils. "Just a little disguise, so if anyone asks, you look like you could have a cold. Checking on you is my best excuse for being here. If I need one."

147

Alexander let me do what I had to and then nodded his huge head up and down like he agreed with me. "Maybe you could sneeze a little, if anyone asks?"

He snorted against my arm, his moist breath spotting my sleeve. "Yes," I said. "Just exactly like that. Good Alexander. What a nice horse." I patted his neck. "Susan was right about you. So smart."

Now if I had to tell someone I had come to check on Alexander because Susan was afraid he had a cold, he would back me up.

I walked back through the barn.

"I won't hurt you, babies," I said, taking a cut-up apple from my everything bag and bribing the nearest animal.

I looked everywhere I could think of, and then moved to the next stall, and the next. Then came the one that was empty since Joshua's sad death. It looked as if the stall was being used to store older tack and bales of hay. I took a sample of hay from each bale just in case. Me, I wouldn't know marijuana if it bit me. But Nathan would.

I moved a saddle to get to the last bale. As I set it on the hay, something crackled. I stopped and turned the light that way. Rats I didn't need. Not even if it was only a mouse.

Nothing moved. I nudged the saddle again.

Crackle.

Something was odd about that saddle. I looked closer. Torn. The leather gaped at one side of the front flap, exposing what I think Susan had called the knee padding. I grabbed the saddle, never mind what she'd called it, I wanted to know what made the noise. I hadn't heard a noise like that from *our* saddles when we were riding the other day. Creaking and squeaking I could understand from leather, but a crackle?

I dug into the tear and felt something. My heart jumped into my throat and my fingers slipped against a bundle. The packet?

This bundle was what had crackled. It did it again as I strained to pull it from its hiding place. Suddenly, a shower of white powder coated my hand and spilled across the hay-littered floor. I just stared, shined the light on the gleaming white trail, and felt my breath stop in my lungs.

148

This was what I was looking for. This was the real money-maker, I could tell. Another point for my side. I only wished I could remember what the score was.

I pulled the leaky packet from between the leather flap and the padding and tucked it into a spare plastic bag I had in my everything bag. Then to the bottom I pushed it, so it shouldn't be seen or fall out. Next I sprinkled a lot of loose hay over the fallen powder so that it was all hidden from view. I checked the rest of the saddles in the barn. None were torn. Nothing crackled.

I had a moment of panic. How would I prove that the powder came from here? Would the police think I put it there myself? I didn't have too good a history with them, what with the murder and me and my Susan being in the wrong place at the wrong time.

Feh! They could test what had fallen to the stall floor. That would show them it had been here. As I sifted more hay over it and put the saddle like I had found it, I noticed two or three cigarette ends on the ground. Smoking in a stall I knew you didn't do. In a barn even. Such a fire hazard I didn't want to think about. I picked one up. Just a bit of paper and loose tobacco.

Suddenly, I could see Miss Kentworth taking that bit of tobacco from the end of her tongue as she smoked. If she had been here waiting for something, a drug delivery or money exchange, she would have been nervous, just like when Nathan and I talked to her. Maybe she would have smoked in spite of the danger of fire. I picked up all of the ends and looked at them closely. Was that a trace of lipstick on one?

Of course, students who weren't allowed to smoke might come here to hide their habit. But I had seen no signs of student smoking any of the times I'd been here. No one had been sneaking a smoke behind the barn the night I had seen Mary Louise with the man. Never had I noticed any cigarette butts on the grounds, not even in the fields as Susan and I rode out that day. The only person I'd seen smoking was Miss K. And she, unlike the students, wore lipstick.

I knew that like many teenagers, the girls here probably put

149

on makeup as soon as they were off the grounds. As in most strict English girls' schools, they weren't allowed to wear cosmetics on campus, and lipstick was the most obvious.

Now I knew where I would look next. I checked on Jock, who was still sound asleep, returned his flashlight, and hurried out of the barn.

Thirteen

THE moonlight helped now that the clouds had shifted. Such help I could have used a bit earlier, but now, since there was still activity in some of the buildings, I was afraid I would be seen.

Keeping to the bushes, I crept as close to the administration building as I could before leaving the cover of the shrubs. Like going for a shot deep into the back of the court, I ran toward the shadow of the building.

I flattened against the stucco when a couple of girls passed not five feet from me, laughing, and headed for the dorms. What they were doing out at one in the morning, I couldn't imagine. Weren't there curfews? Housemothers? Of course, it was Saturday night, but since the gates had been locked when I'd gotten here just after midnight, maybe curfew didn't apply inside the gates. I would have to be especially careful.

There was still one light on in the administration building and I hoped the doors would be unlocked. I edged around the corner and onto the porch. It was deep and half-timbered like the rest. I wiped at my face—a cobweb on my skin made me shiver.

My heart sank into my shoes when I tried the knob. It wouldn't budge. Now I would have to circle the offices, looking for another door or even an open window. More chances of being seen. Window ledge after window ledge I passed, always testing the glass for movement. Such rough, dark wood surrounded each opening that I was afraid I would get nothing but splinters for all my efforts. From such old timbers they would probably fester.

It was so quiet out that twigs snapping under my feet sounded like pistol shots as I stepped up to another window on the side of the building. A faint hint of music that must have come from the dorms floated on the night air. I tried a window. Latched.

I moved on.

The side exit was also locked. So cold. My fingers were getting blue. I couldn't say for sure, because it was hard to tell in the dark, but they felt blue. My feet, too, were almost numb from stepping in the occasional patch of crusty snow that still lingered beneath the bushes. I was pushing on my seventh—or was it my eighth?—window when something gave. *Mazel tov!* Now all I had to do was grow about a foot taller so I could get in. I looked around, but couldn't see anything that would make me as tall as I needed to be.

Cursing, I realized I would have to risk another trip to the barn for something to stand on. An overturned feed bucket would be just the thing.

I was halfway across the compound when I thought I smelled something burning. My first thought was for the horses and I broke into a jog.

A voice behind me asked what I was doing on the grounds. I jumped. Ten years it took off my life, a voice coming out of nowhere like that. I turned to see a large shape in the darkness, then sighed when I realized the face and the smoke were familiar. What a relief. "Mr. MacMurray, am I glad to see you," I said, taking an especially deep breath of the tobacco smoke and thinking again of my Morris.

"Might I ask what you're doing skulking about in the dark of night, Mrs. Zindel?"

"You can, if I can ask why you're asking?"

"I'm on a sort of lockup tour for the weekend, security duty, seeing no lads have crept in with their sweethearts, that sort of thing." He puffed on the meerschaum and blew a smoke ring, which immediately broke on the night breeze.

Such a shame, I thought as I watched it. Mr. MacMurray was inhaling that strong pipe smoke. Lung cancer for sure.

I smiled. "Well, I'm glad someone is keeping an eye out. I just saw two girls who seemed to be roaming around rather late—"

"And why are you here so late, ma'am? The gate gets locked at midnight."

"I've been with Alexander. He has a little cold. Susan was so worried about him she couldn't even close her eyes till I agreed to come look. And her with her poor broken arm throbbing away like a hammer on an anvil . . ." I looked sad and shook my head.

"She's been hurt?" Mr. MacMurray looked genuinely alarmed.

I smiled. "Her arm was broken when someone pushed a chunk of wall off Clifford's Tower onto Susan and our friend Janet. Susan rolled down the tower hill and broke her arm."

"Jesus, Mary, and Joseph! That's how the monk was killed during the massacre!" He pulled the pipe from his mouth and waved it for emphasis.

I felt the shock clear to my toenails when he reminded me. I had forgotten that part of the history. Mr. MacMurray was right. "Yes. Exactly like that," I said, my mind a million miles away from our talk. It made Susan's injury seem even more frightening. And connected in some evil way to the ritual that had been performed on Mary Louise's body.

"You should go home and get some rest, Mrs. Zindel. Y' don't look well."

"I'm fine. Just a little longer. I must be able to assure my granddaughter that her favorite horse is all right." I gave him my Joan Crawford look, like in *Mildred Pierce*, he should know I was as determined.

"I'll walk y' to the phone box, if y' like?"

153

"Oh, no. It's late, and I'm sure you have your rounds to finish. I'll be gone in a moment."

"If you're certain? I need to tell the dorm mother to keep the music down in the west wing. It's disturbing Miss Kentworth."

I nodded. "She must need all her rest with what's been happening lately."

"Oh, she wasn't sleeping. She was trying to work on the books. Weekends are the only time she has for paperwork."

"So, you see, we're not the only ones up late." I said, hoping to make my own errand less suspicious.

" '. . . and miles to go before I sleep,' I think your Robert Frost put it?"

I nodded. From Robert Frost I didn't know, but Shakespeare, that was something else again. " 'Sleep that knits up the ravell'd sleave of care,' " I said, giving him a quote from England's own great author in return.

"Let me know when you get ready to leave. I'll unlock the gate."

I nodded.

He left and I hurried toward the barn.

Before I was halfway there I found a bucket someone had left out, and I was on my way back to the unlatched window.

I struggled, even with the bucket for help, to wiggle up over the sill. Finally, I fell with a thud onto the hardwood floor of the original kitchen.

Huge. Larger than they would have had to keep just for making tea or lunches for the staff. They could almost have used this for the main student kitchen. I wondered why they hadn't converted it to offices like the rest of the rooms.

It would be tricky finding my way. And if Miss K was still working, I'd have to be very careful that she didn't see me.

I crept from the kitchen into the hall with only one or two false tries. I could see the main entrance about forty feet ahead. Unless the dark had me completely turned around, Miss K's office was just two doors the other side of that. If the light I had seen in the building earlier was from Miss K working late, then I would have some waiting to do.

The hall looked long, dark, and lonely. I thought of the penlight in my purse, but didn't dare use it. I tried to summon the kind of courage it took to walk onto the court at the beginning of an important tennis tournament. I had only taken one step toward her office when it happened.

A blur of dark material like the swirling garments of all three Macbeth witches, and then such a pain in my head. *Oy!* Everything went blacker than the inside of that building.

I felt a cold draft. My eyes fluttered open. From somewhere behind me came a thin light and a thicker chill. I tried to look in that direction, but my stomach rolled. Like on a ship. I swallowed against the sickness building in my throat and put a hand to my aching head. Such a lump.

It was a minute more before I could move. By that time, I was half-frozen. At last, I was able to see that whoever had hit me had left by the side door, the one that had been locked when I'd checked earlier.

Slowly, I got to my feet. Hanging on to the wall, I edged over and closed the door quietly. At least if I left it unlocked, I wouldn't have to jump back out the window with my aching head. And the cold, I can tell you, was doing my arthritis no good. Who could have hit me? And why? Maybe Miss Kentworth would have something to say. Painfully, I edged down the hall toward her office, no longer willing to wait until she left.

Carefully, I peeked into her waiting room. No light came from under Miss K's door now. I crept closer. Had she left? Had *she* conked me on the head on her way out?

When I put a hand on the knob, my palm was so damp with nerves it slipped against the cold metal. I took some napkins from my everything bag and then tried again. Success. I peeked through the crack. Empty. I stepped inside.

I dug in my everything bag for my penlight and clicked it on. Housekeeping hadn't been here, I could tell. Miss K had thrown papers all over the floor; such a messy worker? I wouldn't have thought . . .

I caught my breath. A pale hand poked out from in back of the desk. I moved closer. The arm and the shoulder, then the

155

white, staring face of Miss Kentworth filled the circle of my light. If I had been sick before, my stomach really gave a lurch now. Saliva rushed in under my tongue. I swallowed. Then swallowed again.

Fighting the pain in my head, I leaned forward and felt for a pulse. Nothing. Not that I had expected it from the angle of her head. Even to my amateur eye her neck looked broken.

Chilled with more than cold now, I stood staring and feeling the icy sweat prickling on my neck, my back, and down my arms. I stepped to the desk and switched on the lamp. Bright, but Miss K wasn't going to complain.

Suddenly, I snapped it off again. Mr. MacMurray had had a call from the headmistress only a short time ago. That must mean the killer had only just done this! I felt weak all over to think that Miss K's murderer had been sneaking through the same hall, covered by the same darkness that hid me. Now I was certain that my attacker—he, or maybe she—was also a murderer. I stood shivering in the dark, grateful that I was not lying in that hall with a neck bent like Miss K's.

I patted the desk top. I felt the phone. Without waiting a moment, I dialed O and asked for the police. "This is Mrs. Frances Zindel at Taddington School. I'd like to report a murder. In the administration building. Miss Kentworth, the headmistress." Shaking, I hung up.

Pulling a knitting needle from my everything bag, I stood behind the door and waited. If the murderer came back, I would be ready. A monster this murderer must be, and strong enough to snap the neck of a woman Miss K's size—five nine or taller, and no petite, bony thing, but what I would call *zoftig*, nice, but on the plump side.

As I stood in the dark, my mind raced. Should I leave? What if the killer came back? I talked to myself a little. "Don't be silly, Fanny. He hit you on the head to escape." The sound of my voice in the darkness gave me a little courage, made me able to think more clearly. He was probably long gone. Good riddance.

At first I couldn't wait for the police to arrive. Then I thought of the packet of drugs in my everything bag. I shouldn't have taken them. I knew it now. I should have left them where they were and led the police to find them.

It was spilt milk. Who knew I would have such a reason to get the police here so soon? Panicky, I flicked on the light. I couldn't take the chance of the police finding the packet on me.

Where could I hide it? The flowerpot, maybe? No, I thought. Too messy. I'd get dirt all over. Even if I was careful, I'd get it under my nails.

I looked at the bookcase. In one of the old movies, I had seen the hero cut out the center of a book to make a hiding place. I dug through my bag. The knife I had with me was too dull, better for spreading cream cheese on a bagel. To use my scissors on each page would take forever.

Scissors!

Suddenly I knew. I looked at the overstuffed chair. Within moments, I had the cushion off and I was making a cut along a seam at the back edge. I dug in my everything bag for my needle and thread. Thank goodness, I had some of that invisible thread, the stuff that was like very thin fishing line. It would match any color.

I stuffed the pills and the white-powder packet inside the pillow and did my best to even out the lumps. Then I whipped the edges back together so that you could hardly see the mend. My mother had insisted on a young lady being good in handiwork. In my mind, I thanked her, and not for the first time.

Already it seemed like hours since I'd called the police. Where were they? I checked my watch. Seven minutes only. Not so long. I glanced around the office while I waited.

I could look for clues. But considering I'd only been here once before, I wouldn't know what was unusual.

Then it hit me. One thing I could check. I dug in my everything bag until I found the plastic bag with the cigarette butts I had found in the stall. Those maybe I could match with Miss Kentworth's.

I moved one of the sheets of paper off the desk ashtray. Good, it had been a stressful evening for Miss K—besides getting murdered, I thought. She had smoked a lot of cigarettes today. The Waterford crystal ashtray set into the leather holder contained a thick layer of gray ash and at least a dozen crumbled white ends. Several still held traces of her lipstick.

I pulled out the bag I had marked: *Butts from the barn.* Bingo! Looked like a match to me. The lipstick on those ends seemed to be not only the same color as on these butts, but also the same shade that still tinted Miss K's dead lips.

Carefully pushing aside a small mound of half-burned tobacco and gray ash, I took two samples from the Waterford. I put them in a separate bag and labeled it with my marking pen. *Butts from Miss K's office.*

I had barely put my evidence away when I heard a commotion at the main gate. A policeman was rattling the grillwork and shouting. Mr. MacMurray was running toward the police car with his keys clanking. He was shouting back. I watched the police car pull up to the administration building.

I opened the window and leaned out. "In here," I called to the officers. "This way."

A crowd of students was gathering and one of the uniformed men held the girls away from the door. I saw Mr. MacMurray using his broad shoulders to push toward the entrance. He was taller than either policeman, and when he shouted at the girls, they listened. A flock of pastel-robed young ladies fluttered down the steps like flower petals in a wind. Some in curlers, some in braids, others with their hair loose about their shoulders, all squealed and chattered.

The policeman rushed through Sara's outer office, banging open the connecting door. Lucky I was still by the window or I'd have been flattened. "That's how I found her, Officer," I said, pointing at the body. "I haven't touched anything except the phone. Miss Kentworth was dead when I got here." I'd also touched the ashtray, but I'd had a plastic bag over my hand. I wasn't going to volunteer anything extra.

He nodded and checked the body. "Neck snapped, looks like," he said, and walked to the window to shout at his partner. "Call for an investigation team, Clive." He glanced at the brass plate on Miss K's door and then turned toward me.

"Officer Gallagher, ma'am. Are you the headmistress's secretary?"

"Who, me?" I shook my head. "I'm Fanny Zindel. I made the phone call."

"Then what were you doing here at this time of night?"

My mouth hung open a moment. This was the time for my excuse. "I was here checking on my granddaughter's favorite horse. He has a cold. I thought he should have his temperature checked, but I couldn't wake the stableboy.

"Since one of the teachers had said Miss Kentworth was working late, I thought I should report it to her. As soon as I came in the building, someone clunked me on the head and down I went like a raw dumpling sinking to the bottom of a soup pot."

"Someone struck you?"

"You bet!" I said, moving closer to him and showing him the lump. "See. Such an egg you don't even get from a goose. Feel it."

"That's not necessary, ma'am. I can see the blood in your hair."

"Blood? I'm bleeding?" I must have looked a little pale at the news, because Officer Gallagher helped me to a chair. Little did he know I was plunking my *tuchis* down on the illegal drugs. I shifted uncomfortably on the lumpy cushion. Oh well, by the time I sat on it for a while, the cushion would look even more normal. It crackled and I froze, hoping no one else heard it.

"Take it easy, ma'am. Did you see who struck you?"

I shook my head very gently. "Just a dark blur."

"And where were you when this happened?"

"On my way to Miss Kentworth's office, of course."

"No, ma'am. I mean where exactly? Here in the office?"

I hesitated. "No. Out in the hall."

"Show me."

I got to my feet and with his hand on my elbow—I was grateful for the support, I can tell you—I led him down the hall. "Here. I remember because when I came to, that door was open and blowing cold air on me until I nearly froze."

"You closed the door, ma'am?"

159

"Pneumonia you maybe think I'd like better? Of course I closed it. Born in a barn I wasn't."

Officer Gallagher sighed and flipped his notebook shut.

"What's the matter?" I asked.

"You touched the knob, right?"

"Oh," I said, suddenly understanding and ashamed of myself. I should have known better, someone who was once asked to join Mossad. Of course, I had been hit on the head, so I wasn't thinking too clearly.

"Well, what's done is done. We'll take your fingerprints just to check."

He walked back to Miss K's office and I followed.

He glanced at his little notebook. "Who's this teacher you spoke with? The one who told you the headmistress was working late?"

"Mr. MacMurray, the gentleman at the door. The one who helped your partner keep the students back."

He looked me up and down. "You stay here. I'm going to fetch him."

A moment later, he was back in the office with Mr. MacMurray.

"Then you were the last person to speak to Miss Kentworth," the policeman said, as he and MacMurray came through the door together.

Mr. MacMurray nodded. "Yes, sir, about half-past midnight it was."

"You saw her?"

"She rang me up. I had the grounds duty."

"So you were supposed to make sure no one was illegally on the premises?"

"Yes." I saw him looking at me. I backed up and sat carefully on the drug cushion again.

"You saw nothing strange?" he asked the teacher.

"I did see Mrs. Zindel, here, and I asked her what she was doing on the grounds so late."

Gallagher looked directly at me. "What time do the main gates get locked, Mr. MacMurray?"

I think I blushed a little as they spoke.

160

"Half-ten during the week, around midnight on Friday and Saturday nights."

"Then you must have arrived before midnight, eh, Mrs. Zindel?"

I hoped the red creeping up from my collar didn't show. "I . . . uh . . . didn't get here in time. But you see, I had promised my granddaughter. She has a broken arm, and Alexander, her horse, has been sick," I added, hoping for sympathy. "So I walked along the hedge until I found a space."

"You admit you broke into the school?"

"What broke? A branch of the hedge, maybe. It was a small space. The grounds aren't fenced."

"But the gate was locked, ma'am."

"But a promise to a sick child is a promise Fanny Zindel keeps."

Gallagher sighed. I could tell he was annoyed with me. "What time did you break into the school, ma'am?"

I shrugged. "Maybe Mr. MacMurray noticed. I ran into him on my way to the barn." So I wouldn't mention it had been my *second* trip to the barn.

Gallagher looked at the teacher. "You check your watch, sir?"

"It was about a quarter till one."

"So, you went to the barn and then what?" He eyed me sternly.

"I thought Alexander should have his temperature taken. I knocked for the stableboy. He didn't answer. So I came looking for the headmistress."

"And how did you know she'd be about at this hour?"

"I told you," I said, glancing again at the math teacher. "Mr. MacMurray had mentioned she was working late."

"You saw a light in her office?"

I could feel the sweat trickling down the side of my neck. "I . . . don't remember."

"Mr. MacMurray, here, had to unlock the front door to let us in. Maybe you'd like to tell me how *you* got into the building?"

I shrugged. "The side door was open."

161

"Not when I checked, it wasn't," Mr. MacMurray said.

I squirmed in my seat a little. It cracked again. I would have squirmed a lot if I had known what the other officer who came to the door was going to say. Maybe then the crackling would have drowned him out.

He carried the feed bucket in one hand, his flashlight in the other. "I found this bucket upended under a window."

Gallagher looked at me. "So, you came in the side door, but someone obviously used this to crawl in a window." He waved the bucket by its wire.

I looked at the floor. What was I going to say now? If I didn't admit coming in the window, they would get a false idea about the real murderer. What if Miss K had let the killer in? That would mean she knew her murderer.

What if the killer had a key? I looked at Mr. MacMurray and then felt ashamed of myself because he'd always been so nice to me. Of course, killers could be nice, sometimes. I would have to tell them.

"Mrs. Zindel, did you come in that side door?"

I shook my head. I prayed that honesty was the best policy, like we always try to teach our children. "All right, I did come in the window, Officer Gallagher." I looked at him, pleading. "I just had to talk to Miss K. I knocked, but I guess Miss Kentworth didn't hear me. It's a heavy door. My hands," I held them up, "are arthritic. They've been hurting, so I can't knock very loud."

Red and chapped my hands looked from the cold. I hoped the swelling near some of the joints showed him I was telling the truth. Well, almost the truth. Miss K wouldn't have heard me if I had knocked. After all, the dead don't answer their doors.

Gallagher looked over at the officer who had found the bucket. "Go over to the barn, Clive. See if one of the horses is sick."

"Alexander's the big gray one," I said, quickly. "His name is on his stall. A little brass nameplate."

Gallagher gave me a frown. "Mrs. Zindel, I am afraid I will have to take you in for questioning."

"Questioning? Me?"

"I'm afraid so, ma'am. You did break in. You did say you found the body."

"Yes, and I told you why, and I have a lump on my head from the killer."

"And maybe you're that killer. Maybe that lump on your head came from a fight you had with her." He gestured to the fallen Miss Kentworth.

I felt my mouth drop open in shock. I couldn't think of a thing to say as I followed him out to the squad car.

Officer Clive joined us. "There's a big gray horse in there all right. Looks like his nose is running." Clive took off his hat and scratched his head. "Do horses get runny noses, sir?"

Gallagher shrugged. "Don't know. We get back to the station, you call the local vet and ask."

An exciting drive it was with me trying to talk sense into Gallagher and his partner, Clive, and them trying to ignore me.

At last, we were at the station and I hoped I would soon be safely back at the hotel.

We went inside and sat down. The clerk offered us tea, but I was still too upset to drink anything.

"As I tried to tell you on the way over, Officer Gallagher, I couldn't have killed the headmistress. An old lady, my size, with arthritis in her hands so she can't even break crocheting wool any more, should snap a neck? On a woman the size of Miss Kentworth?"

"We'll have to wait for the coroner's report to give us the cause of death."

"Officer, while you are questioning me, who couldn't possibly have done the deed, the person who did do it is getting away."

"One step at a time, ma'am." Gallagher got up out of his chair and took some keys from the top of his desk. "Please come with me, Mrs. Zindel."

"Come where?"

"I'm going to have you wait in the back until the report comes in."

"In jail? You're going to put me in jail?"

"Calm down, ma'am. It's not an arrest. I'm not booking you. This is a small station. We have other people to question and I'll need the front for that."

"I get a call to my embassy," I said. "To my granddaughter. To my cousin, Lady Doris Bond."

"If I decide to arrest you, you'll get your call."

He led me into the back of the building. I saw iron bars and small cells. It made my stomach tighten and my head pound. A doctor I needed, not a jailer. I stepped through the cell door and sat on the small cot. The door clanged shut and the officer left.

Fourteen

FROM inside I could hear Nathan's angry bellow. Then Gallagher roared back and things got quieter. The quiet stretched on until it got on my nerves, what nerves I had left.

The door flew open and an angry Nathan was framed by the bars of my cell. Oy, was I going to hear him *kvetch*. Just from his expression, I knew he'd complain. It made me sorry I'd given his name to Gallagher when he'd asked me if there was anyone who could pick me up from the station.

The policemen were questioning poor Mr. MacMurray even more closely than they had me. I could still hear his voice between Nathan's shouts.

I knew Nathan must really be tired. He'd left his pajama shirt on under his coat. "You know I'm not an early riser. What kind of trouble are you in now?"

"No trouble. They just wanted to ask me a few things about Miss Kentworth's murder." I saw his eyes grow wide with shock.

"Whose murder?" he asked through gritted teeth.

Gallagher spoke up. "Miss Gwendolyn Kentworth, headmistress at Taddington Girls' School. Found at about twenty past one by Mrs. Zindel here."

165

Nathan glanced up at the policeman and then back at me. He was still frowning. "And what was Mrs. Zindel doing there?"

Gallagher didn't even have to look in his notebook. We'd been through it so many times. "She said, sir, that she was checking on her granddaughter's horse. He had a cold. So, she said she went to the headmistress's office."

"The headmistress was working so late?" Nathan asked.

"I was surprised at that, too, sir. Mr. MacMurray, on grounds duty, indicated that he had seen Mrs. Zindel walking about and mentioned to her that Miss Kentworth was still in her office."

"Then I'm correct in assuming you have Mrs. Zindel here as a matter of convenience to writing your report?"

The officer looked uncomfortable. "Well, sir, not exactly. It seems that Mrs. Zindel, here, entered the building by rather unorthodox means."

"Unorthodox?"

"I used a feed bucket to climb in through an open window, Nathan." I rushed on before he could start shouting. "No one heard my knocking, not the stableboy when I tried there, not Miss Kentworth later. That's when I got hit on the head."

"Hit on the head?" Nathan looked as if the same had just happened to him.

"It seems, sir, that no one would have been able to knock up the stable lad. He was sleeping one off in his room." Gallagher flipped a page of his notebook. "Had the devil's own time—excuse me, ma'am—wakin' him ourselves, we did."

"How did Miss Kentworth die?"

"Well, we won't know all the details until they can do a full autopsy, you understand, but it appears as if her neck was broken."

"Appears? *Gottenyu!* Snapped like a twig! You should only have seen the angle of her head, Nathan." I bent my head as far onto my shoulder as I could. "Like this, only worse. If that wasn't a broken neck I don't know what—"

"Fanny! Enough, already. You're a medical examiner now?" Nathan snapped.

166

I lowered my eyes and closed my mouth.

Nathan looked pointedly at his watch. "So, may I take Mrs. Zindel home, Officer?"

"I suppose I should hold her for breaking and entering, but she seems to have been on the grounds with Mr. MacMurray's blessing! And since the headmistress is the deceased, there's no one to press any charges!" He shrugged. "Go on, you two, I've got a report to write."

Nathan took my arm, a lot more firmly than I thought necessary. He dragged me out before Gallagher could change his mind.

"Ouch!" I said, as soon as we were through the door.

"You deserve much worse. I should turn you over my knee and paddle your *tuchis!*"

"Nathan Weiss!"

"Don't you 'Nathan Weiss' me, Frances Zindel. What were you doing on those school grounds? The truth!"

He handed me into the car and stomped around to the driver's side. "Well?" He cranked the engine and lurched from the curb.

"I told you. I wanted to check on Alexander—"

"Bunk! Hogwash. You went to see that stableboy, didn't you? In spite of what we discussed."

I gulped. "Well, maybe I stopped by his room when I was checking on the horse. I mean, he would wonder what I was doing in his barn so late."

"Yes. He would. So would I. But I'm afraid I know. You went after those drugs, didn't you?"

Him I couldn't fool. I nodded.

Nathan slammed his hand down on the wheel. "Dammit, Fanny!"

"Now, Nathan," I put a hand on his arm but he shook it off. "I found he had a lot more than those pills in his barn. Just like I thought!" I said, folding my arms across my chest and raising my chin a little.

Nathan pulled to the curb and slammed on the brakes. "You did what?"

"I found some white powder stuffed in a torn saddle. And a whole extra bottle of those pills in his nightstand. These didn't even have a label. So much for your idea that he was just small potatoes, Mr. Know-It-All! What do you say to that?"

"I say you should be in the slammer, Mrs. Zindel. How in hell did you get those drugs past that copper?"

I smiled. "I didn't. I hid them before he got there."

"What! Hid them?" Nathan looked sick.

"Yes, I sewed them into a chair cushion in Miss K's study." His reaction was not what I expected. Proud he wasn't.

He gripped his head in his hands. "Oh, Fanny. You didn't."

"I did. And quite a smooth move, I thought. Much better than to get arrested for possession."

"Fanny,"—he shook his head—"the police will seal that room for God knows how long. It's a murder site." He started the car again and drove on toward the hotel.

"So? They won't find what they don't know is there."

"Maybe not. But now we can't get to our proof, either, unless you admit your guilt to the police."

"Oh." My pride, like a cake when you bang the oven door, took a fall. "The police would be angry, right?"

"Angry? Fanny, you're in enough trouble breaking and entering. Now, you want we should tell the police that you've moved evidence of a drug deal and hidden it at the scene of a murder?"

"It wouldn't look so good?"

"No, Fanny," he said, pulling into the parking lot of the hotel, "it wouldn't. You should never have moved the drugs. You should have left them where they were and led the police to them." He sighed. "I guess all this tampering with evidence would get you about ten years."

"But Nathan, I was afraid someone would come for the drugs before I could get back with the police. Then all those drugs would already have been in the hands of innocent children."

He sighed. "Fanny, now how are you going to prove the drugs were ever in the barn?"

"Easy." I beamed. "I thought of that, Nathan, honest. All the police have to do is look at the dirt in the stall beneath the saddle rack. The packet had a hole. There's plenty still there, believe you me. I covered it with loose straw."

"I suppose I should only thank *HaShem* for a small favor." He climbed from the car and came around to let me out.

"So, what do you think, Nathan? Who would have killed Miss K?"

Nathan stopped in his tracks. "Wait a minute, Fanny. If you didn't go to that office because of Alexander, why did you go?"

I hesitated. "Look what I found in the stall, right under the drug saddle." I showed him the three cigarette ends I had taken from the barn. "I remembered from when we were in her office that day, that she didn't use cigarettes with the filter. See there's even a little lipstick on this one." Then I showed him the ones from the ashtray. "And look. They seem to match these from Miss K's office, right down to the lipstick."

Nathan smacked his forehead with his palm and groaned. "My God, Fanny, you suspected the woman had something to do with a major drug operation and you went in to chat with her about it? A coffee klatch, maybe?"

"No, I didn't think she'd be there. When Mr. MacMurray said she was working late, I thought I'd wait in the hall until she left. Then I'd search her office. I wanted cigarette butts from her ashtray to compare with these." I held up the bag from the barn.

Nathan groaned again and hurried me through the lobby and into the elevator. "You're impossible, Fanny."

"What impossible? Susan's reputation is at stake, my son is going to be sued for Joshua's worth, and half the town thinks Mary Louise was murdered by at least a Jew, if not my granddaughter. I should relax and enjoy the conference, maybe?"

In a huff, I opened the door to my room, stepped inside, and closed it firmly behind me. Nathan should only know I was upset with him. All this *shandeh*, this shame, on the Zindel family, and I should sit around on my hands doing nothing to set the record straight? Nathan of all people should know better. So soon he forgot Israel, maybe?

I set my everything bag on my cot, then shrugged out of my

169

coat as quietly as I could so as not to wake Susan and Janet. Poor Susan, I thought, all this *tursis*, trouble, and a broken arm as well. I looked over at her bed.

My heart jumped out of my chest as I stared at the hollow where her head should have rested on the pillow. Her bed was empty! I grabbed my bag and coat and rushed down the hall.

"Nathan!" I cried, pounding on his door. "Is Susan in there with Geoff?"

Nathan opened the door, his face pale. "I was just going to ask you the same thing. Geoff's gone."

Fifteen

OME ON, Fanny. I'll take you right back to the station."
I held up my bag and coat. "I already have my things."

Nathan locked his door.

"Wait! We can't go to the police," I said.

"Why not? She's missing."

"Nathan. It's bad enough Susan had no proof of where she was when Mary Louise was murdered. Now I should go and tell the police that I don't know where she was when Miss K died?"

Nathan stopped. "Good Lord! You don't think she could have had anything to do with it, do you, Fanny?"

"Nathan Weiss! Your mouth I should wash with soap!"

He looked sheepish. "Sorry. I guess that's what the police would ask." He unlocked his door and we stepped back into his room.

"She couldn't snap a neck like that any more than I could." I held up my arthritic fingers in front of his face.

Nathan gave me a look. "Geoff seems like a sturdy fellow. Plays soccer and all of that."

"He's a nice boy from a good Jewish family."

Nathan shrugged. "He's a nice boy in love with your grand-daughter. Maybe he blames Miss Kentworth for all Susan's troubles."

"I won't even think it." I put water to boil in the electric kettle. "Even if it crossed Geoff's mind, Susan is with him. She would never let him." I took some cookies from my everything bag and set them on a plate. My hand touched the bag with the hay samples. I pulled them out.

"I suppose you're right, Fanny. I was just playing devil's advocate, again. But they're still missing. What the hell are we going to do?"

I sat thinking. The teakettle whistle sounded, making me jump. I poured two cups and handed one to Nathan. "Eat. You'll need your strength," I said, pushing the cookies toward him. Maybe a little food would help my head, which was beginning to ache. The lump, also, wasn't any smaller, I can tell you.

"What are these, Fanny?" asked Nathan, looking at the bags.

"I thought you'd tell me."

He opened a plastic bag and sniffed. "Good clean alfalfa, Fanny. Nothing else." He looked at the rest. "Not in any of them."

I shrugged. "It was a try."

We sat munching and sipping for a moment. So quiet. "Where would Susan go in the middle of the night?" I asked, taking two aspirin from my purse and swallowing them with a little of the tea. Such a headache.

"You think they would have gone to Geoff's?"

I shook my head. "Susan knows better. His parents are still in London. She knows how it would look."

"Sometimes when kids want a little privacy, they don't think about that."

"Privacy they had here in your room, on your balcony, only a few hours ago. Privacy they had when they went out for coffee together." Suddenly it hit me. "Nathan! What were we talking about when the kids were on the balcony?"

He shrugged. "I don't remember."

"I'll tell you what. We were talking about the insurance and Joshua's murder."

"Oh, Fanny, you don't think—"

"I do. I think my Susan would go to Taddington to make sure the same thing didn't happen to Alexander." I jumped to my feet, sloshing the tea from my cup.

"Fanny, Alexander isn't worth a small fortune like Joshua was. The school would have nothing to gain. Assuming that was even their intent with Joshua, which"—he shook his finger at me—"by the way, we haven't proved."

"Susan thinks Alexander is worth the world. More valuable than Joshua, not less."

"That may be so, but you can't very well go back to the school at this hour. Besides, they'll have a policeman there now."

I paced the room. Nathan was probably right. If they thought a killer was loose in the school, they would surely post guards.

Suddenly, I had an idea. I took my address book from my everything bag. After a few moments of searching, I found the number Mr. MacMurray had given me when he'd promised to keep me informed of anything he found out about Mary Louise.

I dialed. The phone rang several times before a sleepy voice yawned a hello into the receiver.

"Mr. MacMurray? Fanny Zindel. I'm sorry to call you so late, but it's an emergency."

I heard a lot of throat-clearing.

"It's all right, Mrs. Zindel. I only just returned from the station. What can I do for you?"

"This may sound strange. But I need to ask a favor."

"What?"

"Could you check the barn? I need to know if Alexander is all right. Naturally with all the commotion, I never got anyone to call a vet." I held my breath and waited for him to answer.

"You want me to go check on a horse? Now?"

"I know it's a lot of trouble. But my granddaughter is

173

frantic. If Alexander needs a vet, I'll be happy to pay for one to come out. The police said the stableboy was drinking. I don't think he would be much help if the horse is really ill."

"Mrs. Zindel, it's after half-three in the morning—"

I cut in quickly. "That means that poor animal has been without help for hours, now. Please Mr. MacMurray, I'll make it up to you, I promise. Just see if he's still on his feet."

He sighed. "No need to make it up to me, ma'am. I'll give a look and call you back. Give me your number again, will you?"

I read him the hotel phone number and gave Nathan's room number. "My daughter is a veterinarian. I know a lot. If he's not on his feet, we may need a doctor."

"Right, Mrs. Zindel."

"He'll call us," I said, hanging up the phone. All I could do was pace.

At last the phone rang and I nearly knocked over the night-stand grabbing for it. "Yes?"

"Mrs. Zindel?"

"Yes, Mr. MacMurray, how's the horse?" I held my breath.

"Well, he . . . he seems to be missing."

"Missing?" My worst fears were coming true. I knew in my heart Susan had taken him. Now they were all out there somewhere. Susan, Geoff, and Alexander, wandering in the dark and frightened out of their wits. And with Larry and Judith due here in less than nine hours. "Thank you for checking for me, Mr. MacMurray."

"I'll make a report right away, ma'am. I'm sure he can't have wandered far."

"Ah, no. Please. As a personal favor to me, Mr. MacMurray, could you not do that?"

"Not report him missing?" He sounded alarmed. "Why not, Mrs. Zindel?"

"Well, I think I know where he may be. Believe me, he's in good hands, but it will take me a little time to find him."

"I don't think I can do that. He's school property, y' know. And I am in charge of the grounds security this weekend." His voice had changed. It had an edge.

"Oh, please, Mr. MacMurray. If I tell you what I think, will you help me?" I was begging him. I heard the desperate note in my voice and hoped it would affect him.

"Well . . ."

"Because I think Susan took Alexander to protect him."

"Protect him?"

"I think she's afraid the school might have him put down for the insurance money."

"What a thoroughly horrid idea, Mrs. Zindel. It makes this night even more of a misery."

"Mr. MacMurray, I'm forced to trust you."

"I'm a trustworthy man, Mrs. Zindel. M' word is m' bond." I could hear the pride in those words.

"I think the school is involved in an insurance scam."

There was a long silence. "An insurance scam?"

"Yes. The school was planning to sue Susan's father for the cost of Joshua. I learned that the insurance company is reluctant to pay. But Miss Kentworth never mentioned insurance. I'm sure she would have accepted money from both sides. The school has had some financial difficulty."

"Great Christ! I had no idea."

"So you'll help me?" I hurried to press him while he was sounding uncertain.

"I could only delay the report until Monday morning. My shift ends then."

"Oh, thank you Mr. MacMurray. I knew I could count on you to help."

His brogue thickened and I had to listen carefully to understand him. "Y' know I canna be sure the stable lad won't make his own report?"

"I understand. Anything you can do will help."

I hung up and looked at Nathan. "He'll do what he can. But we've got to find Susan!"

"Geoff's," Nathan said, and grabbed his coat.

I followed him out the door.

It was a long drive to Leeds, over an hour under good conditions. On dark roads that were unfamiliar, it took even longer. Geoff's family lived on the far side of the town and we

175

wasted a lot of time finding our way through the empty streets.

A few roundabouts, a few wrong turns, and we were lost in the industrial section. Huge, gloomy buildings and warehouses. Factories waiting for workers who wouldn't appear until Monday morning. No one to ask directions from.

At last, we found an open gas station and corrected our course. It was after five when we got to Geoff's home on the outskirts. A nice neighborhood it was. But crowded. Not many single houses, mostly like our townhouses at home. I began to worry.

As we neared the address, the homes were individual houses again, but still without much land around them. My nerves stretched tight.

When we finally got there, I was crushed to see that Geoff's house was dark and the doors and windows were locked. We walked all the way around the house.

I was even more upset to see that there was a small patch of front yard and no backyard to speak of. No place for Susan to have hidden Alexander.

"Well, Fanny, any ideas?" Nathan held the car door open against an icy spring wind. I ducked inside, hoping for warmth, shaking my head and blowing on my fingers. Numb I was outside and now inside, too.

"I guess we go back to the hotel."

Even the pink of the sunrise didn't help our dreary return to York. The fields looked cold and foggy. Everywhere along the road there were trees empty of leaves. Patches of grimy snow lay in the shadows and hollows.

We drove through York. I glanced around the quiet city. As on the morning when Susan and I had walked to Market Square, nothing moved except a delivery man with his Sunday papers.

Nathan insisted we go for coffee and rolls in the train station. The hotel restaurant wouldn't be open yet. It was too early, he said, to get anything more, but he was cold and miserable and didn't want to wait until full breakfasts were served. I agreed with him. Maybe a croissant would settle the gnawing in my stomach.

176

Impressive. In the station, with its high ceilings and Victorian styling, our heels echoed on the marble flooring. The polish reflected back wobbly images of me, my arm through Nathan's. The marble market they must have cornered to build this.

A shabby-looking young man with a shaggy black-and-tan shepherd mix at his side carried his guitar toward one of the train entrances. He set up for the day. A melodic picking of his steel strings followed us and echoed off the high ceilings and marble columns.

Most of the small shops were still closed, their iron gates pulled down and locked to metal rings in the floor. A newsstand was just opening; the gate rolled up with a roar. Beyond that, we found a coffee bar in service and sat on the high stools, resting our elbows on the chipped Formica counter.

Despite my worries, I was hungrier than I realized. I had two apple croissants and three cups of decaf before I warmed up. Then I realized how exhausted I was. All night I had been up running around.

"We need some rest, Fanny," said Nathan, voicing my own thoughts.

I nodded and fought back a yawn.

At the hotel, Nathan walked me to my door and waited until I was safely inside.

Wearily, I shrugged off my coat and dropped my everything bag on the floor near the bed. It landed with a soft thump and I glanced over to make sure I hadn't disturbed Janet.

Gottenyu! Was I dreaming even before I was in bed?

My Susan was sound asleep, cuddled up as if nothing had happened. Her poor injured arm, its cast shining whitely in the moonlight, rested easily on the pillow above her head.

Sixteen

WAS it possible I had misjudged my granddaughter? Had she been restless and just walking? No, Geoff had been missing, too. And Alexander!

Suddenly, a soft *tap-tap* at the door. I hurried over.

"Fanny, Geoff's sound asleep in my room."

I nodded and stepped into the hall, closing the door quietly behind me. "Yes."

"You aren't surprised?"

"Susan is also asleep, like a little angel. Now what?"

Nathan shook his head. "I guess we don't have proof that they had anything to do with Alexander's disappearance, just a strong suspicion."

I sighed. "No proof, but the feeling in my *kishkes*," I said, putting a hand on my stomach.

"So? What do we do now? You want me to wake Geoff?"

I shook my head. "It's Sunday morning. Let them sleep. They'll be up soon enough for the closing of the conference. And Susan has to face her parents today."

Nathan rolled his eyes. "And you have to drive." He looked at me. "The closing?"

"Yes, right after the Catholic mass. We'll have 'Expressions of Heritage and Hope' at the tower. Then the speeches from the delegates, presided over by the archbishop of York. About mine, I haven't even thought, I can tell you."

"You have to give a speech? And no sleep tonight? You're the one who should go to bed, Fanny." Nathan gave me a concerned hug.

"*Feh!* Sleep now I couldn't. I don't need nearly as much sleep as I used to. Neither do you, if I recall a night or two in Israel?"

He smiled and hugged me closer. "All right. What do you want to do? Me, I could still use a real breakfast."

"I might have a bite, just to keep you company, but I have to think about my speech."

By the time Nathan had had his omelette and several cups of coffee, I had decided. I would tell how much the *B'nai Brith* delegate from the U.S. of A. appreciated the memorial. I also knew what I would do about Susan.

"You decide yet, Fanny?" Nathan set his cup down so that the waitress could refill it. I nudged my cup her way also. Now that I knew I wasn't going to get any sleep, real coffee with caffeine I could use after such a long night.

"Yes." I held back until the waitress left. "I'm going to ask her."

"Ask her?"

"Yes, Susan would never lie to me." I folded my napkin and set it by my plate.

"Maybe I should talk to Geoff?"

I shook my head. "No. She's my granddaughter. I'll handle it. Thank you, Nathan."

He nodded. "Good luck." He went back to his coffee and his paper.

I stood up and marched back to the room.

No elevator. Too slow anyway. I wanted to get this over with. I trotted up the stairs and down the hall. This no sleep stuff wasn't bad for my arthritis. You don't sleep lying in one position all night, you don't feel stiff in the morning. Maybe I should try to sleep a little less in the future. Maybe all this sleeping was more than just a waste of time. Maybe it wasn't even good for me.

I was glad to see Susan was awake when I came into the room. Janet also, but she was in the bathroom already. I could hear the water running in the tub. Good. I needed a little privacy with my granddaughter.

"Susan, you slept all right?" I said, smiling at her.

"Sure, *Bubbe*." She ran a brush through her long hair, the dark curls springing back as soon as she finished the stroke. "Did you sleep well?"

"Funny you should ask, *Susa-le*. I never got to bed all night."

She looked startled. *"Bubbe,* what's the matter?"

"I had a little trouble. More than trouble. Another murder."

"Murder!" She was shocked. "What happened? Who got murdered?"

I paused a moment, Nathan's first words coming back to me with a sharp pain. Could Susan or Geoff have been involved? "Miss Kentworth was found dead last night in her office."

Susan sat down on the bed as if her knees had turned to chicken soup. I felt relieved. I was sure she had no idea ahead of time about Miss K. About Alexander, however, I wasn't so sure. *"Susa-le,"* I said, sitting next to her and putting an arm around her shoulders, "did you know Alexander was missing?"

Susan drew in a breath, but then smiled. "Oh, he probably just wandered out into the paddock. He used to get out of his stall sometimes. He's such a smart boy. He'll be back around breakfast time."

I was a little worried that Susan seemed to have such a story all made up. Could I be wrong about her taking the horse? I didn't want to accuse her falsely. "You think it's all right? He's just gone for a little walk, maybe?"

"Well, I'm not real sure, *Bubbe,* but he has done it before. Let's call the school and see if he's come back for his food."

"Are you sure you didn't have something to do with this?"

She looked away from me for a moment. *"Bubbe,* how could I? Geoff and I were just hanging out—"

"Susan, I know you were upset when you overheard Nathan and me talking about Joshua's death maybe being on purpose for the insurance. Did you think you needed to protect Alexander, maybe?" I had to interrupt her; my granddaughter had been on her way to spinning a real lie about herself and Geoff if what I suspected was the truth. I didn't want to hear it come out of her lips.

"Susan, did you take that horse?"

"Oh, *Bubbe,* what could I do?" I saw her turning a little bit red. She fiddled with the hem of her sweater, twisting it in her fingers.

I put my hand over hers. "Susan, I know you would never lie to your *Bubbe.* Tell me, did you take Alexander from his stall?"

She looked up at me, her green eyes huge and filled with tears. Like a pot boiling over she sobbed and threw herself into my arms. I held her for a few moments while she cried and told me how sorry she was to even think of trying to lie to me. She apologized.

"So," I said, when she calmed down a bit, "what did you do with him?"

She dried her eyes and gave me a look. "I can't tell you. I'll admit I took him. But it was just to keep him safe. He's okay where he is. I won't say more."

"Susan."

"Bubbe, you can't tell what you don't know. And no one can blame you for his being missing."

I sighed. Protecting me she was. From what? A headline maybe she feared: SIXTY-FIVE-YEAR-OLD GRANDMOTHER ARRESTED FOR HORSE THIEVERY? "Geoff helped you?"

"I won't make Geoff an accomplice, either." She got that stubborn look on her face, like when she was little and wouldn't eat one of her vegetables for Judith. Stubborn like I used to be, too. And still was; Nathan would agree.

Susan got up and paced a little. "I'll tell you as soon as I know he'll be safe back at the school. I promise." She held up

181

her hand in a Girl Scout–pledge position and then crossed her heart.

She seemed so serious, so eager, so young! It tore at my *kishkas* to look at her. I put out my arms and she fell into them. "All right. But if the police get into it, you'll have to tell them where he is."

"The police!"

"Well, school property is missing and someone has been murdered. I imagine someone will make a report, sooner or later."

Susan gulped. "Maybe everyone will be too upset about Miss K to notice?"

I shook my head. "Mr. MacMurray already knows. I went to the school last night. I'm the one who found Miss Kentworth. I was seen on the grounds and I had to say something. I told them I came to check on Alexander for you."

"You found Miss K dead?"

I nodded.

"Did they think you killed her?"

"They did at first. Because I have such a good motive. Miss Kentworth expelled you from school and is suing my son. And because I had to admit that I sort of broke into the administration building."

Susan gasped. "Broke in!" She clutched my hand. "Why?"

"Well, better you shouldn't know everything just now, but I needed to see Miss K's office and I thought it was necessary. Then when I found her, things just got out of control."

Susan shook her head. "Oh, *Bubbe*, it's a real mess, isn't it?" She started to cry again. Not sobbing, just big tears rolling silently down her face.

"Believe me, if I had known my granddaughter was going to pick last night to start her career as a horse thief, I never would have begun mine as a burglar." I took both her hands in mine. "Susan, I'm afraid that you were in the wrong place again. You were on the school grounds when a murder was committed."

"But *Bubbe*, I didn't do it. I didn't even know about it until you told me."

"I know that. But if anyone, God forbid, saw you at the school . . ."

"All right. I'll tell you that Geoff was with me. That's all I'll tell you. But he's my witness."

"He was with you when you were caught on the grounds illegally at the time of Mary Louise's murder. Geoff, being in love with you, doesn't make a very believable witness."

Susan shrugged. "No one saw us."

"You can be so sure?"

"I'm sure. We went out the back and through the fields."

I sighed. Air I needed. I felt as if I hadn't drawn a good breath since I'd walked into the room. "All right. Let's get the other horse thief and get some breakfast. I have a speech to give."

"A speech?" Susan got her sweater and hurried to keep up with me.

"For the closing ceremony."

"Can I watch?"

"Of course. But first you have to have a real breakfast. Energy after a night of horse thievery you could use, I'm sure." I smiled so she shouldn't think I was nagging. "You'll also need it to face your father and mother."

She frowned and shook her shoulders as if she could throw off her fear. She put her arm through mine. We collected Geoff and went to the restaurant.

I was shaking when I gave my little *spiel*, my talk, about how much the Jews of America appreciated this memorial conference. At last I got through it. I saw Susan, Nathan, and Geoff cheering me as I stepped down. Someone else had been there cheering me. Someone I hadn't expected to see here.

Janet stood at the very back of the crowd, dark glasses covering her bruised eye and her face pale even from this distance. She moved like she was much older than I knew she was—like she was my age, maybe. I looked for Kenneth. Had he done something to frighten her again?

I made up my mind we were all going to walk her back to

183

the hotel. When I returned to my seat with Nathan, I told him what I was worried about.

"We'll take care of it, Fanny."

I was anxious for the rest of the speeches to be over. Such *shpilkes*, I could hardly sit in my chair. At last there was a too-long speech from the Reverend Malbys and it was over. I jumped from my seat and hurried through the crowd.

Barely in time. I caught Janet's sleeve just as she was about to duck into a shop.

"Janet, wait."

She turned and there was a funny look on her face at first. Not anger. More like guilt. Why?

"Oh, Fanny. I have to talk to you. Not here. Let's get away from all these people."

"You just give me a minute," I said, and hurried back to tell Nathan and the kids where I was going.

"I don't think it's safe, Fanny." Nathan gave me his stern look. "Why don't you come to the Jews in Medieval York exhibit at the Minster Library, like we planned. Bring Janet."

"We'll be fine. Janet just wants to get something off her chest. You give us a little time. Keep an eye on the children. I'll meet you back at the room."

Nathan shook his head. "I'd sooner argue with a bear trap."

I let his remark roll off me and hurried back to Janet. "So, what's the matter?" She was really worrying me. "Is it Kenneth?"

She jumped like she'd been shot. "What do you mean?"

"Did he get crazy again? Chase you?"

Her face seemed to relax, but the bruising showed through her foundation. I should have offered to cover it for her. I had had practice with stage makeup. "No. It . . . it was the police. There's been some trouble."

"At home? You need a ride to the airport, maybe?"

She shook her head. "Wait till we're alone, please."

Janet walked quickly, leading me through the narrow streets. I could hardly keep up. A tennis game was more relaxing. Finally she darted down a long walkway between houses. "Where are we going, Janet? Back to Los Angeles by way of Nome, maybe?"

She smiled, a tight unpleasant pulling back of her lips. Then she walked on. "There's a place by the river. Just ahead."

I followed. We came out from the alley behind houses to a quiet, reedy bank on the river Foss. Pretty it was. Janet sat down and patted the ground next to her.

"All right," I said, bending my knees slowly so they shouldn't twinge and settling down like an old horse at her side. "Talk."

She looked uncomfortable and her hands twitched nervously in her lap. "I hardly know where to begin, Fanny."

"At the beginning is usually the best," I said, making a little joke, nodding at her.

She gave me another tight smile. Almost painful to see.

"Well. Did you hear that there'd been another murder at Taddington?"

I nodded. "Bad news travels as fast as good. Faster."

"Well, I . . . there's something I've kept from you. I'm sorry, but it seemed the right thing to do under the circumstances."

"Circumstances? I know you for a little over a week and, already, we have circumstances?" I looked at her, waiting.

"Fanny. I've inherited Taddington. I'm Janet Taddington Percy."

If I hadn't been sitting I would have fallen down. "You? How?"

"My mother's family owned Taddington. Founded the school."

"I remember you saying your sister went there—"

"Yes. That's why I don't ride. My sister was kicked in the head. She's . . . she was never right again. We had to put her in a full-care facility. I think she's why I'm a therapist." Janet wore a look of such pain it broke my heart.

I reached for her hand.

"I did tell you I had business here in England, besides the conference. My mother died about six months ago. I came over then and the school was nearly under. I put every penny I had into saving Taddington."

"The money from your joint savings account with Kenneth?" I guessed.

185

"Yes. But it was my money." She looked angry now. "Kenneth really did spend his part and more on young girls. Now I have to try to sell Taddington before I lose everything. I'll need money to fight my ex in court. He's going to try to sue me."

"Oh, you poor thing!" I said, gripping her fingers hard in mine. "But why did you keep owning the school a secret?"

"My mother had made arrangements for the school to carry on as always under Miss Kentworth. I didn't want to tell you I was the owner because . . ."

When she paused I jumped in. Who knew I'd be sorry? "Because you knew I might ask you to help my Susan!" I dropped the hand I was holding. This one didn't need anyone to hold her hand. She was one tough cookie.

"No. It's true I didn't want to be asked to undermine Miss Kentworth's authority, but I did help you. I took the letter to your son off her desk when I was there. I saw to it that it was never mailed." She handed me the envelope.

Did I ever feel like a fool. "I'm sorry, Thank you, Janet. But why did you want it to be such a secret?"

Janet sighed. "I'm here incognito. There's been other trouble at the school. I think my mother made a dreadful error in her selection of Miss Kentworth. It is suspected that she may have something to do with the high incidence of drugs at Taddington. I wanted to snoop. Undercover, so to speak. Find out if she was on the up-and-up." Her eyes pleaded with me.

"Snooping, believe me, I understand. I was asked to join Mossad only this summer," I said.

Janet stared at me. "Mossad? You're an agent?" She looked a little alarmed.

"I turned them down. I wasn't sure I wanted to go to work at my age. I like to travel, but on my own schedule." She seemed calmer. I guess she, like most people, couldn't imagine me as a spy.

"I, too, want to slow down, Fanny." It was her turn to pat my hand.

I gave her a hug, "There's no reason I can't change my mind

whenever I want. I could be an agent like that!" I snapped my fingers so she would know how fast.

"Good for you, Fanny." She laughed. "Let's forget all this gloomy stuff."

I looked into the water. Hardly moving it was, unlike my thoughts, which ran like white water over rocks. Should I maybe offer to help her figure out if Miss Kentworth had been guilty? Was her problem solved now that Miss K was dead? Could Janet have possibly thought murder was a way to settle her problem with her headmistress?

I looked at Janet for a long moment. No. I didn't think she was a murderess. I had seen a few assassins in Israel and I hoped I knew enough to tell. I nodded. "I have to get back. Susan's parents are flying in and we're all meeting at Doris's at noon."

"Oh, Fanny! I should have given you those papers sooner. I never thought Susan had anything to do with that horse being hurt. Mary Louise was a very careless girl." Janet had an unpleasant look on her face as she spoke of Mary Louise. "She couldn't follow the rules."

I raised my eyebrows. "You knew Mary Louise?"

"Only from all the reports Miss Kentworth sent me. Let's just say that that girl figured prominently in a number of them. Gwendolyn was never firm enough with her. Had some sort of phobia about offending the vicar. Came of being a country girl who rose above herself, I think." She shrugged the thoughts away like a cast-off coat. A little harsh she sounded, but she was probably still in shock.

She reached for my hand. "Fanny, it's spring break starting tomorrow. Thank heavens. Maybe the police can clear this all up before most of the students come back. Anyway, if Susan wants to return after break, I'd be happy to have her."

I was stunned. I hardly knew what to say. "I don't know, Janet. I'm grateful, but I think her parents will want to take her home."

She smiled, patted the hand she held. "I understand. I just wanted you to know I was on Susan's side. Tell her I think there was a horrible miscarriage of justice."

I stood up. "Thank you." We started back down the path. "There is one thing."

Janet stopped walking and turned to me. "What's that, Fanny?" She looked a little concerned.

"If Susan has to go back to the States and leave Alexander it will break her heart. I just wondered if . . ." I paused a moment.

Janet grinned and jumped in. "Of course we can sell you Alexander. There are lots of horses for Taddington, but only one for Susan."

Tears filled my eyes and I hugged Janet so hard I nearly sprained my elbows.

"Good. Settled, then?" She held out her hand and gave mine a firm shake. We had bargained on something important.

Then we walked back to the hotel, Janet showing me all sorts of interesting things about the side streets and "snickelways." Those were the small rabbit-warren-like alleyways between walls, fences, and buildings that were the shortcuts people took through the town.

She told me they were paths and lanes for foot traffic only. Some were "snickets," mostly unpaved and between fences; some were "ginnels," mostly paved and between buildings. "Footsteps, except soft shoes, echo in a ginnel, but not in a snicket," she said, smiling at the lore of her city.

Some of the snickelways she showed me led through arches so deep they were nearly tunnels and they came out into mansionlike courtyards. Others, Janet said, were generally unknown even by the citizens of York. Some led to the medieval wall that surrounded the town.

One of these we took, and walked the path at the top of the wall for a time before coming down again and continuing to the hotel.

I was silent. So much to think about. I still wished Janet had said something earlier. But being an almost-agent myself, I could certainly understand that she couldn't very well check into Miss Kentworth's activities if everyone knew she was the owner and here in England.

Such a lot of headaches came from being the owner of any business dealing with the public. I remembered the woman who had bothered Miss K about some sort of donation. Didn't I know what time-wasters people asking for money were? I had had enough doors slammed in my own face when I had worked for *Hadassah*. Now that I thought about it, there were plenty of reasons for Janet to keep her identity a secret.

When I didn't find Susan in our room, I went to Nathan's. There they were, all three of them, sitting around *noshing* and watching TV. A regular party they were having. It made me feel like a villain to have them all stop laughing and look grimly my way.

"Good news," I said, hoping the more cheerful mood would return. "Janet owns Taddington." You could have heard a mouse hiccup. Susan's mouth gaped open.

"What do you mean, *Bubbe?*"

"I mean that her family founded Taddington. She's really Janet Taddington Percy. Janet inherited the school from her mother and now that Miss Kentworth is dead, she'll have to run it until a new headmistress is found."

Nathan looked angry. "You mean she was in control all along and—"

I cut him short. "Yes. And she's welcomed Susan back as soon as spring break is over." I looked at my granddaughter. "She says she never sent the letter to your parents; she never believed you had anything to do with the troubles at the school."

Susan whooped and threw herself into my arms, almost knocking me to the floor. "I can see Alexander again!"

I held her away from me for a moment. "You probably could, *if* he weren't missing."

"Oh, *Bubbe*, you know I can bring him back now. Everything is fine."

Nathan glared at her. "You bring him back, you as good as admit that you stole him in the first place."

"Oh, Nathan, don't be such an old bear. Janet will understand when I explain it all. She owns Taddington." Susan gave him a lopsided grin and he melted.

Susan hurried to the phone.

"Wait," I said. "Before you do another thing, you get ready to see your parents."

Susan deflated like a balloon someone had stuck a pin into. "*Bubbe.* I knew you shouldn't have called them."

"You've forgotten a little something called murder, maybe?"

Susan was frantic. "*Bubbe!* They're going to drag me home. I'll never see Alexander again." She began to cry.

This I could do something about. I couldn't keep my good news any longer. "You go like a good girl. *Bubbe* has arranged for Alexander to go, too."

She shrieked. Such a *geschrei.* "Go, too? What do you mean?"

"I mean Janet said she would sell me Alexander. You can take him home with you. We just have to make sure the police will let you go and your mother doesn't insist you die of shame first." I smiled as I said it so that she should know I was kidding. Well, maybe not completely kidding. Judith was probably already having a conniption.

Susan returned to the phone. This time she dialed. With a breath you could have knocked me over when I heard her say: "Aunt Doris! The coast is clear."

Nathan and I listened in amazement as Susan told us of how she had smuggled Alexander to safety and phoned Aunt Doris to bring a horse box to collect him and keep him out of sight until things got straightened around.

"So, that's how you managed to get back to the hotel and into bed while Nathan and I were chasing all over the country-side looking for Geoff's home."

Susan nodded. "I'm sorry, *Bubbe,* I just couldn't take any chances with Alex's life." She put her arms around me. "I would rather go to jail than see anything happen to him."

"I hope it occurs to you, young lady, that you almost got that wish," Nathan said sternly. "Just get that animal back to the school before they have something more to arrest you for."

I nodded and picked up the keys to Nathan's rental. "Geoff, you and Nathan can have a nice lunch and we'll see you when we get back."

Susan rolled her eyes dramatically. "If I live through it, Geoff."

He hugged her and kissed her gently. A sweet kiss, I thought. Such a nice young man. I led Susan out to the car.

Seventeen

Hardly had I set the brake on the rental when Judith flew down the steps like Lady Macbeth on the way to wash her hands. Such a pleasant expression she wore, like an owl about to pounce on a snake. One of the tabloids flapped from her talons.

Susan didn't even have a chance to get out of the car on her own. Judith reached through the open passenger door and grabbed her daughter by the arm. "What is the meaning of this, Susan Rebecca Zindel?" She waved a particularly gory tabloid picture of Mary Louise in Susan's face.

"Mom! You're hurting my arm with your nails. Cool it! I haven't done anything." She pulled away from her mother and ran into Larry's arms. "Dad."

My son soothed Susan and hugged her close, pressing kisses into her hair. "I know you didn't do anything, sweetheart. We're going to get this all straightened out."

"I'm so sorry, Daddy. You know I would never hurt an animal. I don't know why they want you to pay for Joshua."

"England or not, I know the law. They've got a fight on their hands when they go against Lawrence Zindel."

"Oh, Larry, for God sakes, you know you can't practice here. And the goddamn horse isn't the question." She waved the tabloid. "This scabrous rag is accusing my daughter of a ritual murder!" Her voice rose in volume and pitch until it ended in a shriek.

I stepped in. "Judith, calm down. It doesn't name names. My blood pressure medication you're going to need soon. As if anyone really thought someone Susan's age was responsible for that"—I pointed at the tabloid—"Susan isn't even in jail."

Judith turned on me. "Jail!" she screamed. "Frances Zacharina Zindel, why the hell is it every time you and Susan get together it's a disaster. First Israel with kidnapping, murder, and spying, and now, this humiliation with the blood libel. How the hell can I face my sisterhood? What will people say?"

I was still cringing at her use of my middle name. Served me right, I guessed, for all the times I'd called her Judy. "I don't know what *people* will say, but *I* say you're making a mountain out of a molehill, as usual, *Judy*."

She glared at me.

I went on. "And Larry, the horse thing is settled already. Janet, Taddington's owner, gave me back the papers that requested you pay for Joshua. She doesn't think Susan had anything to do with it."

I must say my son looked relieved.

Doris came out of the house and hugged Susan. "So we can put Alexander back now, huh?"

"Oh, yes. Thank you, Aunt Doris. Thank you so much." The two of them walked arm-in-arm toward the barn. I knew then I was right to cash in a bond. What else was a savings for?

Doris looked over her shoulder at me. "We're going to check on Alex. Fanny, you take everyone into the house. My cook has outdone herself on lunch. I'll be right in."

Lunch, I don't have to tell you, was a nightmare. Not the food, it was delicious. A real Jewish table: gefilte fish, borscht, a kosher brisket with beans, and apple strudel for dessert. I ate until I was bursting, I can tell you.

Unfortunately, Judith and Susan couldn't enjoy. Susan was unhappy with Judith's *kvetching*, and Judith was unhappy with her broken nail. One too many times she had rattled that tabloid in my *Susa-le*'s face. That last time, her longest talon snapped like a twig.

If I had thought she'd been screaming before, I was wrong. She cried like an animal with its foot in a trap. She jumped from the table and ran around the house like a *meshuge* looking for her file.

"Too late for a file!" she cried. "Where in this Godforsaken place can I get a new acrylic?"

Doris remained calm. "It's Sunday, Judith. Monday morning I'll drive you to see my hairdresser. She has a nail girl who can fix anything."

Judith looked at Doris as if she had just signed over the crown jewels and all of Easley House. I sighed with relief. More of Judy's hysterics I didn't need.

"Come, Susan," Doris said, "we'll get my groundsman to load up Alex and we'll drive him back to the school."

"Bubbe?" Susan turned hopeful eyes on me. "Can't he stay here if you're going to buy him?"

Judith's head came up like a bird dog spotting a quail. "Mother Zindel, what are you going to do with a horse?"

Something told me she suspected, but so she shouldn't get gray hair wondering, I told her. "I'm giving it to Susan. A birthday present. Or did you forget your firstborn child just turned seventeen?"

"Forget? I could forget twenty-one hours of pure hell bringing her into this world? Of course she's seventeen, but where do you think she'll put a horse?"

I smiled. "You can make a little room out back, Judy. A nice stall and maybe a riding arena where all those roses are now." I waited for the explosion.

"Tear out my roses? Now you want me to tear out my prize-winning roses?" She swooned into a chair.

"Not all of them, Judy, dear. Just enough to make room for Alexander."

"I think that will work nicely, Mom. We have plenty of

room, Judith." Larry smiled and gave me a wink. "You'd like that, wouldn't you, honey?" He put an arm around his daughter.

"Yes, Daddy! Thank you." She ran to hug me, too. "Thank you, *Bubbe.*"

I hugged her back. "Then, if it's all right with your Aunt Doris, I'm sure I can fix things with Janet."

"Maybe I could stay here with him?"

Doris smiled. "Of course you can stay."

I patted Susan's arm. "Aren't you forgetting someone?"

Susan looked at me, puzzled.

"Geoff?" I whispered, "he's waiting with Nathan to see if you live through this."

Susan looked shocked at her mistake. She had forgotten. And such a nice young man. A shame. "Okay, *Bubbe,* you're right. I guess I have to go back and stay with you until Geoff's visit is over."

I nodded.

"Thanks, anyway, Aunt Doris."

Doris smiled at Susan. "You know we'll take the best care of your horse, little one."

"I know." She flew into her aunt's arms and hugged her. "Let's go, *Bubbe.*" She glanced at her mother. "I can't keep Geoff waiting, Mom."

Larry looked over at me. "Mom, you make sure I can reach you at all times. I'm going to look into this blood libel thing with Robbie Patterson, Doris's barrister friend."

I nodded.

"And I want to meet this Geoff while I'm here." He looked sternly at his daughter.

I told Susan that we'd have to stop at Taddington on the way back to the hotel. I needed to thank Mr. MacMurray and tell him everything was all right about the horse.

He wasn't hard to find. He was in his quarters, packing for the spring break. He would be going home to take care of his mother.

I could see the relief on his face when he knew he would not have to file a report with the police. I thanked him and gave him one of the little gifts I had bought each of Susan's teachers. Mr. MacMurray's gift, of course, was the most personal because I knew him best. Some wonderful aromatic tobacco, just like my Morris used to smoke.

"Thank you so much, Mrs. Zindel," he said, tucking it into a corner of his travel bag. "I know Mum will enjoy my smoking this around her. She loves this smell of pipe smoke. I think it reminds her of Dad."

I smiled. "Susan will probably be going home to the States with her parents, but I wanted to thank you for your time with her."

His grin parted his beard. "It's been m' pleasure, really."

When we arrived at the hotel, Nathan and Geoff were waiting anxiously.

"So, what happened?" Geoff asked, hurrying to help Susan from the car.

"My mother had a cow. Then *Bubbe* told them not to worry about Joshua because Janet had dropped it. Then the best part. *Bubbe* told Mom she was buying me Alexander for my birthday." She began to laugh and her green eyes sparkled at Geoff. "Then Dad told Mom she could rip out her roses to make room for him!"

Nathan gave me a look and put his arm around my shoulders. "I see your hand in that, Fanny," he whispered. "I hope you're not pushing Judith too far."

Susan and Geoff went off to the Railroad Museum. I knew she wanted some privacy while she told Geoff that she'd be leaving soon.

Nathan walked me back to my room and we had coffee sent up. We needed to talk.

"So, Susan's returning then. Good."

"Oh, I don't know, Nathan. Now that Janet's in charge—"

"Fanny, there's been two murders. One of them a girl Susan's age. The police don't even have a suspect unless you count yourself and your granddaughter."

"We know that's nonsense." I stood up and began pacing.

196

"Exactly my point." He leaned forward.

"What point?" I asked, as he poured the cream.

"You know you didn't do it. You know Susan didn't do it. Whoever did it is still running around loose."

It hit me so hard, what he was saying, that my knees buckled and dropped me on the corner of my bed. "*Gottenyu!*" I said. "I must be stupid."

Nathan put a hand on my shoulder. "Not stupid. Just distracted. You and Susan both cared more about saving Alexander's life than about the murders."

Now I felt ashamed. "How could I forget what some crazy did to that poor girl? Or to Miss Kentworth?" A tear slipped down my cheek and Nathan caught it on his fingertip.

"That's what I love about you, Fanny."

"What? That I forget such a thing as murder?"

He shook his head. "Just that you focus much harder on life and making it better, saving it."

"Oh." I smiled at him. "Still, we don't know who killed them or even why." I felt uneasy again.

"Well, I think I know about Mary Louise. The why."

"So? You're going to let me die of curiosity like the cat, maybe?"

He gave me a look. "Fanny, the cat didn't die of not knowing, the cat . . . oh, never mind. I think Mary Louise was cheating someone. You were sure that Mary Louise was 'holding back a packet' on someone. We know Mary Louise sold drugs to young men. We even know she used sex to get them hooked. Harry Parker probably wasn't the only one."

"Probably not," I said, sighing at the thought of such things among young girls.

"Remember you told me the stableboy bragged about the quality of his drugs?"

I nodded. "We know the pills he was selling were full strength, just like he told me." What was Nathan getting at?

"Well, suppose that it wasn't just his pills?"

"*Nu?*"

"Fanny, what if somehow he was also getting a better quality of heroin?"

197

"They have a choice? Like meat in a supermarket? U.S.-D.A. Choice or Prime maybe?" I was shocked.

Nathan chuckled and patted my shoulder. "Well, sort of, but U.S. inspectors don't come into it."

"I should hope not!"

Nathan ignored my comment and went on explaining. "The drugs like heroin and coke are almost always severely cut by the time someone like Jocko gets them."

"Cut?"

"Diluted, Fanny. They put in all sorts of things—anything whitish—milk solids, sugar, talcum powder. Coke mixed with baking soda and dried is what crack really is."

"So, how could Jock say his drugs were any better?"

"That's just it, Fanny. What if he *did* get ahold of a shipment that wasn't very heavily cut? And what if Mary Louise or her source got some?"

I put my hands to my head which was beginning to ache.

"Then Mary Louise could do some cutting of her own and make herself twice as much money on the same amount of merchandise."

Light flooded into my brain. "Nathan! You mean like these fast-food joints that put lots of oatmeal and stuff in their ground meat?"

He nodded. "Exactly. And if Mary Louise's source found out she was cutting quality and keeping all the profits . . ."

"Bingo!" I said. "I wanted to kill a couple of fast-food places myself for what junk they put into my grandchildren!"

"Then think how angry you'd get if they also stole from your pocket at the same time."

"They do, Nathan. They do," I said, thinking of the exorbitant prices such places charged for junk.

He hugged me. "I love you for your ethics, Fanny."

"Ethics-shmethics, we got a murder to solve. Mary Louise's friend told me that Mary Louise had 'held out a packet' from Miss K. Now Janet just told me that she suspected Miss K of having something to do with the drugs at Taddington. Maybe Miss K killed Mary Louise!"

"Fanny, take it easy. It's possible. But Janet had no proof

against Miss Kentworth. And if Mary Louise did hold money back from Miss K, it could have been from the prostitution ring we know Mary Louise ran, possibly with Miss Kentworth's sanction."

"Oh. Well, either way, Miss Kentworth probably murdered her. Who cares whether the money was from the prostitution or the drugs?"

He took a sip of his coffee. "We have no proof that Miss Kentworth was involved in either of Mary Louise's activities, Fanny."

I sighed. "Yes, it's possible that it was only because Miss Kentworth had a crush on the vicar that she let Mary Louise get away with murder." I stopped when I heard my sad choice of words. "I mean let her have special privileges around school," I corrected hastily.

Nathan patted my shoulder. "I know what you meant. But if it's any consolation, I would have voted Mary Louise most likely to have murdered Miss Kentworth. A shame she predeceased her."

I shook my head. "A shame Mary Louise died at all, but she probably wasn't strong enough to snap a neck anyway." I drummed my fingers on the nightstand. "We *have* to find out if it was Miss Kentworth who Mary Louise worked for."

"You're getting all upset over this, Fanny. Forget it for a while. We need more information." He took me in his arms and held me close as he lay back against the bedspread.

Suddenly this was going again where I had no wish for it to go. I pulled free and sat up. Nathan pulled me back, but I resisted. "No, Nathan, please. I thought a lot about this. I can't. Cut out to be anybody's mistress, I'm not."

There. I had said it. Nathan looked stricken. "Fanny, that's not how I see you." He took both my hands in his. "I don't want you to feel uncomfortable, but marriage at our age, and with me living thousands of miles away, is a bit unsatisfactory, don't you think?"

"For over thirty years I didn't think marriage was ever 'unsatisfactory,' " I said, stiffening and pulling my hands from his.

"Fanny, we're both adults. Two mature, consenting adults, who love and respect each other."

"It won't work, Nathan. I'm not comfortable with an affair. All my life that has been something *other* women did—other not very nice or respectable women."

Nathan looked away. "You think I don't respect you if we give each other a little pleasure in our lives? You're wrong. I love you, Fanny."

"I know. And I feel the same. But what we don't feel the same about is having an affair."

"Fanny, I can't offer you anything more just now. My life is in Israel. Yours is in the States."

I looked at him. My heart felt like it was breaking in a dozen pieces. I knew this might change something between us forever. "Then I guess we'll just have to wait until one of us can fix that. You're not really an agent anymore, Nathan."

Nathan went to the minibar and poured himself a drink. He gulped it before answering me. "I'm not ready to give up Mossad completely. I still have my uses. I still matter. I still get a paycheck. That's important to a man, Fanny."

I nodded. "Maybe when you retire, Nathan."

"Fanny, I won't tolerate pressure like this. You're trying to make me choose between you and something that's been everything to me." He stood up. "I'll see you at dinner."

Just like that, he left. No hug. No kiss.

My room felt dark and cold. I flung myself facedown on the bed. It had been so long since I had had a good cry. The only thing I resented was crying over a man who was so completely typical. Morris and I had had a good sex life. I was no prude. Such fun we used to have together. I had enjoyed being made love to and giving my husband pleasure.

Naturally, when Morris and I got older, things slowed down a little; it was expected—what with his heart trouble and my change of life. Still, we cuddled a lot and had other things between us, a family, a life, years of love. That was what was important. Nathan and I had none of that, yet.

I stopped crying and asked myself a hard question. How would I feel if this meant the end of my relationship with

Nathan? I sniffed and blotted my cheeks with a tissue. That would hurt.

One thing I now knew for sure: I didn't really know Nathan well enough to *want* to marry him. Not that he had asked. And maybe he would never ask. That hurt, too.

I tossed my soggy tissues into the wastebasket, put on a fresh coat of lipstick, and set about straightening my things. I would have to speak to the desk about extending my stay. Now that Larry and Judith were here, I knew I didn't want to stay at Doris's.

Down in the lobby, I waited for the clerk to check whether I could stay in my room when I heard a high-pitched voice behind me asking for Miss Percy's suite. The voice seemed familiar somehow.

I turned and recognized the same woman who had fled Miss K's office the day Nathan and I confronted the headmistress about Susan's trouble.

"Maybe I can help you," I said. "I'm her roommate."

"Are you indeed?" The thin face peered at me, the nose sharp and straight, the brown eyes suspicious behind the wire-rimmed glasses.

"Yes. Who should I say called?"

"She's not in?"

I shook my head. "If it's urgent, you might try Taddington School. She's taken over as headmistress."

"Not for long, I should think. You may tell her that Miss Johnson's solicitors are questioning the lack of livestock at her supposed agricultural school. Now it will be her turn to abide by a court decision." She handed me a business card with a her name and small animal tracks across the front— Four Pause Rescue Center.

"Oh," I said, looking at the card, "You're the one my cousin, Doris Bond, brought the rescued kitten to."

"Lady Doris Bond?"

I nodded. "Yes. The other day on the way up to see her, I found a kitten half-starved and frozen along the road. She highly recommended your organization."

Miss Johnson's sharp features seemed to soften and she

smiled at me. "Your cousin is a remarkable woman. She and Janet's mother, Wilma, did a lot of fund-raising for us." She sighed deeply. "Such a loss, Wilma's death. I know your cousin did not take her passing easily."

So that was whom Doris had known. "Let me treat you to a cup of tea and you can tell me how the kitten is doing," I offered, anxious to know more about the connection between Four Pause and the school.

We moved from the desk to the hotel restaurant, and as soon as we were seated and had given our order, Miss Johnson, who insisted I call her Emily, eagerly told me stories of the kitten that Doris's gardener had brought her. Miss Hypercat had, it seemed, needed some special nursing. Miss Johnson had taken her home with her and fallen in love. The kitten had pretty much taken over Miss Johnson's entire home. Typical.

Gradually, I led the conversation back to Janet and the troubles with the school. I was stunned to hear the terms of the will: if Taddington ever failed to uphold its agricultural program, the property would revert to Four Pause. It seemed Wilma's rescue work would go on long after her death.

As Emily told me all this, her brown eyes seemed to stare at some private vision that only she could see.

"It will be so nice to have the extra acreage for my orphans," she said, a sweet smile on her thin face.

"Well, I know they'll replace the horse as soon as the insurance pays off on Joshua's death," I said, trying to soften the blow for Emily. It was obvious that she was cooking her chickens into a nourishing soup even before they were out from under the hen! It was no time to tell her Janet was selling Alexander.

"And the school is such a help to youngsters like my Susan who want to work with animals as a profession. There aren't many places to train for vet school in the States. Or here, for that matter." Maybe she would feel more kindly toward Taddington if she knew what it meant to other animal lovers. After all, since Janet seemed determined to keep the school running, Miss Johnson's dreams of expansion would have to find some other route besides through Taddington's acres.

"Mrs. Zindel, that school has been faltering for years. It should have come to me when Wilma died. I don't know how Janet and her Miss Kentworth managed to keep solvent, but now, what with the scandal and the good families leaving, Taddington will have to revert to its rightful heirs—the homeless animals we all love!" With that, she thanked me for the tea, stood, and—still staring into space—strode out.

I felt so anxious I could hardly wait to pay my check and talk to the police. Emily Johnson certainly seemed to be more than a little fanatical. If she saw Janet and Miss Kentworth as obstacles between Taddington's rightful animal heirs and their inheritance, what might she do?

At the very least, Miss Johnson would have to be considered as much of a suspect as Susan and Geoff. Maybe, like me, she didn't have the strength to break Miss K's neck herself, but who knew whom she had working for her at her kennels?

I headed for the police station, unaware that seeing me was next on their list, too.

Eighteen

OFFICER Gallagher let me go through my whole story before telling me that they had already brought some- one in for Miss K's murder.

"Who?"

"Funny you should ask, Mrs. Zindel. He claims you're his only alibi."

"Me? An alibi?"

Gallagher looked over his shoulder at his assistant. "Bring him out."

I waited, my thumb deepening the depression on the Irish marble worry stone in my everything bag. Smooth it felt, and cool, which was more than I could say about myself.

Then the guard brought in the prisoner. Not a real surprise, but *my* worst fears. I felt my knees lowering me to the chair without an order from my brain. I wondered if Jock had already told them things I preferred they didn't know.

" 'ow's your arthritis, Mrs. Zindel?"

Hot I felt. My neck, my cheeks, to the roots of my hair. "Hello, Jock," I said.

"You know this lad, then?" the policeman asked.

I nodded. "He's the stableboy from Taddington."

Gallagher gave me a look and flipped open his notebook. "I thought you said you went to see Miss Kentworth because you couldn't raise the stableboy."

"That's right," I said. "I could hear him snoring right through the door."

"I wasn't asleep until after I had a nip or two with you first." He rubbed the back of his neck with a work-rough hand and raked his hair with his fingers. "What the hell you put in those drinks?"

I smiled at the officer. "It was just a friendly little glass of scotch to keep out the chill. I wanted to repay him . . . for . . . being so good to Susan, my granddaughter," I added, lamely. "And as he said, keep my arthritis from hurting me." I leaned forward and rubbed my knees. "A swallow now and then does help these old bones." I tried my frail look on Officer Gallagher. He ignored me.

Jock glowered. "The day a lady drinks Jocko under the table—without some help—is the day the whole bloody world will end!" he shouted, waving an arm at me.

The assistant pulled him back.

"So you admit you were in the barn twice, not once."

I glanced at Jock's frightened face, and nodded slowly. I knew I was making a bargain with the devil himself, but I had to count on the fact that Jock wouldn't be any more anxious to tell the police about our little drug trade than I was.

"And that was before you went lookin' for Miss Kentworth?"

"Yes."

Gallagher flipped the pages of his notebook back and forth and glanced at me and then at the stableboy. He turned to his assistant and sighed. "Let him go."

The stableboy gave me a grin. "Thanks, Mrs. Z. See y' around."

As soon as he was out the door, Gallagher turned his attention to me. "Mrs. Zindel, I seem to have a real problem with your statement. When exactly did you arrive at Taddington on Saturday night?"

"I'm not really sure. It was too dark to see my watch."

"What was the first thing you did? The *truth* now," he warned.

I swallowed and took a breath. "I went to the barn to see the horse. Before I could get to the stall, I met Jock. We talked and I offered to pay him to take extra special care of Alexander. We did have a drink on the bargain. My arthritis and the cold, as I explained." I looked at Officer Gallagher, but he didn't comment. I hurried on. "I was starting to leave when I met Mr. MacMurray. In telling him the purpose of my visit, I realized that I had failed to see the horse with my own eyes."

"That's when you went back to the barn?"

"I did."

"And how was it that Jocko was already dead drunk asleep?" He consulted his notebook again.

"I'm sure I don't know. Perhaps he'd been drinking before I arrived and what I offered him tipped him over the edge. Anyway, when I saw that Alexander really looked under the weather, I wanted to tell someone. That's when I went looking for Miss Kentworth." I sat upright, pleased with myself. That had worked out very nicely.

"So, you went to the barn three times?"

"Three?"

"Well, at some point you had to get that bucket. Or did you assume when you went looking for the headmistress that she might have need of a midnight snack of oats, perhaps? I mean, with her working so late and all." Officer Gallagher smiled wickedly at me.

I reddened. "Well, I didn't have to go all the way to the barn a third time. Someone . . . uh . . . must have left the bucket lying out."

"Real handy for you, eh?"

"Well, it was there, so I used it." I shrugged.

He flipped a page in his notebook. "And you felt you should break into the building, even though y' knew Mr. MacMurray was on the grounds because y' couldn't raise anyone knocking?"

I nodded. "I had about as much hope of finding Mr. Mac-

Murray again in the dark as you would finding Jock on a sober day," I finished, angry at his sly sarcasm.

"So, you were in the barn, according to Jock; Jock was in the barn, according to you; Mr. MacMurray, according to you, was out on the grounds. I guess your alibis for everyone have run me fresh out of suspects." He slapped the cover of his notebook shut and tossed it on his desk. He gave me a look that told me he didn't believe a word.

"Not quite," I said. "There's Miss Johnson."

"Who?" Gallagher looked pained.

"The owner of Four Pause. It's an animal-rescue organization. Miss Johnson is supposed to inherit Taddington. She admitted to me this afternoon that Miss Kentworth was the only one keeping the school within the terms of the will."

"What will?" He retrieved his notebook and began scribbling.

I looked at him. "Why the will left by Wilma Taddington that gives the school to Miss Johnson, *if* the agricultural program is discontinued or, if the school goes broke."

"So this Miss Johnson was there that night?"

"No. Of course not. At least, I didn't see her. I just think she has a good motive."

Gallagher slapped his forehead with his palm and collapsed into his desk chair. "Wait a minute. You're telling me that some animal-rescue lady stands to inherit all the Taddington acreage?"

I nodded. "I'm also telling you that she saw Miss Kentworth and Janet as obstacles to that inheritance."

"If this Miss Kentworth owned Taddington, who is Janet?"

"No. No." I shook my head. "Gwendolyn Kentworth was just running it for the new owner, Janet Taddington Percy. She was doing too good a job."

"You're losing me, Mrs. Zindel."

I sighed. "It's very simple, Officer. Janet Percy inherited her mother's school about six months ago. Miss Kentworth, the headmistress, had found a way to keep the school running at a profit. That means Miss Kentworth actually kept Miss Johnson from inheriting."

207

"This Miss Johnson, she big enough to snap that lady's neck?"

"Well, I don't think so. She's a thin little thing," I admitted. "But she could have had help. Hired someone."

Gallagher laughed. "You a big mystery fan, Mrs. Zindel? Maybe see a lot of flicks? Watch a lot of telly?"

I glared at him and gave him my best Columbo squint. "You thought my granddaughter might have had help from her boyfriend. How is this any different?"

He looked at me with new respect, I thought. "You give me the information. I'll look into it."

I had done all I could. I left the station and hurried back to the hotel, hoping to catch Susan and Geoff so we could all have dinner together. After our little tiff, I didn't feel like facing Nathan alone.

I was crossing over Lendal Bridge when I felt someone grab my arm. "What?"

I saw the grinning face of Jock. He held me tighter and walked with me down the steep stairs and toward the water's edge. "I'll scream if you don't let me go," I said, tugging experimentally at my arm. He tightened his fingers.

"And I'll tell the coppers you're a junkie, Mrs. Zindel. You just pay me what you owe me for the rest of those pills and we'll forget this ever happened."

"What are you talking about?" I fingered the extralong hatpin, wondering if I would need to use it.

"That full bottle you took from me nightstand once you slipped me that Mickey in my drink, that's what I'm talkin' about."

He gave me a shake that rattled my teeth in my head. "All right. How much?"

"Four pounds each. I figure there was about twenty pills in that bottle."

"Four! I only paid you—"

"That was before you caused me all that trouble with the coppers."

"I gave you an alibi for murder. You should thank me."

He shrugged. "Maybe you're right. But four each is the last

offer. *And* you keep your mouth shut from here on out." He dug his fingers into my upper arm and I couldn't help the squeak that I gave from the pain.

"All right." I counted eighty pounds in traveler's checks into his dirty hand.

"You think I'm stupid? I can't cash those. Come on," he said, and marched me up the steps and back toward town.

Outside a curio shop, he pulled me to a stop. "You're goin' in to buy something small. You get them to cash those things for y'. Or else. I'll be waiting right here."

I nodded. Into the shop. Trouble. I couldn't talk the clerk into cashing eighty dollars' worth for one small purchase.

It took some doing to talk the clerk into letting me spend twenty and cash two fifties. Thank heavens I had still needed a parting gift for the gamesmistress, Ms. Westenbury, and for Mr. Craig, the Latin teacher.

At last, I was back out on the street with my packages and my cash. Jock hastily took the money. "See y' around, Mrs. Z."

I certainly hoped not.

Shaking with relief, I hurried back across Lendal Bridge and practically ran for my hotel.

As the elevator doors opened, I almost bumped into Mr. You-Know-Who.

"Fanny!" he said, "I've been looking everywhere for you. Are you all right?"

"Me? I'm fine. What should be wrong?"

He put a hand on my shoulder. "You look a little pale. I'm really sorry about our misunderstanding. You know your friendship means a lot to me."

I smiled at him and patted his cheek with my hand. "And yours to me, Nathan. I'm glad you don't hold it against me."

Nathan was about to say something more but a greeting from Susan and Geoff coming into the lobby from their museum trip made him fall silent. I hoped there wasn't something else on his mind.

"*Bubbe!* Nathan! We're starved. Can we go to dinner a little early?"

I glanced at Nathan, but the moment had passed. "Of course," he said. "I'll treat. The hotel or a restaurant in town?"

"You decide. I'll run up and see if Janet wants to join us."

"Don't bother, Fanny. I stopped by your room on my way down. She's not in." Nathan offered me his arm and I took it. Susan and Geoff led the way into the hotel restaurant.

"I'm too hungry to make it much farther, *Bubbe*," Susan said, grinning at Geoff and pretending to faint into his arms from hunger.

Dinner and a walk after took up most of the evening. Susan and Geoff decided to stop off at the concert hall, so Nathan walked me back to the hotel.

It took all my courage to tell him about my last brush with the police. When I finished telling about Jock, and his demand for money, Nathan was furious.

"I asked you if anything was wrong, Fanny. You lied to me."

"Well, it was over, Nathan. There was nothing to be done."

"You still should have told me right away."

"In front of the children?"

He sighed. "Always an excuse, Fanny. Okay. You go up to the room and stay there. I'm going to go check with my contact. Maybe this new information will give him a lead."

I'd had too much excitement for one day to argue with him. The room and a hot bath sounded fine to me.

Nathan kissed me on the cheek and waved as he walked back out of the hotel.

Janet was standing over an open suitcase when I entered our room. "You're leaving?" I asked, surprised and a little hurt.

She held an envelope out to me. "I'd written you a note. I'm just glad I don't have to leave it for you." She came over and gave me a hug. "Good news, Fanny, the police have finished with Miss K's rooms and I can move out to the school. Thank heavens, I'll have spring break to get ahead on the paperwork."

"They solved the murder?" I asked.

Janet smiled. "Not exactly. But they have their motive. I

was right about her. The police now know her murder had nothing to do with the school itself."

"So? What did it have to do with?"

"I was right about Miss Kentworth and drugs. They found some in her office." Janet looked almost pleased. "They were hidden in a chair cushion. Can you believe it?"

I sank down onto the bed, my mouth opening like the mouth of a carp out of water.

Janet didn't even see my reaction. On she went, while I thought only about how my actions had ruined a dead woman's reputation. Worse than *Lashon Hara*, that was.

"Apparently, she had quite a lucrative little sideline for herself. I think Mary Louise was helping her and then they had a falling out."

"Falling out?"

"Well, the police have just about proved that Mary Louise and some of her little friends were luring in drug customers with their more obvious charms."

I tried to look surprised and a little shocked.

"Oh, don't worry, Fanny. The police promised me the reputation of the school will be protected at all costs. After all, why should the actions of a few cheap little sluts sully the name of Taddington and its more socially prominent students?"

I didn't have an answer for her, so it was lucky she didn't expect one. I sat like a stone as she rambled on, folding things into her suitcase and talking about the plans she had for her mother's school.

"You're not going to return to your practice back home?" I finally managed to ask.

"Oh, yes. Eventually. But I've taken a leave of absence until we can find someone really suitable to replace Miss Kentworth. Someone prestigious." She paced around the room with a thoughtful look on her face. "It's my own fault. I knew a year ago my mother was getting too old to make sound decisions. The Taddington girls' families will simply have to understand that now that I'm in charge, mistakes like mother's Miss Kentworth will never happen again." She

211

punctuated her sentence by slamming the lid of her suitcase, clicking the latches shut, and brushing off her hands as if she'd just finished a particularly unpleasant task.

Somehow this didn't seem like the Janet I knew. After all, her mother must have done a quality job to have taken the school this far. It hurt me to see Janet being so harsh.

"Yes," I said. "I'm sure you'll straighten it all out."

Janet hugged me, repeated her offer of keeping Susan in school, picked up her suitcase, and left.

I had other worries. My own foolishness certainly rivaled or bettered that of Janet's mother. What if the drugs I had hidden in Miss K's office were Jock's? Sure, I had found the cigarette butts, but circumstantial proof only, they were. Who would have thought that the police would have found the drugs so quickly? I had hoped to get back there for them before that happened.

Could it be that my actions had not only blackened the reputation of a woman who could no longer defend herself, but might also have misled the police in their efforts to find her murderer?

Nineteen

ATHAN, I'm in terrible trouble," I said almost before he could get his door open.

"Fanny, what's the matter? You look awful." He led me inside and sat me down on the bed. "You want a drink?"

"Just some water." I settled back against the pillows and the headboard. Good to have someone care for me.

"You're going to need something stronger than water. You look like you just saw every ghost in York." He poured a nice gin and tonic from the minibar, with a twist of lime, just like I like, and handed it to me. "Drink," he said.

So I drank. A long swallow. It seemed to help.

"Now, what's this trouble you're in?"

I took a deep breath. "You know I hid those drugs in the cushion in Miss K's office?" He nodded and I went on. "Well, the police found them."

"Did you think they wouldn't?"

Guilt rushed through me. "I had hoped to get them back before that happened. But that's not the real problem, Nathan. They think that's why Miss K was killed." I set my drink on the nightstand and wrung my hands. Lady Macbeth and I suddenly had a lot in common.

"Fanny, you know it's more than likely that she *was* in‑volved—"

"But, Nathan, what if that leads them the wrong way after a killer?"

"Fanny, if she was involved in the drugs, that will be a good start for them. You know she gave Mary Louise a pretty free rein and—"

"*Feh!* That's what the police think. That's what Janet thinks. But if it was just something a lonely spinster does because she had a crush—"

"Fanny." He held up his fingers one at a time to count off what we did know. "You went to Miss Kentworth's office because you found those cigarette butts in the stall near the drugs.

"My contact said that Taddington had been in borderline bankruptcy for years.

"The first time it's been solvent has been the six months since Janet inherited. And we know drugs were uncommonly heavy around Taddington and Gresham." He was holding up three fingers by now. I knew more were to come.

"And you talked to that boy from Gresham who said Mary Louise had lured him into drug use," I added.

He nodded. "And you discovered Mary Louise had held back either money or an actual packet of drugs from Miss Kentworth. To say nothing of the fact that they were close enough for the headmistress to help her obtain an abortion."

That was six already. Either Nathan didn't want to hold up another hand, or he'd given up that method of keeping track.

"Wait, Nathan. Janet told me she used her money to help the school when she first inherited. Maybe Miss K wasn't involved with anything illegal. Is it possible?"

He shrugged. "Anything is possible. But I thought you mentioned that Janet was keeping quiet about her position because she suspected Miss Kentworth of funny business.

"Look, Fanny, if it's good enough for the police, to guess that Miss Kentworth and Mary Louise fought over a drug business, then who are we to say different?"

"But then if Miss K killed Mary Louise, who killed Miss K?"

214

"Fanny, that's police business."

Nathan had a point. A good one. Maybe even great. But something still nagged at me. Two somethings. But one of them I couldn't quite bring into my mind.

"I still can't imagine that Miss Kentworth would kill Mary Louise and then do those horrible things to the body."

"That isn't the typical MO for murder, unless it's the first of an anti-Semitic series."

I nodded.

"Anyway, the mutilation is not a typical woman's MO. You're right about that," Nathan agreed, refilling my glass.

I didn't remember finishing my drink. "Something else bothers me, but it's right on the tip of—"

"The only answer is that someone else must have mutilated the body," Nathan said, shocking my thought deeper, where I couldn't get at it.

"Two murderers?"

"Well, one murderer, one defiler."

I shuddered. The thought of someone running around loose who could do that to the body of a beautiful young girl was even more frightening than the idea of a loose murderer. "But Nathan, that still doesn't tell me what I should do about the drugs I hid in that office. Even if she was involved, it could still mislead the police about her killer, couldn't it?"

Nathan shrugged. "I don't know what to tell you, Fanny. From what you told me about your last encounter, Officer Gallagher didn't seem too forgiving of you changing your story on him. But I do think you're going to have to tell him and turn in those cigarette butts as evidence."

I sighed and sipped. "I guess you're right." I sipped again and set the glass on the table. "I'll have to face Gallagher's anger again. At least he didn't arrest me for it, last time." The detail that had been bothering me nudged. I twirled my glass on the table, spreading the wet ring against the surface.

I jumped up. It came to me. Something Miss Johnson had said. I had to find Susan. "Wait a minute, Nathan."

Quick as food disappearing at the *Kiddush* after the Sabbath service, I hurried back to my room. Susan and Geoff were just coming in.

"*Susa-le*, I have to ask you something." I stopped her in the doorway.

"Sure, *Bubbe*. Anything." She smiled and hugged Geoff's arm.

"How long was Miss Kentworth at Taddington?"

Susan got that little crinkle in her brow between her eyes as she thought. Just like her Aunt Deborah when she had a serious case to doctor. "It hasn't been that long, *Bubbe*."

"Try to remember, *Susa-le*. It's important."

She looked at Geoff. "How long have we been going together?"

He gave her a pouty, hurt look. "You mean you don't know by heart? I'm crushed."

She slapped his shoulder, playfully. "Come on. Tell me."

"Five months and two days."

"No hours and minutes?" Susan asked, faking a pouty, hurt look of her own back at him. "*I'm* crushed." She looked at me as Geoff gathered her in a bear hug. "Miss K was made headmistress a few weeks before I started going with Geoff."

"You're sure, Susan?"

She nodded. "Yes, because the old headmistress wasn't so strict about the boys coming on campus. They couldn't come in the rooms, but the grounds were all right. That's how I got in trouble with Miss K. Her rules hadn't been in effect that long when Geoff and I got caught kissing at the gate."

"Thank you, *Susa-le*," I said, and turned to go back to Nathan's room.

"Wait, *Bubbe*. Why did you want to know?"

"Tell you when I work it all out. Go. Watch a little television, cuddle, enjoy."

I burst through Nathan's door. "Now I have more trouble."

"More already? You've only been gone two minutes."

"Why would Janet lie to me?"

He lifted his hands into the air, palms to the ceiling. "I give up. Did she?"

"Yes! No reason. That's why. She makes a big deal out of telling me that Miss Kentworth was hired by her mother, who

216

was practically senile. I find out from Susan that Miss Kentworth only came to Taddington about six months ago—right when *Janet* took over. And Miss Johnson mentioned 'Janet's Miss Kentworth,' just like that. In those words."

Nathan looked thoughtful for a moment. "Well, would you want to be linked with a drug-running headmistress?"

"But to blame it on her mother? A dead woman? Why? And who am I that she should make up a lie for?"

He rubbed his brow with his fingers as if trying to smooth away the worry lines. "Well, you are a friend; I think she was just embarrassed, Fanny."

"Maybe. But maybe not." I began to pace.

"Forget it for now. Come, have a late dessert with me."

I agreed. "Maybe a little something will act as brain food."

Nathan laughed, got his coat, and took my arm.

There weren't many restaurants open on Sunday night, but finally we found a pub on one of the side streets that was still serving. I had tapioca pudding. Nathan had coffee and shortbread cookies, which he shared with me. I couldn't think of a nicer evening. I was glad we had patched up our quarrel.

When I woke the next morning, I was still troubled by the situation with Miss Kentworth and Janet. I knew I was still troubled because I hadn't slept well. Susan was already up and out, so when I finally dropped off, I must have slept harder than usual.

My hair, which I usually braided before bed, was *farplonteren*, as if I hadn't even bothered to brush it the night before. Such a tangled mess. It took me the better part of an hour to get them all out and put my hair back in its tidy bun.

Maybe it was good it took me so long because I always think clearly when I'm brushing my hair, blood to the scalp and, God willing, the brain. Unfortunately, I didn't like what I was thinking. What if Janet hadn't had enough money for the school from her divorce? She'd admitted needing money now to fight Kenneth in court. What if she and Miss Kentworth had both decided drug money was a necessary extra? It would certainly help Janet hang on to Taddington's valuable acres.

My stomach felt tight to think of Janet involved. Janet was a friend. Such things you didn't like to think about friends. Still, that was the only way I could make any sense out why she might lie to me.

I had to have Nathan check on that will. If Janet was allowed to sell the property, it might be worth it to her to do anything to keep it going. I didn't think she would ever make a fortune just running it as a school. Maybe I was wrong. I'd have to have check that out, too. Were schools over here a profitable business? I knew Susan's fees were high. We knew there had been donations, at least, of one valuable horse. Had there been others?

I grabbed my bag and hurried to Nathan's room. I knocked till my knuckles were sore, but that didn't make him answer. He wasn't there. I would have to wait.

Disappointed, I returned to the room. The phone was ringing off its hook. Such an angry sound the ring over here had. As I picked it up, and heard the voice at the other end, I realized the word *angry* fit.

"You want to do *what*, Officer Gallagher?" Could he have read my mind? I knew I had to go to him this morning about the drugs in Miss K's office.

No. He repeated his demand and I felt as if my tongue were stuck to the roof of my mouth. I didn't want to answer him but I knew I had to. "All right, Officer, we'll be right down."

I hoped all three of them would be at breakfast. If not, I hoped Nathan would know where the children were.

"Excuse me," I said, as I almost ran down an elderly man leaving the restaurant. I wedged myself into the room and looked frantically along the row of tables. Not so crowded, now that many of the conference members were on their way back to wherever they came from.

At last, I spotted Susan and Geoff holding hands at a private corner table. Their heads were together and they didn't look as if they would welcome me, but I had no choice.

"Susan," I said, plunking my everything bag down by an empty chair and smiling at Geoff, who jumped to his feet to help me. "Thank you, I'm sure." I gave him a smile.

My granddaughter I couldn't fool. "What's wrong, *Bubbe?*" Her green eyes looked frightened.

"I heard from Officer Gallagher," I paused and gave her a look so that she could prepare herself. "He wants to see all three of us at the station house."

"More questions?" The words came out soft and panicky. I knew she was thinking about her adventure with Alexander the night Miss K was murdered.

"Don't worry, Susan. I'll be right with you. He needs to ask us some questions. And he wants to take our fingerprints."

"About what?"

I lowered my eyes. "Someone told the police they saw you on the grounds the night Miss K was murdered. They said they saw you near the administration building."

"*Bubbe!* You know that can't be. I was only at the barn. You know. You were there. You would have seen me if anyone did."

"If we were there at the same time, maybe?"

Susan looked into her lap.

"All you'll find there is your napkin, Susan. Tell me, did you go anywhere near that building?"

She lifted her chin, gave me a hard stare, and said: "No. I went to the barn through the fields and I left the same way."

"All right, Susan. We know you took Alexander after the police were on the grounds because Officer Clive had seen him when he checked to see if I was telling the truth about him. Were you on the grounds very long before you took him?"

She shook her head. "Who would wait around when committing a theft? We came across the fields to the barn, grabbed Alex, and rode back out the way we'd come. I didn't even stop for his saddle."

I sighed. "Thank heavens you weren't any earlier. Not only wouldn't you have had an alibi, I wouldn't have one either."

"I was with her, Mrs. Zindel. I can vouch for her." Geoff said, eagerly.

"It will all have to come out, now." I looked at Geoff. "You being there isn't such a help, I'm afraid."

"Why not?"

"Well, Susan isn't strong enough to snap a neck by herself." I didn't know how else to put it to him.

"Oh, God," he said, sinking back into his chair. He looked almost the color of cold ash.

"In fact, you'd better call your parents."

He looked uncomfortable. "I already did," he said. "After talking it over with Mr. Weiss, I called to let them know I'd be staying on with Susan so that we can have some time together before she goes home. My folks have gone on to Switzerland for a skiing holiday."

I sighed. "Then until we can reach them, you're our responsibility."

Susan pushed her breakfast away. Not that I called what she had taken a real breakfast.

"No. You eat. Better you should face Officer Gallagher on a full stomach. Who knows when you'll get lunch." Privately, I hoped we'd be through by then. Maybe the fingerprints would clear us quickly, but the way Officer Gallagher had spoken to me on the phone, I imagined we'd be lucky to get dinner.

The police wanted to fingerprint us because something had showed up on the gold star—Susan's Star of David.

"Susan was in the hospital," I reminded the clerk as she pressed my fingers into the inky pad.

"Yes. But she admits the star is hers. If it's her print, then that's normal."

I gave Gallagher a look and the clerk pressed Susan's fingers against the pad. "Whose print do you think it is?"

"We don't know. That's why we need samples," Gallagher said.

"We're suspects again?" I blurted, indignant at the way everything was going backwards.

Officer Gallagher stopped being pleasant. "None of you ever stopped being suspect." I decided I didn't like him after all. Job or no job, he seemed to be enjoying the scares he threw into us.

As I'd feared, we were there longer than lunch, especially when I told him I was changing my statement again. I gave him the cigarette butts and told him that the drugs in Miss K's office had actually been found by me in the stables.

I don't have to tell you, he hit the roof. The pages in his notebook were flapping so fast I could almost feel the breeze. Finally, he got it all down.

"Until the lab report comes back on those cigarette butts, I can no longer assume Miss Kentworth had anything to do with those drugs. Therefore, she might have been killed for another reason." He looked at Susan and Geoff. "Like vengeance."

It was nearly two by the time Officer Gallagher made his decision. The rest of his information wasn't a comfort.

"Mrs. Zindel, I think I'm going to have to hold these two."

"What hold?" I was really frightened.

"Well, that witness said Susan was in the right place and her young man, here, says he was with her. They can't prove the witness was wrong. We all know your granddaughter had a motive, and her boyfriend has the strength."

"Officer Gallagher, do you really think that Susan and Geoff came to the grounds early enough to kill Miss Kentworth and then waited around until after you and your partner were there and gone again before leaving with Alexander? No! Even a fool would leave right after the murder."

One hand crept up and rubbed his red neck. Fanny: one, Officer Gallagher: zero.

I pressed my advantage. "You know Alexander was still in his stall until just before you drove me to the station." Fanny: two, Officer Gallagher: zero.

He nodded. "All right. But I want those two to stay in their hotel room in case my witness has further proof."

"So you still suspect them? Against all logic?" I could hardly believe my ears.

"Not *against* logic, Mrs. Zindel. *With* my witness."

"You are making a big mistake, Officer Gallagher." I slid the handles of my everything bag up my arm and clutched my purse.

221

"Be glad I'm not arresting the lot of you. I could hold you for changing your statement to the police, you know." He leafed through his dreadful notebook. "I seem to have two or three versions here. When I get 'em typed up, maybe you'd better decide which one to sign."

As angry as I was, I felt a flush creeping up my neck. I certainly couldn't say anything to that. "Come on, Susan, Geoff."

I glared at Officer Gallagher, but edged from the jail while we still could. Finding Nathan was now at the top of my list, right after I took the children back to the hotel.

A while it took me to find Nathan. In the meantime, there was some good news and some not so good. The good: we were all cleared of the Mary Louise murder. None of our prints—nor Mary Louise's—matched the partial print on the star. The not so good: Gallagher was still convinced that Geoff and Susan were strong suspects for Miss K's murder.

At last, Nathan answered my knock on his door.

"Nathan!" I said. "I'm so glad you're back." Quickly, I filled him in on what had happened. He seemed a little shocked that Gallagher was being so stubborn.

"He can't *really* think the kids have anything to do with it, can he?"

"Apparently, he does. So I have a few questions for you." I gave him my list.

"Okay. I already know that the private schools that aren't government run can be lucrative. That doesn't mean that Taddington is. Certainly not so soon after you say Janet had to pour a lot of her own money in. But I think you're right that her surest avenue of wealth is to sell the place, if the will permits. I'll find out."

"Don't get so involved you forget the early supper with the family, Nathan." I headed for my room to change clothes for dinner.

"Right, Fanny."

As I dressed, I thought about Larry's nice offer. Sweet it was for him to include Geoff and Nathan in this family dinner.

I wondered why Judith had agreed to eat early. Her I would have figured for holding out until later, when she could wear something much fancier.

First thing this morning, Doris had taken Judy to get her nail fixed. Now she was ready to face the world again. A little unhappy Judith sounded to learn we had to eat in the hotel restaurant. But she brightened when she realized the hotel restaurant was an elegant one. I have to say I was a little angry with her that she didn't get more upset about Susan and Geoff having to stay at the hotel.

I shouldn't have worried. Larry got angry enough about it for both of them. Only with a lot of fast talk did I calm him and convince him that fighting with Officer Gallagher over such a small thing wasn't worth it right now.

No one had a really wonderful time. Unfortunately, Judith was about what Nathan had expected, no better. Larry, usually pleasant enough to make up for Judith twice over, wasn't very good company because he was still so angry.

Nothing Nathan could say to him calmed him any. His upset was nothing compared to Judith's. She sobbed and dabbed at her eyes through most of the meal. I noticed, spitefully, that she never managed to shed enough tears to ruin her makeup.

Dinner ended early and on an unpleasant note, with Larry raging about his meeting with Robbie Patterson first thing in the morning. He was determined to find some charge with which to make Gallagher's life a misery.

As soon as Judith and Larry left with Doris, Nathan was on his way. He said he would find answers to all our questions and for me not to worry. Easy for him to say, going off to do something about it all. Harder to sit and wait.

While Geoff was in Nathan's room changing out of the good clothes he'd worn to dinner with Susan's parents, I comforted Susan.

"But *Bubbe!* Did you see how Mom kept looking at Geoff? I know she and Daddy think it's all his fault that I'm in this trouble. I know it!" She started to cry and I put an arm around her.

"I can't say you're wrong, Susan. But Nathan is investigat-

223

ing some more. By tomorrow morning we'll probably have everything cleared up and your parents will see more clearly."

"Mom? See anything clearly? *Bubbe*, you've got to be kidding."

Geoff knocked and came back into the room.

"Take it easy, *Susa-le*, all any of us can do now is wait," I said, waving off Geoff's concern and turning on the television.

The children switched channels for a bit, while I worked on my crocheting. Not much to choose from. The hotel's cable channels had mostly reruns from the U.S. The two government-run British stations both had talk shows.

Finally, Susan stood up, stretched, and yawned. "Can we go down and get some coffee, *Bubbe?* I need the exercise."

"Of course," I said, "but stay where I can find you."

Not twenty minutes after the kids left, the phone rang. I put down my crocheting, hoping it was Nathan with news. News it was, but not from Nathan.

Officer Gallagher had found someone else to use as a witness. 'Corroboration' he called it. A second girl at the school swore up and down that she, too, had seen my Susan at the administration building the night Miss Kentworth was killed.

I gasped. "It's not possible! We had that worked out, Officer Gallagher, you and I."

"You had it worked out, Mrs. Zindel. I still had my doubts. Make sure the children are there when I arrive."

My heart sank into my shoes. "Arrive?"

"I'll be there in ten minutes." He hung up and I nearly dropped the receiver trying to cradle the phone. I was shaking like a fat lady on an exercise machine.

This couldn't be happening, I thought. But it was.

I took a deep breath and dialed the front desk. The clerk said he would send someone into the restaurant to get Susan and Geoff.

Moments later, my beautiful *Susa-le* and her boyfriend burst into the room. "What is it, *Bubbe?*

"Bad news, I'm afraid." I sat the both of them down on the bed. "Officer Gallagher is on his way over."

"For what? More stinkin' questions?" Geoff asked.

224

I shook my head. "Another girl claims to have seen Susan at the administration building. Now they have what they call 'corroboration.'"

"What?" Susan jumped up off the bed. "That's a lie!"

I put my hand on her shoulder. She shrugged it off and started to shout something. There was a knock at the door. All of us froze.

I pulled myself together enough to answer the door. Officer Gallagher stood there with two of his men. He glanced over my shoulder. "Excuse me, Mrs. Zindel," he said, and stepped past. "Susan Zindel, Geoffrey Barham, I'm going to have to take you in. I must warn you that anything you say can be taken down in evidence."

My mouth dropped open. "Wait a minute, Officer Gallagher. You can't do this."

"I'm afraid I must, Mrs. Zindel. Can you arrange legal counsel?"

I nodded. "I'll call Susan's parents, immediately. They're in Easingwold with my cousin, Lady Doris Bond."

"You do that. Come along, you two."

Susan threw herself on me, sobbing. "*Bubbe*, please. Don't let them do this."

I rubbed her back and told her to stop crying. "I'll take care of everything, *Susa-le*. You just go with Officer Gallagher and do what he says. I'm sure your father will insist on knowing who these girls are who are telling such lies." On the last word I glared at the officer so he should know I didn't believe his story for a minute, 'corroboration' or no 'corroboration.'

So quiet the room was with Susan and Geoff gone. At a loss, I went to the phone and tried Nathan's room. I would have walked down there, but my knees were shaking so hard I had to sit.

Just as well I didn't go. No answer.

Now the hard phone call. I dialed Doris.

If I had thought Judith was hysterical before, I was wrong. I could hardly finish talking to my son before she was drowning us out with her *geschreis*. My Larry. Such a good son. He told me not to worry, not to lift a finger. He would be back

225

in York as soon as Doris could bring him. Then he would take care of everything.

I tried to do what he said. I picked up my crocheting and threw it down again a dozen times until the yarn was so knotted and so many loops were dropped I was going backwards instead of forward with it.

Once more I dialed Nathan. Nothing.

Janet, I thought, maybe I should call her at the school, see if she knew these girls, the ones who had lied. She had moved onto the grounds now. Maybe she'd seen them talking to the police, could point them out to me. I dialed the number she had given me for her private rooms.

No answer there, either. She was probably in the kitchen or over at the office catching up on Miss K's paperwork. I dialed the main number, but it was already after nine and I didn't really expect Taddington to have a receptionist on during spring break.

Finally, I couldn't stand it anymore. I hurried from the hotel. In my head, I could hear Larry ordering me to relax and let him handle it. But I couldn't. If I was to help Susan, it wasn't going to be by sitting on my *tuchis* in a hotel chair.

At the front desk, I left a message for Nathan telling him about Susan and Geoff, also where to find me.

Then, I went out to wait for my cab.

Twenty

"TADDINGTON School," I said, settling back in my seat. As we drove, I thought about all the doubts my questions had given me over Janet. I was still curious about her and her refusal to admit having hired Miss Kentworth herself, but all that could wait. Susan was more important. I knew if I could find those girls, I could get the truth out of them.

From my everything bag, I pulled out the little tape recorder. So much for my big band tape. Tommy Dorsey would have to be sacrificed. I took out cellophane tape and put a small piece over the notch so that I could record over the music. Then I set the recorder at the top of my bag, right under my crocheting. I turned the volume all the way up. If I found out who those girls were, I wanted to be able to flick on the machine without being seen. I hoped the crocheting wouldn't muffle their voices.

Of course, I had to warn myself not to get my hopes up. It was possible that these girls did not stay on the school grounds for spring break, but had reported to Officer Gallagher from their homes.

The cab turned into the gates and eased to a stop at the administration building. The one remaining stone spire of the old abbey ruin at the rear of the grounds was lit by the headlamps as we came around the bend in the drive. The grounds weren't as well lit during the break. But it wasn't so dark that I didn't see that familiar figure striding toward my cab as we stopped.

Gottenyu! Nathan. I jumped out, tossed the driver a ten-pound note, and hurried to meet him.

"What are you doing here, Nathan?"

"I got your message when I phoned the hotel. My God, Fanny, this is awful." He put his arms around me and hugged.

I hugged back. Hard. I fought tears. There was more important business than crying like a silly old woman. "Come on, Nathan. I can't wait to see if Janet knows who those 'corroborator' girls are."

Puffing nervously on his pipe, Nathan hurried me along the walkway. "You know they might not be here, Fanny. Spring break."

"I know Nathan. But if Janet knows *who* they are, she can tell us *where* they are," I said, pulling open the door to the administration building.

Nathan smiled and shook his head. "You never should have turned down the Mossad job, Fanny."

"Who turned it down? I just haven't given them my answer yet."

I heard Nathan chuckle, but I didn't turn to smile at him. The hall looked dark. "I don't think Janet's in here."

We entered the waiting room for Miss K's office. It was empty. Nathan pushed open the door to Miss Kentworth's office, but it, too, was empty. "Let's check the kitchen and then try and find her rooms," I said.

There was no one in the kitchen so we went out onto the grounds. Nathan drew on his pipe. "Let's ask someone where her suite is."

"Fine," I said. "Who?" I looked around the empty yard.

"We could try the barn or the library."

228

"The library." I didn't want Nathan to run into Jock. As mad as he'd been about the way Jock had strong-armed me on Lendal Bridge, I was afraid Nathan would lose his temper.

Just as we climbed the stairs, a student came hurrying out. We asked if she knew where Janet Percy, the new acting headmistress, was.

"I haven't seen her, sir. But Miss Kentworth used to have her apartments on the second floor at the back." She pointed to the rear of the library.

Nathan smiled at her. "Thank you. We'll check."

Around the back of the building we went and up the dark wood staircase. The door at the top was ajar and we entered a long hall.

It wasn't hard to find the only occupied suite up there. Soft classical music was pouring from a lighted and open doorway.

Nathan knocked and stepped inside just ahead of me.

"Janet? Janet Percy?"

There was no answer. I moved in front of him. "Janet?" I called. "It's Fanny and Nathan."

Still no answer.

"Let me," I said, moving toward the other room ahead of him. "What if she's changing?"

He nodded, but followed closely.

Sure enough, the adjoining room was a bedroom. I caught my breath. Such a mess it couldn't have been only from Janet moving in so recently. "Nathan," I said, "something's wrong."

He was at my heels before I could move. "You bet something's wrong. This place is a wreck."

I looked around at the suitcase flung to the floor, clothes spilled everywhere, along with the hangers that had fit her garment bag so nicely. Tea had been made, but the cup was smashed on the floor, and the electric kettle was lying under the window on the rug. From that she wasn't going to get hot water, she was going to get a fire if I didn't unplug it.

I picked up the kettle. As I turned, the gauzy curtain caught against my coat and lifted away from the frame.

"Don't move, Fanny." Nathan hurried forward. He took the curtain in two fingers. "Step out of the way."

"The glass is all smashed, Nathan!" Automatically, my hands pulled the cord from the pot as I followed Nathan's glance out the broken window.

The window wasn't the only thing broken.

"You think she's dead, Nathan?" I stared out at the twisted figure on the flagstone patio below. Janet Percy lay in a pool of blood too large to allow life to go on inside that body.

He nodded. "We'd better check, though."

I followed him back along the hall and down the dark wood staircase.

Outside, the air was chilly and I shivered inside my coat.

We approached Janet's body on the flagstones. Around her face in a red halo was the blood I had seen from the window. Worse it looked up close, like a tomato aspic left too long in hot water before being dumped from the mold. "I think we'd better call the police," I said.

"No, Fanny. I'll call. You take my car and go back to the hotel."

"Me? Why?"

"What do you think Officer Gallagher will say if he finds you here with another body?"

I shrugged. "A better alibi than being with a Mossad agent a person couldn't ask."

Nathan let out an exasperated snort. "We'll go over and call from her office," he said.

We sat in the office together. I was on the chair, now without its lumpy cushion; Nathan perched on the edge of Miss Kentworth's desk. We waited for the police. Again.

It seemed to take forever.

"Shouldn't we just search her rooms a little, Nathan?" I asked, when the waiting began to get to me.

"You want to tamper with the scene of the crime, again?" he asked. "And you want me as your accomplice?"

I hung my head. "We might find something that could help Susan."

230

"Fanny, if we can find it, so can the police. Besides, if all these murders are connected, and probably they are, then this one, being committed while Susan is in jail, is the perfect alibi."

I brightened at that. "Maybe my Susan won't have to spend the night behind bars," I said.

"Probably not, Fanny. I think this will help Larry get the children out immediately."

I jumped up and hugged him, then let go quickly when I heard sounds outside in the yard.

The police cars squealed their way up to the front of the building. I could hear yelling and doors banging. I shuddered at the thought of confronting Officer Gallagher, whom I was beginning to consider a family member.

Nathan's pipe went out. I could tell because he drew on it several times in a row and no smoke billowed up. He leaned over the desk and tapped the bowl out in the Waterford ashtray.

I stared at the little lump of partly burned tobacco and tried to shut out the pounding footsteps of my own personal *dybbuk*, haunting spirit, as Gallagher and company beat their way down the hall. In my mind I could see the ashtray as it had been the night Miss Kentworth died. A dozen cigarette butts had been clustered around a similar little lump of partly burned tobacco.

"Does it always do that?" I asked.

"What?" The door to Sara's office flew open, banging against the wall with a crash. I waited to hear the glass of Miss K's office door breaking, but it didn't.

"Make that little pile of tobacco," I prompted.

Nathan looked where I pointed. "The dottle? Sure." He turned from me and stretched out a hand to the red-faced Irishman, who puffed and shouted. "Officer Gallagher, thank you for coming so readily."

"You again, Mrs. Zindel? By all the saints!" He gripped his

231

hair with his pudgy fingers and seemed in danger of pulling it all out.

"No need to tear your hair, Officer," I said, giving him a smile I hoped he could see wasn't my friendliest.

"You're here. Another dead body is here. There's a need!" He puffed some more in my direction but I pretended not to notice.

"*Feh!* Mr. Weiss was with me every minute. This one you can't blame me for. My granddaughter, I hurry to mention, is still in your care."

He glared. "Maybe this one was killed before I came to arrest her," he said, smiling like a shark about to gulp a minnow.

I showed him my teeth, but a smile you couldn't call it. "The body is in the back. The blood is just beginning to congeal. Like aspic it looks. Go figure. With the blood not yet dry, how could Susan or I have done it and driven back to the hotel in time for you to find us there?"

"Let me take you to the body," Nathan said, stepping between me and Officer Gallagher as if he feared one of us might injure the other soon.

"Stay here with her," Gallagher said to the young cop who had come in with him.

They walked out, leaving me to fidget. Well, I wouldn't. I took out my crocheting and placed my Israeli folk-song tape in the carrier. So cheering.

It wasn't long before Nathan and Gallagher were back.

I pulled off my headset so I could hear what they were saying.

"You can go, Mrs. Zindel."

I looked at Nathan.

He handed me his keys. "Take my car, Fanny."

"But . . ."

"No 'but's. You go back to the hotel and you stay there."

"Nathan, what about—"

"Fanny, we'll discuss it at the hotel. You *will* be waiting when I arrive."

"I—"

232

"I think you'd better do what he suggests, Mrs. Zindel."
Gallagher's eyes could have chilled soda!

I picked up my things and walked from the room. I wasn't
going to get anywhere with the two of them against me. At
least they could have let me hang around and eavesdrop.

I unlocked the rental and climbed in. Suddenly, I gripped
the steering wheel and took deep breaths. Deep like when I
was about to go on stage. I waited for the nausea to pass. My
friend Janet lying smashed in a pool of blood was almost more
than I could take. Maybe there were things going on that I
wondered about, but such a death shouldn't happen to a dog.

I put the car in drive and pulled out onto the street. On the
wrong side, naturally. A motorist honked viciously and
swerved to miss my front fender. Upset or not, I would have
to pay better attention.

I lurched onto the left and pressed the accelerator. Too
hard. The car leaped ahead. What had Nathan rented? A
bucking bronco, maybe? I slowed and drove on.

I was nearly to the hotel when I realized that Officer Gallagher was awfully short of suspects. Mary Louise, Miss Kentworth, and now Janet, all of whom had caused me to have
doubts, were now dead. I pulled to the side of the road and cut
the engine. I had to think.

Was it possible for those girls who had lied to the police to
have any motive for the killings? Mary Louise and Miss Kentworth? Maybe. But Janet? Never. They probably hadn't even
known her yet.

There was one suspect everyone had ignored. I remembered Miss Johnson, the cat lady, and her trancelike confi-
dence at tea. She had been so sure that she would inherit
Taddington now. Why?

Officer Gallagher had been so unpleasant when I had suggested her as a possible suspect. He shouldn't have been. If we
were looking at motives, Miss Johnson had the last one. She
alone would profit now from Taddington's acres. I started the
engine. I knew how to get Officer Gallagher's attention. He

was going to listen to me on this one. He would have no choice.

I drove to a service station, gassed up the car, and looked up a number and address in the phone directory. I dialed the number, jotted directions, and hung up.

Then I dialed another number. I left a message about my intentions with Officer Gallagher's desk clerk.

My next stop would be Four Pause Rescue Center.

Twenty-One

THE directions led me out the same road as we had used going to Doris's. I put my tape player on as soon as the traffic thinned and the road straightened. Dark and boring, even with trying to keep to the left.

As I neared the turn to Easingwold, I slowed and watched for signs. There it was. The small street with the line of trees. I maneuvered the car into the lane and was nearly rear-ended by a truck.

The huge delivery van roared on toward Easingwold while I pulled to the side to finish shaking before driving on. I would have gone back to the hotel that very moment, but I couldn't be sure Officer Gallagher would investigate Miss Johnson on his own.

With a sigh, I clicked on the interior light and memorized the rest of the directions. Reading and driving in this country would only get me killed.

Easing back onto the road, I made one turn after another and finally saw the sign that read: FOUR PAUSE RESCUE CENTER.

"Okay," I lectured myself, "remember, just a look to see if she's alone." Alone, I knew I could handle her, maybe even trick her into a confession. If she had someone there who looked like they could snap a neck, I would make a note of that, too. Then I would turn it all over to Gallagher when he arrived.

I shut off the engine and let the car roll quietly to a secluded spot beneath some trees. I would walk the rest of the way. I could always use the kitten for an excuse if things got sticky.

Once again, I set up my tape recorder and placed it under my crocheting. I changed the tape back to Tommy Dorsey. If I had to ruin one, I could retape Dorsey from my records at home.

I crept toward the buildings. Hearing meowing and an occasional bark from one long, low structure, I decided to start with the kennels. Maybe one of the helpers was the strong, silent type, strong enough to have helped Miss Johnson with the murder.

I tried the door at one end of the building. Open, but creaky. I eased it wider, holding my breath against the sound. I should have known the animals would make enough noise to cover it. Maybe too much noise. I waited a moment to see if anyone would come to check.

Nothing. They quieted.

Inside, the light was so dim it was gloomy. My heart went out to all the pathetic little creatures who had to live in such cages. Then I remembered the ones who didn't even have a warm home and food like this and I felt worse. I was almost to the break in the row when I heard scuffling sounds from up ahead.

Dropping to my knees, I huddled against an empty kennel and thought about crawling inside in case a vicious animal had escaped. I listened for the sound of doggy claws on the cement floor.

No dog appeared, yet the scuffling sound continued. Now there was a thump. Then another. I crept forward on my knees. This was why no one had noticed my entrance.

At the far end of the building, I saw two huge figures, dim silhouettes struggling with each other. A fight. I inched forward. The larger man—wearing the galoshes of a kennel worker—was shoved hard, the force flattening him against the wall. I heard the clatter as he let several metal feeding dishes fall from his hands.

In what light there was, I could see his face mouthing something. Hear I couldn't possibly, the dogs and cats were making such a racket because of the fight.

His attacker, his back toward me, must have been shouting awful things because his victim was cowering and looked extremely frightened, both hands out in front of him for protection. What I was understanding from my recently acquired lip-reading skills were the same words over and over.

"Stop!" he mouthed. Then, "Don't kill me!" At least I was fairly sure I was lip-reading correctly. Naturally, at the Tracy Clinic, where I had volunteered twice a week, nobody forms words like *kill,* or *murder.*

Now I didn't know what to do. I honestly didn't believe my knitting needle or even my extralong hatpin would be much good against someone who could put such fear into a man the size of the victim. But I couldn't let murder go on before my very eyes.

I set my everything bag down against a wall of wire mesh and scouted the kennels around me for a better weapon. A two-by-four, perhaps, or . . .

I spied a full bag of cat-litter and thought I might blind the killer long enough for the intended victim and me to escape. I reached for the latch.

I had only taken my eyes off them for a moment, but unfortunately, that moment was followed by a sound like the smash of a watermelon dropped off a balcony. I looked back to see the kennel worker on the floor, the attacker bending over him.

I'm ashamed to say I didn't rush forward immediately, but I certainly had no way to handle the attacker on my own. Thank goodness the man on the floor let out a pathetic groan. I knew he couldn't be dead.

The man pulled something shiny from the wrist of the fellow on the floor. Then he dragged him into one of the kennels and snapped a lock on the run door.

I collected two fistfuls of cat sand. If the attacker discovered me, I would try to blind him with it. Fortunately, I didn't have to use it. As soon as he had what he wanted from the kennel-man, he fled out the far door.

I dropped the sand and hurried to the run. The man was getting some color back. But get in and help him, or let him out, I couldn't. The run next to him looked empty so I entered it to see if I could, at least, press a handkerchief against his bleeding scalp. I knelt down and reached under the chain link. No matter how I twisted my arm, I couldn't seem to do him any good. Unfortunately, while I struggled, two mother cats and a kitten wandered from the run I was in. I wasn't fast enough to stop them.

I stood up and hurried from the cage. If I was going to keep the attacker in my sight, I'd have to be quick.

When the unconscious man on the floor moaned I looked back, stepping hard on the tail of a mother cat. Thank God it wasn't the kitten. Such a crunch would have killed a baby.

I desperately wished I could collect the mama cats and the kitten and put them back where they belonged, but I was losing time. They would be all right here in the building, assuming I could get out the door without them following. Where had that kitten gone anyway? I couldn't see him anywhere.

I gave up on the animals and collected my everything bag. *Gott in himmel!* So heavy. That's where the kitten had gone— my bag. He was curled up on top of everything and sleeping like he'd never get enough of it. So, he could stay, the little stowaway. There was no time to find a safer place for him.

I hurried after the attacker.

On my way through to the next building, I managed to shut the two mother cats in as I slipped through. I would have to put the kitten somewhere safe before I needed to use my tape recorder. Besides, my bag weighed a ton!

Where had the man gone? Had I lost him after all? I heard the animals telling me that someone had entered the next building.

I hurried to it and eased open the door. Runs and kennels.

So many homeless. I heard the soft mewing from my bag and thought, more lives, and there aren't enough homes, let alone good ones. Suddenly, I was furious with people who just let animals make more animals. This was why I donated so much time to rescue groups and had had so many pets under foster care in my home. I marched forward and gripped the handle of the next door, which had not quite fallen completely shut.

Out into the night and the cold, which was getting quite fierce. I tucked my scarf tighter around my neck and sucked my mouth and nose into its warm folds. Next there would be snow, the way my luck was running.

I headed toward the smallest of the buildings, where I saw a light come on and then go out again. I hoped Officer Gallagher had my message by now and was on his way.

Surely in this building I would find the offices. I would call Gallagher again from the first phone I came to. In addition to finding out whom I'd been following, I hoped either to prove he was the killer or find incriminating evidence against Miss Johnson.

The small building was still a shelter. More cages and one giant aviarylike wire area with at least fifty cats inside. They were lying around like miniature lions on logs and perches. I heard muffled thumping coming from a small utility closet.

I hurried over and gave the knob a yank. Locked tight. Another adult cat, probably the office mascot, came over and wound herself around my ankles and meowed pitifully. She was anxious to peer in my bag, curious about the baby. Perhaps she was reminding me I'd have to find the kitten a safer place.

"First things first," I told her. I pulled my penlight out of my pocket and rapped on the closet. More thumps and muffled moaning.

Shining the light around the walls, I looked for a key.

Suddenly, a hand clamped over my nose and mouth and I was falling backwards.

Twenty-Two

I WAS dragged. I could feel a huge male chest at my back and strong arms wrapping around me, fighting to get me across the room away from the utility closet. I tried to get my foot up and rake it down the shin of my attacker as Sadie and I had learned in self-defense class, but I was being forced along too fast.

One good scrape plus my heel digging on his instep and whoever it was was going to get the shock of his life. As I tried to get my feet under me, I could feel the office cat near my legs, frantic to get to my everything bag and the kitten. The everything bag dangled from my elbow, its straps twisting with my struggle. I only hoped the kitten would be all right.

Suddenly, lights flashed on, nearly blinding me. The attacker thrust me from him so hard I fell against a desk and only just caught myself. Well, I had been looking for the office, hadn't I?

I turned, ripping one of my knitting needles free of my bag as I did.

Such a shock.

Facing me from across the room, a gun pointed neatly at my

chest, was Kenneth, Janet's pitiful excuse for an ex-husband. "What in the name of God are *you* doing here?" I don't think I really expected an answer, but the words just slid out of my mouth—a lot like losing your grip on a soupy noodle.

"That was my sentiment, exactly, Mrs. Zindel. You first." He gestured with the gun.

"I came to talk to Miss Johnson. I left a kitten here and I wondered how it was doing." It wasn't so far from true.

His face turned a mottled ugly red with white blotches, making him look as if he had a disease. "You're looking in about a kitten in the dead of night?" He smiled, telling me he knew better.

I wished he hadn't used that particular expression. "Yes. I couldn't come sooner. Tomorrow I'm leaving England, and won't have time."

He shook his head. "The truth, Mrs. Zindel. I know you and Janet were close. You were her confidante. You followed me here. You recognized me that night in the hall of the administration building. You've been after evidence against me ever since! Instead of hitting you on the head, I should have killed you when I had the chance.

"No matter," he said, taking his pipe out of his pocket and gnawing nervously on the stem like a rabbit nibbling a carrot.

"*You* killed her!" I said, not thinking too clearly. Murderers get more dangerous when you mention their errors. I tried to make up for my mistake by sliding my hand in under the kitten and the crocheting to switch on the tape recorder. "It was the dottle from *your* pipe in Miss Kentworth's ashtray."

He looked away and went on as if I hadn't spoken. "You don't know what happened. Janet was an accident. An accident." He seemed to be trying the word out on his tongue and liking the taste of it.

"Then you won't mind explaining to the police."

The gun he thrust in my direction. "Shut up! She stole from me. Everything. And she laughed at me. Called me stupid. Me, with three degrees!" His eyes looked unfocused and he seemed ready to explode. I kept my mouth shut. "Said those girls were just after the money I spent on them. Fooling me, just like she did, by lunching with that friend of yours. The way he embarrassed me in the restaurant. That rock should have hit him on the head like I planned."

I gasped, but kept quiet. If he was going to admit to hurling that rock off the tower, I wanted him to continue, to keep on confessing. The reels on my tape recorder were turning.

He seemed about to light his pipe, realized he couldn't and hold the gun on me, and stuffed it back in his pocket. "That Miss Kentworth," he said, spitting the name.

I nodded.

"She started it all. The drugs. Using the young girls to lure the customers. She wanted more than her headmistress's pay. But she was ruining the school. Destroying Janet's heritage; the only thing she had worth any real money."

"And so you killed Miss Kentworth? To protect your ex-wife's inheritance?" So excitable. I would have to soothe him somehow, if I wanted to keep that gun from going off in my direction. "I don't understand."

"I did as soon as I figured out what was going on between Kentworth and that little slut. The one your granddaughter had the run-in with."

I just nodded and made what I hoped were soothing noises.

"Mary Louise was cutting into Miss Kentworth's profits by cutting the drugs. That's what really started to draw attention to the whole thing. That scandal alone would have closed the school. Then the stupid bitch had her kill that horse. I guess she figured it would punish the girl. The insurance money would keep the school going so that she could continue run-ning her drug business.

"Then there was the relationship Mary Louise threatened. They were an item, you know, Miss Kentworth and the rever-end." He smiled then, like a dirty little boy telling sex secrets behind the barn. I think I had never hated anyone quite so much.

"That stiff old vicar and that dried-up, drug-dealing old maid! Really quite humorous when you think about it." He laughed and it seemed his crazy cackle would never stop bouncing off the plain, white walls of the office. "Except that it was a danger to Janet's inheritance."

242

"The inheritance you planned to sue her for?"

He just laughed harder, but tears started down his cheeks. "And win, too. I would have."

The thumping from the closet had stopped. I hoped the reason was exhaustion, not something more permanent. I tried to keep my mind off that. "I can understand that you had to kill Miss Kentworth to protect the inheritance, but why did you kill the girl?"

He turned an even red now, anger filling in the lighter blotches. "I never touched the little slut. Maybe Miss Kentworth got tired of her meddling in the romance. Maybe she told the vicar his darling daughter was dealing drugs and prostituting and *he* did her in to save face. But *I* didn't kill her."

"Did Miss Kentworth provoke you in some way? Was that an accident like Janet?" I hoped I was giving him an easy out.

Maybe he would fall in love with the idea of accidents; those he would think he could talk his way out of with the police. Good, then he wouldn't have to kill me. A neck you can snap in anger. A gunshot wound in an old *bubbe* would be harder to explain.

He looked up at me, confused, as if for the moment, he didn't know why he had ended up here with a gun on me. "I went to Kentworth's office to beg her to consider what she was doing to the school. She laughed. Then she tried to tell me Janet had set it all up. All the ugliness, the drugs, the prostitution, everything. I snapped her neck." His face crumpled like a cardboard box left out in the rain. "I had to stop her. If Janet ended up penniless . . ."

"I know," I said gently. "You would be penniless, too."

He sighed and tears began to run down his face. Unfortunately, the gun never shifted. It still pointed at my chest. The office cat twisted herself through my legs and I picked her up, setting my everything bag on the floor as I did so. I hoped that the recorder had picked up more than the occasional mew of the kitten who hid it from sight.

"I went to her. To Janet, to tell her what I'd done for her. Helped her protect the school so she wouldn't lose it to Four Pause."

243

I said nothing. He had started and I didn't want him to stop. Not while my tape was turning.

"She laughed at me. Me, a college professor! Told me that if it weren't for Gwendolyn and her drug business, she'd have lost Taddington long ago to Miss Johnson.

"I went nuts at the thought of losing everything."

Smarter not to point out to him that before he could have counted Janet's inheritance as his own, he would have to win in court. "So you fought with Janet?" I suggested, when he didn't continue right away.

He nodded. "We fought. I didn't mean to kill her. I loved her. Those other women were nothing to me. But she refused to listen." The tears were dripping onto his jacket lapels now. "Suddenly, she came at my eyes with her thumbs and when I pushed her away, she just . . . kept going. Out the window. Onto the bricks below."

The moment I had been waiting for. Outside I heard the sound of sirens. He must have heard it, too. The nose of the gun dipped just a little in alarm.

Quick as a flash, I hurled the office cat at him, apologizing to her even as she flew toward Kenneth's face, her claws ready for what claws did best. I lunged for my everything bag. Careful not to hurt the kitten, I groped for the small can of hairspray and tore at the cap. The gun went off and I hoped Janet's ex had missed anything living.

Pointing the hairspray directly at Kenneth, who was still screaming and hitting at the poor cat with his free hand, I let loose and got him in both eyes.

He dropped the gun and grabbed his face, batting the cat away and trying to rub the stinging stuff out of his eyes with both fists. He screamed and swore at me in blind hurt and rage.

I scrambled after the gun and turned it on him.

That was how Officer Gallagher found us when he entered. Nathan was with him. They let Miss Johnson out of the closet and sent the medical crew for the man Kenneth had beaten unconscious.

Miss Johnson told us that Kenneth had planned to take the

man's Medic Alert bracelet. Her kennelman was a Pakistani who had been mute since witnessing the slaughter of his wife and children almost four years previously.

"Ramuhr was that murderer's ideal scapegoat," she said, sitting stiffly in her office chair and straightening the papers on the desk as she spoke. She kept her eyes off Kenneth who sat hunched, his hands cuffed behind him. "His medical bracelet, which Mr. Stein planned to drop somewhere near Janet's rooms at the school, would, when found, have fooled the police into thinking that I was so desperate to inherit that I suggested Ramuhr go a little beyond his basic job description."

Miss Johnson cleared her throat and sipped water before continuing. The gag had, no doubt, left her mouth feeling like sandpaper. "I suppose I was going to be accused of having ordered him to put Janet Percy out of my misery—so to speak." She allowed herself a little smile at her clever wording.

"Thank you, Miss Johnson. I'll have your statement typed up." Officer Gallagher finished jotting in his green notebook and looked up at me. "Will you be going home soon, Mrs. Zindel?"

"Susan and her parents will go home right away, but there are some other things to keep me for a while. You want I should let you know where you can get in touch?"

He shook his head. "Actually, I just hoped you'd go home and quit tripping over the dead and nearly dead," he said, sadly. "It makes for such a lot of extra work on our part."

"*Feh!*" I said, patting his slumping shoulder. "I didn't find any this time. I kept several people alive, including myself, and brought you the solution to your murders." I turned and started from the room. Some people have no sense of what is right. Didn't he owe me a little thank-you, maybe?

"Mrs. Zindel."

I stopped and put a smile on my face before I turned back to him. "Yes, Officer?" Maybe he'd seen his mistake.

"I'll want you to make a full statement at the station in the morning."

My smile faded. I could feel it running from my face. "In the morning," I said, a little stiffly. Then I drove back to the hotel. Nathan stayed to clear things with Officer Gallagher. Good. I had done enough.

I clapped on my headset and listened to my Israeli folk songs. What was left of my Tommy Dorsey tape had gone to Officer Gallagher along with Kenneth's confession. Some of it had been muffled but most was clear.

Such a lot I had on my mind I hardly thought about the troubles of keeping to the left and I was back in York before I knew it.

Susan and Geoff were waiting for me in the hotel room. Nathan had gotten them out of jail as soon as he'd finished reporting on Janet's death.

"Nathan just pointed out the obvious and mentioned false arrest suits. The only problem is, they have found that none of the suspects' prints, Jock's included, match up with the partial print found on my star," Susan explained.

"This is a problem? For such problems we can thank *Ha-Shem!*" Then I thought a moment. "Maybe tonight's suspect will match," I said, and told Susan and Geoff all that had happened since they had been arrested.

"*Bubbe*, I'm so glad he didn't kill you!" Susan said, throwing her arms around me.

"And I'm glad he didn't kill you, while trying to smash Nathan with that rock at the tower.

"Me, too."

"In fact I could celebrate with a late snack. I forgot dinner and I'm afraid the kittens got fur in everything in my bag."

Susan laughed and we all went out to eat.

By the end of supper, Susan looked especially gloomy about it all. "There won't be a Taddington anymore," she said, staring at me.

"No, but Miss Johnson will keep it all up for the animals. So many more homeless babies will be cared for. Taddington could be turned into the finest animal shelter in all England. Won't that make you happy, *Susa-le?*"

She seemed to think a moment and then smiled. "I guess

that's more useful than a rather snooty private school for a bunch of silly girls."

"Present company excepted," said Geoff loyally.

Susan and Geoff walked off happily, arm in arm, well satisfied with that idea. I wish it had been as easy for me. I wondered whether Kenneth had been telling the truth. Was it possible that his print would not match the one on Susan's star?

Twenty-Three

I WENT in early, even before having breakfast, to make my statement for Officer Gallagher. He didn't look well, and some sleep I know he could have used.

The biggest problem was that no matter how they questioned Kenneth, they couldn't get anything that would prove him guilty of killing Mary Louise. As I feared, his fingers didn't match the print.

Unless the police were finally ready to forget the print and accept that Miss Kentworth had probably killed her, or until they were willing to put some pressure on a grieving father about his daughter's private homelife, they were shy one murderer. And they had no idea who had performed the mutilation.

For some reason, I just couldn't see Miss Kentworth killing off the daughter of her lover. She had so many other ways to control Mary Louise, and murder was an end to all that power she had over the girls who had helped her sell the drugs.

I thought about things as I walked down to Betty's Café, where I was meeting Nathan. We were going to plan a little tour of the Lake District together before he flew back to Israel. Just a few days.

With luck and my planning, Alexander would be arriving

248

in the States by the time I flew home. His three-day quarantine would be over, and I would be there in time to see my daughter-in-law's face when they brought Alexander into her yard.

Judith, I knew, wasn't delighted, but I had reminded her that a good mother makes sacrifices. Susan had had a shock; the horse was therapy.

My Larry, he understood better. Hadn't he grown up in my home with his sister, Deborah, always bringing in strays? He'd already called home and was having men come right away to build a nice stall and an arena.

It was all I could do to tear myself from such delicious thoughts when I saw Nathan striding up the street toward me.

Lovely, but a little sad, our last breakfast at Betty's. It passed with hardly a word other than about the trip.

After breakfast, I called Taddington to see if any of Susan's teachers were still on the grounds. I had two gifts left to hand out. Nathan drove me out there to drop off the one. The other, for Mr. Hamilton Craig, I might never get a chance to deliver. If worse came to worst, I could send it on through mail forwarding.

When we neared the room at the hotel I could hear crying. I waved Nathan on to his room and stepped into the middle of Susan's and Geoff's unhappiness. I started back out the door, but Geoff stopped me.

"It's all right, Mrs. Zindel. It's just going to be a long time till summer vacation. My folks said I could visit then." He tried to look happy at the thought, but the current leave-taking hadn't given him much of a stomach for it.

I hugged them both and helped Susan with the rest of her packing. Most of her things were going home in the huge trunk Nathan had *shlepped* down from her dorm room.

At last she was ready. Geoff would ride with her to London. I took them to the train. How my Susan had gotten her mother to agree to letting her have some time alone with Geoff, even just on the train, I had no idea. But Larry probably had put his foot down. He was sensible. He knew Geoff had had nothing to do with the trouble. In London was soon enough for them to meet and reclaim Susan as family.

I was happy for their time alone, but I wondered what

249

Geoff's parents would think about all this. He had actually been arrested, after all.

Geoff wasn't sure if he would tell his parents about our adventure, but he was sure they'd find out, sooner or later. His uncle was with Scotland Yard, so that made that a sure thing. It was this uncle he would stay with for the rest of the spring break so there was no hiding the embarrassment from the family.

Geoff shrugged and grinned at me as he helped Susan on to the train. "So far, what they don't know can't hurt me." He laughed and followed Susan up the steps.

I was all waved out, cried out, and just about to leave, when I saw a familiar figure in the crowd. What was he doing here?

I hurried toward the man in the tweed coat.

24

NEVER had so many people pressed between me and my destination. I fought to keep my feet in the packed station. It was my chance to give Mr. Craig the gift and thank him for his efforts. Latin would be important to Susan in her veterinary studies.

"Mr. Craig!" I called, when I was close enough to be heard over the noise of the station. He didn't turn my way, even though I could have sworn he heard me.

"Mr. Craig, Hamilton Craig!" I called again, pushing along after him. By ignoring a man who glared at me for squeezing past him, I managed to touch Mr. Craig's sleeve. At last, he turned.

"It's me. Fanny Zindel. Susan's grandmother."

"Oh," he said. Warmer welcomes I've had from Judith with a case of PMS.

"I'm afraid I haven't time to chat, Mrs. Zindel. I have to catch the train for London."

"Then you don't have to rush," I said, holding up my schedule. "The next one isn't for twenty minutes yet. I just looked it up for Susan and Geoff."

He looked startled that I should know. Not such a friendly type as he'd seemed in the lunchroom that day.

"So what can I do for you, Mrs. Zindel?"

"I thought I would treat you to a cup of tea, by way of thanks, you know?" It would be so much nicer to hand him his gift across the table. Besides, I had never had a chance to find out how Susan was *really* doing with her Latin. So much a report card doesn't tell you.

He was nervous, but gracious. "Thank you, that is very kind."

We walked to a little coffee bar and I ordered a pot of tea and some cookies.

"I'm glad to hear Susan's getting out of all this mess," he said, helping us to a table. "Rather nasty, it was."

I shrugged and took my seat. "At least she was cleared of everything. A family name is important, you know?"

"Don't I just. It's not going to be so easy for me to shake the scandal of Taddington from my boots, either." He helped himself to one of the almond biscuits and sipped at his tea.

"Have you a new position lined up?" I asked. "I'm sure if you need a recommendation, I could write something about how much help you were to my granddaughter."

"Thank you, Mrs. Zindel, but I don't think that will be necessary."

I thrust one of Morris's cards into Mr. Craig's hand. "If it is, you can reach me at this address." I handed the gift across, as well. "Just a little something to show my appreciation."

"Thanks. Very." I got the feeling I had embarrassed him a little; he smiled and tucked the card and the package in his pocket without even looking at them. "I shouldn't need to call on you. I'm hoping most of the news about Taddington won't have reached London yet."

"I don't really see how it would affect you, Mr. Craig."

"Well, prep-school families are touchy about the people who teach their children coming from sordid circumstances."

I shook my head and poured the last of the tea from the pot. "I would hardly call having the bad luck to be employed at Taddington making you guilty of a 'sordid' background."

252

He sighed. "You don't understand how it is over here. Everything is so proper. I'll have to hope they haven't heard. A murder of a headmistress and a school owner isn't something that they take lightly."

"Well, neither of the deaths should reflect on the teachers."

"As I said, you don't know the British, madam. Both those women were my employers. And if that didn't do it, it's certain having a student like Mary Louise, first a little tart and then a victim of drug overdose, would finish it." He shook his shoulders as if shrugging off the burden of it all.

"I'm afraid my problems will be compounded if the news gets around." He looked at his watch. "Well, it's hard enough to find a good position without being late. Thank you for the gift, and the tea." He smiled and grabbed his things, hurrying out almost before I could say good-bye.

"Good luck, Mr. Craig!" I shouted after his vanishing figure. One of his arms came up in a sort of salute, but he kept on walking.

I brought the empty tea things back to the counter. Suddenly, I had such a shock I nearly dropped them and ruined my good deed. Mr. Craig had used the word *overdose*.

I hurried to the pay phone, my fingers shaking so that I could hardly dial. "Officer Gallagher, who knew about Mary Louise's being killed of an overdose?"

Naturally, he had to waste valuable time giving me a lecture on meddling, but at last he told me what I wanted to know. I gave him an order or two of my own, some information, then grabbed up my everything bag and ran for the train. So I might end up in London with Geoff and Susan, waiting for Doris to appear with Judith and Larry. So, I'd be a little late for my trip with Nathan, even if I could talk Doris into driving me back to York. So this was more important.

Huffing and puffing, I barely reached Mr. Craig's London train as it was starting to pull out. It was already moving when I ran for the door. My everything bag banged heavily against my hip and my purse dangled like a pendulum from my opposite elbow. Thank goodness hours of swinging a racquet had given me the strength to grab the assist rail, hang on, and pull myself up. Nathan would worry until I found time to call him, but it couldn't be helped.

Now, all I had to do was find the right car. With any luck, Mr. Craig hadn't been lying about his destination.

I edged from car to car, looking in every seat, holding my breath, and wondering what I would say to Mr. Craig if I found him. For that matter, what would I say to Officer Gallagher if I didn't? My heart began to pound; I didn't know which outcome I was most afraid of.

Just ahead of me, in a seat to the right, sat the Latin teacher.

I slid quietly onto a nearby bench and pulled out my crocheting. Over my work, I studied the backs of the brochures he was reading and made notes. Maybe this was a catalogue from the new school where he would be teaching. With a pang, I realized I might need to tape over my Israeli folk songs. I took out my Scotch tape and fixed the cartridge so it would record—just in case.

Suddenly, Mr. Craig stood up and walked rapidly from the car.

I picked up my things and hurried after him. As I walked through the aisles, I fought the swaying of the train.

Two cars later, I realized his destination was the bar. He ordered a double scotch and took a sip of it. I slid into a chair at the other end of the car. Unfortunately, I was not invisible. When he turned to look for a table, I saw his eyes widen with shock. He had spotted me. I was about to move toward him when he turned and practically ran from the car.

Nothing to be lost now, I thought, as I ran after him. I flicked on the tape recorder. The reels were turning, the "record" button was in, the volume on full. "Mr. Craig! Wait!" I called, more for the tape recorder than for the man who had just entered the next car.

I hurried along, trying to keep up, but with the motion of the train, and my bags, he was again leaving the next car ahead of me. Maybe he would only stop when he ran out of train. I gripped my bags more firmly and put on speed.

Unfortunately, in the next free space between the cars, he

was waiting for me, a gun in his hand. "You caught it, didn't you, you nosey old bitch."

"I don't know what you mean," I said, trying for a light, friendly tone. "I'm sure I don't know why you have a gun pointed at me."

He laughed. "Don't play innocent grandmother with your crocheting. The minute I mentioned Mary Louise's dying of an overdose, I saw you react."

"Nonsense. Everyone hears about youngsters getting into drugs. Then they'll take anything from drain cleaner to oregano for a thrill. That's what gets them in trouble." I tried to sound worldly and a little bit bored. "Since everyone knew about the drugs at Taddington, her overdosing was practically expected."

"Good try, Mrs. Zindel. The papers never said anything about how she died. They just played up the mutilation." He looked a little sick as he mentioned it.

Suddenly, I knew. "It was you I saw her with in the doorway of the administration building, wasn't it?"

"What?" He looked a little confused.

I looked for the emergency cord and delivered my next line. "You were in love with her, weren't you?"

His jaw tightened. I could see the muscles twitching beneath the skin.

"It was *your* child she was carrying, wasn't it?"

I watched him carefully. Was that a bead of sweat trickling from his hairline near the temple? "A man could get furious at a woman who murdered his child. Maybe angry enough to—"

Such a glare he gave me now. "At the risk of sounding brutal, Mrs. Zindel, shut up!" He moved the gun to his left hand, used his right to grab my shoulder, and spun me toward the opening. It was suddenly quite depressingly clear that he intended to throw me from the train.

I looped my arm through the handrail and hung on. "Two murders you're going to be guilty of now, Mr. Craig?" With my elbow hooked on the rail, I locked my hands together at the wrists like a trapeze artist and hung on for dear life. I prayed the recorder was still picking up. All I needed now was a tape full of train noise to be found on my body.

I felt his fingers wrap mine as he tried to loosen my hold. "I told you to shut up, but no, you had to keep on, digging at me. Don't you think I've suffered enough?" His face was red with fury and he was barely able to hold the gun as he tried to loosen my grip on the rail. "That damn little whore. I wanted to marry her, have a family. Give her respectability. My name!" Suddenly, he stopped pulling on my arm. Silly me, I was relieved. My biggest pain was my everything bag, poking my hip, crushed between my body and the wall.

He took a step back and pointed the gun at my breast. "It would be simpler if you would just let go. A fall from a train by one of your years would be so much easier to explain, Mrs. Zindel."

"She refused you, like all the rest of them. Her clients." I wanted to keep him talking as I blocked his view of what I was doing. I edged my right hand slowly down into my concealed everything bag.

"Once a slut, always a slut, Mrs. Zindel. And one murder deserves another. She asked me to get high with her, one last time. It was. Hers!" He smiled and waved the barrel of the gun a little for emphasis.

"How did you get her to take an overdose?" My fingers searched the bottom of my bag frantically. Where was it?

"I knew she was cutting the stuff she was selling. I just switched it for some full-strength heroin. She shot it up like always." He laughed and shrugged. "I didn't have to do anything but watch."

His expression made me sick. "You must have hated her a lot to mutilate her body like that. Such a lovely girl as Mary Louise. And you did love her, once." My fingers closed over the tube at last. I began to work it out of the bag, still using my body to block my actions.

"You shut your mouth. I didn't . . . do that to her!" He was nearly in tears. "So beautiful. I didn't actually kill her, you realize? She did it to herself. I couldn't really kill her. At the last, I almost warned her. But when she laughed at me . . ." He

256

shrugged again and I knew from the look on his face he would be reluctant to kill me. It was all I had to go on.

I undid the cap from the tube of Krazy Glue. Good for sticking on loose heels. I hoped it would stick his heel as well.

I acted as if I were feeling faint and slumped against the wall of the car.

"What'er you doing there?" The gun waved dangerously and I staggered as I straightened, dropping the tube on the floor as I did so.

"I'm sorry, Mr. Craig, but it always makes me feel a bit faint when someone threatens to murder me where I stand." I tried to smile at him and stood as tall as I could. "I have called the police, you know?"

That riveted his eyes on mine for long enough. I used the toe of my pump to push the small tube very close to his shoe.

"What kind of a story is this you're giving me?" He leaned forward and I leaned back as much as I could, hoping he would overbalance and have to take a step to catch himself. Then I squashed down on the tube with my foot and pulled it back. The liquid squirted out in a tidy puddle less than half an inch from his toes. Why wasn't he taking a step?

I saw my chance and reached for the emergency cord. There was a squeal of metal on metal and everyone was hurtled from where they stood. All except me. I clung to my handrail for dear life.

Sure enough, Mr. Craig put his foot forward, trying to balance and hit the exact middle of the puddle of glue. I didn't know if it would stick or slide. Either would work.

Slide he did. His feet went up, almost over his head, and he slammed to the floor, the gun rolling from his hand and bouncing toward the opening between the cars. I clung to my rail with one hand and scooped the gun up with my other just as the train shuddered to a halt.

I straightened and used both hands to point the gun at Mr. Craig.

The conductor appeared and his eyes widened as he saw the gun and Hamilton Craig struggling on the floor. I smiled.

What the glue had lacked in power to stick his shoe to the metal, it had found in sticking his coattail.

"Please call the police. Tell them Officer Gallagher of York is on his way. I have his murderer. Just as I predicted."

The conductor backed away with a hasty "Yes, ma'am." I leveled the gun at Mr. Craig. "I just want to know one thing. Where did you get my granddaughter's Star of David to put with the body? And what did Susan ever do to you to make you set her up like that?"

Mr. Craig looked honestly confused. "Setting Susan up? What the hell are you on about?"

I sighed. There was certainly no reason for him to lie to me now. Maybe he hadn't mutilated the body. But that meant someone a lot crazier than Hamilton Craig was still running loose. I shivered and prayed for the police to hurry.

Twenty-Five

*A*s I sat in Officer Gallagher's desk chair and waited for him to finish with Hamilton Craig, I wondered what he really thought of me now. I also wondered if my *tuchis*, my bottom, would ever be the same. Such a chair for an important man like Gallagher? Better we could do in a rest room! Better he could have done for me if he had interviewed me in my hotel room. I had, after all, caught him another killer. A killer who had been about to make a clean getaway.

So, maybe he would offer me a job on the force? Not that I had any reason to stay in England, what with Susan going home. But it would have been nice to be thanked.

"Frances Zindel?"

I turned to see a stranger at the door of the station.

"Yes."

"I'm Duncan Edwards, *Manchester Guardian.* I understand you just caught the bloke as killed that young lady at the school?"

I didn't know what Officer Gallagher would think about my claiming credit for his job right here to the press, but the truth was the truth. I nodded. "Yes. I got his confession on tape."

"You held up the whole London train to do it, I hear."

"I did have to pull the emergency cord to prevent the suspect from shooting me and getting away."

"I hear you did it with Krazy Glue." He laughed and flipped pages in his steno notebook. He reminded me of Officer Gallagher.

"What's going on here, Edwards?"

It was Gallagher himself. I looked up at him.

"Get out of here, Edwards. Talk to the lady on your own time. In your own place."

He towered over the newsman, who scurried, still laughing, from the room.

Gallagher sighed and slumped onto a corner of his desk top. "Still out to humiliate all of England's finest, eh, Mrs. Zindel?"

"Just doing what I had to, Officer. The next dead body you found might have been mine!" I smiled at him.

Reluctantly, he stuck out his hand. "Nice job, Mrs. Zindel. Can I take you to the airport? Please?"

He looked so hopeful that I had to laugh. "No. I'm sorry, although you can drop me at my hotel." He looked crushed. "Mr. Nathan Weiss and I have a tour planned of the Lake District. Besides, you haven't told me who did that ritual stabbing. Such a bad name it gives the Jews."

He smiled. "There's one we have on you, Mrs. Z."

He walked me out to the police car. "You come along and get out of my district—and promise to stay out—and I'll tell you."

"You can go on with your life a happy man, Officer Gallagher," I said, showing him my passage to Los Angeles scheduled for later in the week.

He breathed a sigh of relief, sat behind the wheel, and began to give me all the details. An interesting story, I can tell you.

Twenty-Six

WHEN I had the airport shuttle drop me at my son's Encino home, Susan was out the front door and running down the walk before I could pay my bill. She threw herself on me and I hugged her almost as hard as she was hugging me.

Finally, she let me go and we carried my bags to the house. Larry met me at the door.

"How are you, Mother? Good flight?" He kissed my cheek.

I nodded and felt tears in my eyes for the joy of being home. "It was fine, and the Lake District! Such beauty. I walked my feet off. And so many rolls of film, I'll be a month getting my pictures back and into the album."

There was a shriek from the front stoop and Susan jumped up and down. "He's here! Alex is here, *Bubbe!*"

A large truck was parking a horse trailer at the curb. Susan rushed to the back, working the latches before the driver could get out and help her.

As my granddaughter eased Alexander down the ramp, I heard a gasp behind me. "Hello Judy, glad I could make it for the unveiling." I turned to look at my daughter-in-law. Her face was a study in shock and despair.

261

"He's so . . . so big," she choked, moving out to the curb like a sleepwalker.

I smiled.

"Oh, God," Judy breathed as Susan led Alexander down the drive to his new home in the middle of Judith's now-shrunken rose garden.

It looked nice, I have to say, with the new stall and the white-rail fences of the small arena. Just like a miniature old Kentucky home. I hummed a few bars and gave up watching Judith's face to look at my Susan's happiness.

For almost an hour, Susan was busy walking Alex around to get out his travel kinks, bringing him carrots and making him feel at home, which he was.

Finally, she stopped fussing and came to sit with me on the back patio where her mother had set out predinner snacks and a pitcher of tea. Now the questions started.

I showed her some of the news clippings from the London papers. GRANDMOTHER OF FOUR MAKES ARREST ON SPEEDING TRAIN, read one headline. My favorite was the story in the *Manchester Guardian*, courtesy of Mr. Edwards. SUPER-GRANDMOTHER, FASTER THAN A SPEEDING TRAIN, and a nice story about Mr. Craig's capture.

I had to tell her all the rest of it. Mr. Craig and his part in Mary Louise's death, his attempt to kill me, and the Krazy Glue that had saved my life.

"At least that's settled," Susan said, her eyes staring solemnly into her lap. "I guess we'll never know who stabbed her and blamed me."

"Does it matter so much?" I asked, hesitant to tell her the whole truth. Enough ugliness she had suffered. "They know it wasn't anything to do with you. Let that be an end to it."

But Susan was like a dog with a bone. "I'd like to have my star back, for one thing. Geoff gave it to me."

I sighed. I would have to tell her the rest. It was the only way to justify the fact that I now had her star in my purse. I knew her. She would wonder why the police let me have it.

I dug the packet out of my bag and handed it to her.

"Oh, *Bubbe*," she said, starting to smile as she opened it.

But it didn't last. Before she even pulled it from the wrapping, those green eyes were dark with questions.

I held up my hand. "Okay. Okay. I'll tell you."

Slowly, I explained. It all came out. How the Reverend Malbys had been carted off to a mental hospital. His part had been small but ugly. A million small parts such as his had played right into Hitler's hands. It was his print, on record for his anti-Semitic involvements, that had been on the star.

At a recent sermon, he had begun raving that he was proud of his ancestor, the Baron Malabestia. He had said that the baron spoke to him nightly and told him that since he was a descendant, he would be killed by the Jews. Other dead ancestors apparently told him he had been wrong to invite the Jews to York, wrong to support the conference.

He had begun to rave from the pulpit about banding together with the congregation to drive the Jews from England. At this point, an elder of the church phoned for professional help. Because of the print, Gallagher had already been on his way.

Once at the hospital, the Reverend Malbys had had a full breakdown and, under medication, had revealed his part in his daughter's mutilation. Apparently, he had heard rumors of her pregnancy. These rumors had been amplified by an anonymous letter from one of the schoolgirls. It had named names. Horrified, he had learned that Hamilton Craig, the father, was the grandson of an English Jew and it had pushed him over the edge. His anti-Semitism in full flower, he had hurried to confront his daughter. Finding her dead in her room, he assumed his God had exercised justice.

But apparently it had not been enough for the vicar. Consumed by a need for vengeance and cheated of his need to cleanse his daughter's soul himself, he had seen Susan's star on the dresser, where Mary Louise had left it. It must have triggered something because he said the stories of the medieval ritual murders came to him and he stabbed the body accordingly and left the necklace.

"God, that's awful," Susan said. She held the star on the flat of her hand. "I know Geoff gave this to me out of love, but

263

it really doesn't seem like something I can wear anymore." She searched my face for answers I didn't have. "Do you know what I mean, *Bubbe?*"

I patted her hand. "You know, *Susa-le,* I still have your grandfather's wedding ring. He didn't want it buried with him. Even though he was in pain from the heart attack and dying, he took it from his finger and pressed it into my hand. It was awful to see him that way. But when I look at his ring, I don't only think of his death. At first, that was all I could see through that circle of gold, but now I see back through all the good years we had together before that death."

"Maybe I'll put it away until Geoff comes for summer break. I can wear it again if he fastens it for me."

I smiled at her.

"So, *Bubbe,* you told me all about the Lake District, but you didn't tell me about Nathan." She grinned slyly. "Are things getting more serious?"

I blushed. Such an instinct my Susan had for romance.

"Come on, Gram, spill."

"Well." I shrugged. "To tell you the truth, I do have a little good news."

"Yes?" She leaned forward.

"Nathan is going to see about getting a transfer. He's going to try a temporary assignment in the States."